BEE-COMING

Bee's Flowers Book Two

Corlet Dawn

Corlet Dawn Publishing

To Mark:
Thank you for being my husband and best friend and for
being by my side as I was becoming who I needed to be.
Thank you for always making me laugh. I love you.

Becoming

I must leave so I can become me.

I could stay and be who you want me to be.

I haven't been myself.

Would you want that for me?

Leaving is the best thing I can do.

Just as a caterpillar becomes a butterfly, I must make

the journey.

You could ask me to stay, but that wouldn't be fair to us.

Stuck in who we are now.

I know things must change.

The transformation will bring beauty.

It's what's best for us.

We are all becoming.

Serenity, Age 16

Prologue

They had been working in silence, too consumed with their tasks, and closing the store, to notice their grandma's sudden absence. Stacia was rearranging the merchandise, Rachel dusting the shelves, and Grandma Betty closing the cash register--or so they thought.

The silence was interrupted by the hiss of the overhead speakers turning on. Stacia and Rachel listened with sharp ears, wondering what song their grandma had selected for this dance party. They each grinned to themselves, their already good moods now elevated.

The first few music bars began playing, and each girl started bobbing her head in time to the beat. By the time the first crescendo echoed through the store, their shoulders and hips had joined the rhythm coming from the speakers.

Without speaking a word, both girls danced their way toward the front of the store to experience the music together. Grandma Betty was reconciling the cash register, nodding her head in time to the music while she counted money, hips swaying to the song's rhythm.

They let the euphony bring them closer, mouthing the words to the song, smiling, laughing, making their bodies speak through the music. Rachel raised her duster like a microphone, passing it to her sister and grandma for occasional solos.

They all felt the stresses of the world melt away in these moments. Dancing with each other was so carefree and simple, yet crucial to them. They had danced like this for as long as they could remember, and none of them could comprehend when they wouldn't be able to do this together.

In these moments of dancing like no one was watching, these moments without a care in the world, they felt whole, uninhibited, with a sense that all was right with the world.

As they'd done many times before, they danced through Bee's Flowers' closing duties and then danced some more.

Part One

Daffodil

New Beginnings
Awareness
Self-Reflection
Creativity

1

~Rachel~May 2007

When I gro up I want to own a stor and play with flowurs and bees all day jest like my granma betty.
    Rachel Bee-Wilson, age 6

"**H**ave I told you before that honey helps your brain function?" Grandma Betty asked as she plopped a tea bag into a mug of boiling water to steep. She grabbed the classic bear-shaped bottle of honey and handed it to me. I inhaled the scent of the tea and the warmth from the steam as I let some of the thick, brown sweetener ooze into my mug.

"I'm pretty sure you've mentioned that one before," I replied. "What else do you have?"

"Honey is the only product made by an insect that humans ingest."

I looked at her in disgust for a brief second, wondering if I should get a new cup of tea minus the bug products. "Cool, but gross at the same time."

Grandma Betty shrugged her shoulders, "It's the closest

thing we've got to a perfect food. Nothing gross about that. Now, follow me to the storeroom and tell me what's bothering you."

It wasn't uncommon at any point in time for my grandma to share random bee knowledge. She loved our last name and the fact that the family obtained the namesake after being known in Ireland as "bee whisperers."

We grabbed our mugs and headed to the front of my grandparent's flower store, Bee's Flowers. After a horrible day at school, the shop, and my grandma, were in order.

Bee's Flowers had come to fruition after Grandma Betty resisted her parents' plan after high school. Their plan had limited options like being a wife, teacher, secretary, or nurse. Instead of going to college, she purchased a small cart that she loaded with flowers daily and pushed throughout Denver, Colorado, rain, shine, or snow.

She and a high school friend rented a small apartment, and she set out to gain her independence while working hard in an age when questioning society and working hard didn't match up. She met my grandpa, David, when she tried to persuade him to buy flowers while he was on a horrible first date. They married in a small ceremony before he left for Vietnam. Instead of focusing on her fear during his deployment, she worked harder than ever in his absence. Eventually, she saved enough money to open a storefront.

Many stores had come and gone in the thirty-plus years that she'd owned the shop, and Bee's itself was continually changing as Grandma Betty worked to keep up with current trends. My sister, Stacia, and I had grown up with the shop being an integral part of our lives, a lot of my earliest memories taking place within Bee's walls.

We sometimes went to Bee's to visit our grandma. Most of the time, we were put to work deadheading flowers and dusting shelves, which we didn't mind because of Grandma Betty and the love of flowers she passed on.

She was the fun grandma. She was independent, sassy, and headstrong, and she never hesitated to dance around the store with us to Britney Spears or N Sync. I was certain that she had a crush on Justin Timberlake, a conclusion I reached after she got me to assist her in downloading some of his songs onto her Blackberry.

Grandma Betty pulled out a stool near the cash register and gestured to it.

"Sit," she commanded as she set our mugs down and grabbed an extra chair. Once we got comfortable, she jumped right in.

"What's going on, Rachel?" she asked, never beating around the bush.

"I have my whole life planned," I said. "How can that be a bad thing?"

"I'm not sure I understand what you're talking about," my grandma said before taking a big slurp of her tea, sassy even in how she drank. "Why don't you start at the beginning?"

"I gave Ms. Goodman, my creative writing teacher, a short story to review. She came to me today with a bunch of nonsense about how I've been writing. She made me feel like my life had been too planned out, and I hadn't been adventurous enough. I freaked out and walked out of her class," I said, "It's been a downward spiral ever since."

~

This morning had started like any other day. The end of high school was fast approaching. Since I was finishing at the top of my class, I wasn't putting much effort into schoolwork.

I'd planned my life in detail since I was a child, and it felt fantastic knowing it was heading in the direction I wanted and had worked hard to obtain. Since elementary school, I knew I wanted to teach English. I loved reading and writing and thinking about getting paid to get children excited about the subject was exhilarating.

I had also planned out my love life. My boyfriend, Sean, and I had started dating at the end of freshman year. Next fall, we were starting classes at Colorado State University, and I was lucky enough to be attending with a full-ride scholarship.

We would be living in the dorms at first but planned to move in together eventually, get engaged, and have a perfect wedding. Post-wedding, we wanted to become established as a married couple, secure our careers, and, approximately five years later, have our first baby, followed roughly two years later by a second child. We would have a charming family home, a yellow lab, and a white picket fence.

Since ninth grade, my creative writing teacher, Ms. Goodman, encouraged my teaching aspirations. She would mark my papers with praise and ideas for furthering my writing. With her guidance and support, I felt like a better writer every year, and I couldn't wait to be a teacher, just like her. Because of her guidance, I hoped to complete my first novel shortly after grad school.

I enrolled in her creative writing class every year, and I was currently her teacher's aide, which allowed us to work closely together. Her goal for my senior year was to challenge me, and she'd done so by continuing to evaluate my work while allowing me to review the work of other students with their permission.

Ms. Goodman was stunning, but she was one of those women who didn't seem to know, or care, making her even more attractive. She wore flowing ankle-length skirts and Birkenstock's and smelled like essential oils. One of her nostrils sported a delicate hoop, which seemed rebellious for a teacher. Her guitar lay propped against the wall in the classroom, where anyone could pick it up and strum if the mood struck them. She was unlike the other adults in my life, which made me look up to her even more.

I'd recently written a short romance piece and asked Ms. Goodman to look at it. This morning, when we sat down to discuss it, she asked me if she could be very frank with me. I nodded, expecting a typical critique.

"Your stories are full of potential," she started. "You've

got a wonderful imagination, but your writing seems to revolve around some common themes: boy meets girl, girl and boy fall in love, the girl needs the boy, and the boy needs the girl. They get married, experience minimal conflict, and have a happy ending. Though I see the appeal of a stress-free, planned-out life, I'd love to see you branch out a little with some adventure and strife. I think that romance and love are great, but they shouldn't define someone."

I sat there for a moment, unsure how to take what she'd said, not used to anyone challenging me or my plans. What exactly was the problem with any of those things? Didn't most movies start with love and romance and end happily? Weren't happy endings the kind people strived for, the result that all books and movies told us we wanted and needed?

"Okay," I tried to say calmly, even though my eyes were brimming with tears. I swallowed them back, but I knew she could see how frazzled I was. "I'm not sure what to say right now. I participate in school; it's not like I'm just a boy-crazy little girl--"

"Rachel," Ms. Goodman replied, "I love that you're involved in school. Being the student body president with scholarship-worthy grades, and the head of the prom committee are all great accomplishments that you shouldn't take lightly. I'm only talking about your writing and how it may carry over into your own life. I'm sorry you're upset, but I can't apologize. If I didn't think you could be great, I wouldn't be pushing you. I'd let you continue your predestined path without any advice from me. I couldn't let you finish this year and proceed on your journey without saying what I needed to say. Your writing is progressing in so many ways. You're a phenomenal person and a spectacular writer, no matter what you end up doing, not doing, or writing about."

I tried to turn off my defensive mode, remembering my father's advice about listening to absorb. I'd taken a second to think, focusing on the positive words: potential, great, phenomenal, spectacular. I thought about the trust I had in Ms.

Goodman. I didn't believe that she'd fill my head with false ideas. I decided that the best strategy now was the "exit" type. I'd never dealt well with conflict.

"I appreciate you thinking enough about me to give me advice. It's too much to absorb right now, sorry." I stood up and took the short story from her with shaky hands as I made a beeline for the exit.

"Rachel, let's talk about this," Ms. Goodman called after me, her request lingering in my departure.

Old Blue, my trusty Volvo station wagon, was one of my happy places, so that was where I went as I waited for the lunch bell to sound. Initially, I'd been irritated with my parents when they passed the rickety car down to me after getting my driver's license, but I was upset for vanity reasons because expensive vehicles filled the student parking lot at my Denver high school, mostly purchased by well-to-do parents.

Over time, the car grew on me, and I was taking it to college, where I planned on driving it until it didn't run anymore. Old Blue's bumper initially sported one D.A.R.E. To Keep Kids Off Drugs sticker. Now, the back bumper and windows sported multiple stickers, and it seemed to be a side project for my classmates to plaster my car while I was in class. I loved the eclectic variety of band stickers, tribal patterns, and peace signs that patterned the back of my car. I also liked that it seemed so out-of-character for me.

I hadn't had much time to wallow in pity before hearing a knock on the side window. My boyfriend, Sean, looked at me, confused, as he was usually the first one to the car at lunchtime. I manually rolled down the window instead of unlocking the door.

"Hey," Sean said, leaning into the window. "Everything okay, Baby?"

If I'd been in my normal state of mind, I would've swooned at the term of endearment, but I wasn't remotely in the mood. Instead of answering him lovingly, I looked at him blankly, trying to plan my reply without taking my anger out on him.

"I'm 17 years old and practically a grown woman. How is that baby-like?" I answered icily before I could stop myself.

Too late; Sean, meet anger.

Sean looked at me in surprise, not used to this reaction.

I returned his stare, not blinking, waiting to see if he would give me more ammunition to throw back at him. Sean's best friend, Parker, rescued us from our awkward interaction.

"What's for lunch, dudes?" Parker asked as he hoisted his skateboard over his shoulders.

Sean and Parker were complete opposites. Sean was all pale skin, freckles, and red hair, and Parker was dark-skinned with dreadlocks and big brown eyes. Sean was on the varsity baseball team, and his high school outfit of choice tended to include jeans, a sports-related t-shirt, and a baseball cap. Parker was always up on the latest fashions. Today he'd shown up to school wearing cargo shorts, an Ed Hardy T-shirt, and a Von Dutch hat that complimented the oversized sunglasses that were probably gifted to him by one of his many female admirers. Parker had come out as openly gay in middle school and always focused on breaking down stereotypes, making him one of the most intriguing people at school.

Parker's grandma lived next door to Sean's house. Since they were in diapers, they'd been best friends. When Sean and I started dating, Parker came along as part of the package deal, which I didn't mind as I'd grown close to Parker and now considered him one of my best friends.

Now, I'd lost my patience for them both. "I don't know," I said haughtily, "I'M running to MY house. What are YOU TWO going to do for lunch?"

Parker looked at me shocked and whispered loudly to Sean, "Is she stressed about graduation and pulling a full-blown Britney Spears? Let's hope she doesn't shave her head; it's too egg-shaped."

"I can hear everything you're saying, Parker!" I said as I aggressively tried to shift my car into reverse, loudly grinding the gears instead.

"Ouch," Parker said, grimacing as Old Blue resisted and then purred into reverse.

I glared at them before shifting my car into drive, causing a horrific grinding noise again. As I headed towards the exit of the senior parking lot, my head was spinning, and I now knew why it wasn't okay to drive while upset.

Instead of heading home, I turned on my favorite song, Justin Timberlake's "What Goes Around...Comes Around," driving towards Red Rocks Amphitheater, another of my happy places.

I parked my car in one of the lots, grabbed my water bottle, and walked up the flights of stairs leading to Denver's most breathtaking view. I sat at the top, admiring the view of the city with minimal noise and the scent of fresh air from the mountains. In the peaceful setting, I attempted to break apart what made me so upset about what Ms. Goodman said. I knew I had control issues, but my persistence made me successful. My hard work resulted in a full-ride scholarship to a great school. At 17-years-old, the goals I'd always envisioned were at my fingertips.

I sat there thinking for hours until the light patter of rain drove me to Bee's Flowers, where I knew I could get the best advice.

~

"So that is it in a nutshell. Now I feel like my life is a sham. Sean probably thinks I'm crazy. Speaking of crazy, should I do something wacky and out of character for me?" I asked with a slightly hysterical laugh. "It's all good. Yeah, it's so so good right now." I paused, waiting for her to analyze the situation.

Grandma Betty looked at me and raised an eyebrow. "What did you do to Sean? He has the face of a baby angel and the body of a--"

"Grandma!" I exclaimed as she looked at me innocently.

"Well, he does. I can't wait to see him in his prom get-up tomorrow," she said, winking before taking another slurp of tea.

"Gross, Grandma," I said, smirking. "You can't say stuff like that."

"I'm just trying to make you feel better," she said, swatting at me playfully. "It was either joke with you or make you have a dance party with me to 'Bringing Sexy Back,' and I don't feel you're in a place to fully appreciate J.T. right now."

I shook my head, appreciating her jokes, yet needing her wisdom. "Grandma, I need you to figure this out for me."

"Figure out why?" Grandma Betty stated in Yoda fashion. "What do you need to figure out?"

"I know the direction my life needs to go, and it's all collapsing around me," I felt myself starting to panic.

Grandma Betty placed her hand on my hand. "Calm down, honey. I think you need to ask yourself what made you upset? The part where she told you your life is predictable and lacked adventure or when you realized that she might be correct?"

I looked at my grandma, stone-faced, loving and hating her for rocking the boat. "I thought you'd be on my side," I said with a groan.

"I AM on your side," she said sternly. "You come from--"

"A long line of strong, independent Bee women, just like the honeybee," I interrupted, "I'm aware. You've ingrained that into my head. Once again, what does that have to do with anything?"

"Again," my grandma said vaguely, "What is there to figure out?"

2

~Betty~ May 1969

May 15th, 1969

Miss Elizabeth Bee-
We are proud to inform you that we have selected you as part of our secretarial training program. Please present this letter of acceptance and three reference letters to our offices on May 30th at 8:00 am sharp. Professional dress, with stockings, is required.
Sincerely,
Albert Fitzsimmons
President, Denver Academy Secretarial School

I looked in horror at the letter my mother had placed squarely on my pillow, obviously wanting to make sure that her plan for me post-graduation was as clear as possible.

Graduation was in two weeks, and to my parent's disdain, I hadn't applied to any colleges, a subject I'd avoided speaking with them about for as long as possible since I didn't anticipate it going well. I was smart enough to get into most colleges, but that wasn't what I wanted. I had other plans for my future, and my parents were still not on board.

Since I wasn't the one who applied to the secretary training program, I felt minimal guilt as I crumpled it up and threw it in the wastebasket, hoping my message back to my mother would come across. After a few minutes, I returned and made sure that the paper was hidden, not wanting to make an already touchy subject worse.

I really couldn't believe that it was almost 1970, and my parents were trying to mold me into a woman that would have been better suited to the 1950s. It was a time of movement and growth, and though I loved my parents, I was not interested in going down the path they wanted me to choose.

My parents grew up together in a small farming community just east of Denver, where hard work and neighborliness were important. They'd been best friends as children, and more than that as adults. They'd gotten married at 17 before they ventured away from the farm to Denver, starting their careers there. My mom was a seamstress, and my dad was a mechanic.

My mother, June, was the oldest of nine children. She was blessed with a fiery spirit, which she needed to help keep eight siblings on the right track. My mother was a great storyteller, and I loved to hear all about her rebelliousness. She'd been notorious for wearing pants instead of dresses to school in defiance of the dress code, of climbing trees to hide so she could get out of doing chores in the morning. One of the stories I loved the best involved her falling off one of the family horses while playing around with her sister, breaking her arm for the seventh time.

Hearing those stories made me feel like she should support my desire to forge my path instead of following the one that was expected of young women decades ago. Were we not progressing?

My mother called me down for dinner, and all it took was a glance at her expression to realize she'd probably seen the paper and was about to tell me all her thoughts on my future.

"I got a call from your school advisor," my mother stated as we sat down at the table. "She asked why someone so smart had not applied to any colleges. I told her I had been wondering the same thing, and I still feel college was the best option." She looked at me with expectation.

"You mean secretarial school?" I asked as calmly and respectfully as possible, knowing that getting upset would not improve this conversation.

"What do you mean exactly?" my mother asked as her face changed to a shade of bright red, as her narrowed eyes glinted steel.

"June," my dad said as he placed a hand on her arm, trying to diffuse the situation.

"William, we're having this discussion; if she isn't going to college, she needs to learn a trade," my mother replied as she slowly moved her arm back. My father and I looked briefly at each other, aware that she was mad enough to call my father by his given name instead of Bill.

"Mom, I have a plan," I said, looking as brave as possible, smiling to diffuse the situation. Hopefully, telling her my idea would give her less reason to pounce on me. I knew if she called me by my middle name after calling my dad William that we would need to wait to finish the conversation.

"I went to the grocery store yesterday. While I was checking out, Teresa informed me that Missy Duncan is planning a hitchhiking trip to California before she goes to college. If that is your plan, young lady, you better reconsider."

That wasn't my plan, but I had considered it. I tried to keep a straight face, not wanting her to know. Missy, one of my oldest friends, had asked me to join her on her trip from Denver to the Pacific Coast. Seeing a little bit of the country was intriguing, but I had years of babysitting money, burning a hole in my pocket. I was ready to be on my own and follow my dream which was unique enough that I didn't anticipate it coming true sitting in a college classroom.

"You already know what I want to do," I started, quickly

adding, "Ma'am," for good measure.

"Are you referring to your flower idea?" My mom asked. "Because I thought we already closed that discussion."

"In all honesty, Mother, you may have tried to dissuade me, but it's still what I need to be doing," I said with confidence, about to drop a word that may force her to appreciate how I felt. "You know this has always been my dream."

My mom looked taken aback by my statement, the sharpness in her face fading slightly. When she was a young woman, she sat down at my grandparent's table to tell them she was leaving to follow her dream of living in Denver and becoming a seamstress. Her parents wanted her to follow in their footsteps, but my mother's goals were bigger than farming and raising multiple children. I knew if I could pull at the heartstrings that had driven her towards her dreams, it may work in my favor.

I expected my mom to say something, but she sat in contemplation before standing up, grabbing the dishes from the table, and heading to the sink. I glanced in my father's direction, and he shrugged his shoulders. He was a man of few words, but when he did speak, it counted for something.

"June, Elizabeth," he said after the sink was full of warm water and he'd placed the dishes in the sink to soak. "How do we reach a compromise on this?"

My mother slowly used a dishcloth to wipe the dishes, which was usually my job, but my mother seemed to do her best thinking when she was doing something with her hands, so I left her to it. After a few dishes, she spoke, "I'm going to tell you the same thing my parents told me when I wanted to leave to follow my dreams, if that is acceptable to you, Bill?" My father nodded in agreement.

"You have the right to follow your heart, but we can allow you to learn to fly without our financial support. Your father and I have made it clear that we would help pay your way in college or a training school. If you insist on doing neither of those, you will have to work hard to support yourself. If this flower idea fails, we will be here to support you with whatever comes after that. We wish you luck and love in your venture but will not support it with money."

Inside, I felt many feelings: excitement, fear, apprehension, and hope. I felt like the world was at my fingertips, and it was up to me to make it go the way I wanted. I knew that fulfilling my dream would be hard work, but I was ready to dirty my hands.

My love of flowers started at a young age. My mom stayed busy with her seamstress work, but she still planted a garden every year. I, being an only child, had been her helper. I loved sitting in the dirt, with the sun's warmth on my back, planting vegetables and flowers. I loved that there was such a wide variety of plant-life, and I got books from the library to learn their names and information on how to keep them alive in the dry Colorado soil. More of the planting was turned over to me as I got older until the garden was all mine. I liked the challenge of planting a seed and watching it grow. I felt personally responsible for the well-being of the flowers. I could depend on them, sometimes more than I could rely on people.

It wasn't that I disliked humans; I just felt like there was a lot of evil in the world, and it left me feeling unsettled. There was a sense of unease and discord with the war, the civil rights movement, and the transitional shift towards a new era. Hate was like a noxious weed in our current society, trying to suffocate all that was good and just, wrapping its roots around the stems to steal society's inherent beauty through strangulation.

Flowers would peek their heads out of the soil and angle their bodies to the sun. All they needed was warmth, water, light, nutrients, and gentle pruning. They didn't give up easily, taking what they needed and producing beauty.

The happiness that gardening brought me produced the desire to own a flower shop someday, one called Bee's Flowers. It seemed like fate that my last name was Bee. My fascination with plants also carried over to honeybees. While researching flowers, I learned how important bees were in the life cycle of plants. I would often spout out useless bee knowledge, much to my friend's chagrin. Legend had it that my ancestors had been bee charmers, and that is how we had come to have our surname.

I knew I wanted a shop of my own, but until recently, I hadn't figured out how to go about that with the expense of a storefront's rent. I saved practically every penny I'd earned babysitting throughout high school. With all the nieces and nephews in the area, I babysat a lot. After looking through the newspaper the past few months, I concluded that I would never be able to afford rent in Denver. After going to Boulder last weekend and seeing an ice cream cart in the park, the perfect idea came to me. I didn't need a ceiling right away, just a vessel to sell flowers from.

I'd come home and instantly gone next door to inform my grandfather about my new flower idea. My grandmother had passed away five years ago from a heart attack, and my grandfather moved to Denver shortly after, where he could be closer to family. My relationship with my grandfather evolved from obligation to one of necessity. Over the past few years, he'd become so much more than a grandfather to me.

I ran to his house after seeing the cart, breathless with excitement. I described my thoughts on modifying the design for flowers. "It would need wheels, a handle for me to push, and some pockets for flowers to sit in."

My grandfather wordlessly set down his newspaper, climbed out of his easy chair, and grabbed a piece of paper and a pencil. The lead roughly scratched the paper as he sketched. "Like this?" he asked after a few minutes.

"Yes, except maybe four wheels so it could turn easily," I said after examining the drawing. "Oh, and it would need room for a sign."

My grandfather smiled as he grabbed the drawing from me and went to work on the revision. His idea was to mention my mother's dreams to her to help cushion the blow of my post-high school choices. Now, knowing that my mom was willing to give me a chance, I couldn't wait to talk to him about what had occurred.

"Thank you for your consideration. I agree with your terms. I appreciate the chance to follow my dreams. Now, if we have come to a conclusion that satisfies all of us, I'm going to go see Grandpa," I said, standing up from the table.

My father smiled and nodded. My grandfather and dad had developed a great relationship in the last few years. My grandpa even adopted my dad's nickname for me, Bug. They liked to tinker around in the garage together, always working on cars or some mechanical project.

My mother, now drying the dishes, turned around. "Before you go, I need to make something clear. I'm only upset about college because you are so smart. Your ability to argue would suit you well in a classroom, a hospital, or a courtroom. I know how it feels to dream, but you are so smart that I can't imagine you wasting all of that intelligence on flowers instead of doing something to better society."

I hugged her, appreciating her comments. I just knew I would have to work extra hard to prove that flowers meant more than she thought they did. I walked out of the front door and headed towards my grandpa's house to give him the good news.

3

~*Rachel*~ *May 2007*

The person I chose as my true-life hero is my grandma. She grew up in Colorado and always dreamed of opening a flower shop. She moved out of her house at eighteen years old and worked hard until she had enough money to buy a store. She is not like most grandmas. She likes to make funny jokes, and she also likes to have dance parties with me and my sister, Stacia, even though she's still little. Today, she brought everyone in the class a carnation because they are her favorite even though they are basic. She says that even the plainest flower can sometimes be the most beautiful. I introduce to you my grandma, Betty.

Rachel Bee-Wilson, age ten, at Bring Your Hero to School Day

I sat in the Bee's parking lot after my "enlightening" conversation with my grandma, still not knowing what to do. I wanted her to tell me something to make me feel better, not a Mr. Miagi from Karate Kid vague lesson about "what is there to figure out?"

I made the mistake of glancing at my phone and finding

missed messages from Sean and Parker. I decided to ignore those for a while longer. The most recent text was from Samantha, my best friend, and I decided it was safe to click on hers until I saw all the capital letters. Well, I thought to myself, you may as well jump into the fire.

YOU DITCHED! YOUR COUNSELOR CAME TO GET YOU TO DISCUSS SOMETHING ABOUT PROM, AND THEY COULDN'T FIND YOU! I saw Sean and Parker, and they said you had a freak-out. WHAT is going on? ARE WE STILL GOING TO PROM?!

I hunched over the steering wheel and rested my forehead on the hard surface. I tried to let the desire for rebellion cover up the increasing sense of dread at the fact that I had ditched class, gotten caught doing so by my guidance counselor, and acted like a crazy person in the parking lot with Sean and Parker.

As I drove, I felt like I was in a dream world, considering the morning and what Grandma Betty had asked me: Why was I so bothered by what Ms. Goodman said? If I was so happy with the way my life was heading, would it have upset me, or would I have been able to shrug it off and take it as a difference in opinion? Was I hyper-focused on it now because she had been correct? Did I need some adventure and variety in my life?

My phone started ringing, Samantha's ringtone, "Fergalicious" by Fergie, playing loudly. I pulled over into Sonic when I felt like hearing another song loop would make my already pounding head explode. I decided to get a pity milkshake before attempting any phone calls. Once I had my banana cream pie shake in hand, I called Sam back.

"What in the hell is going on with you?" Samantha said aggressively. I held the phone away from my ear but could still hear her. "Are you sick? Are you pregnant? Could you be pregnant? What have you been keeping from me? Is it drugs? Are you on drugs?"

"Hello to you, too," I answered as I placed the phone back to my ear and took a slow pull off the straw. Heavenly.

"I'm your best friend, and I need to know what's going on," she said.

"Well, let me assure you it isn't any of the things you've mentioned," I said, mouth full of shake, not caring that it was rude.

"Senioritis? I need an answer here!"

"All these years of trying to be the best and follow a specific plan, and here I am, boring and mostly stress-free." I slurped up more of my milkshake.

"Huh, what? What are you doing right now?" Samantha asked.

"Drowning my sorrows in sugary deliciousness," I said, again rudely slurping my shake. If my grandma could drink her beverages with sass, so could I.

"Where are you?" She asked, ignoring my bad manners.

"Sonic," I replied.

"Why don't we meet at the park? I want to know what happened -- in person."

"I'm on my way," I replied, knowing I'd have to speak with her eventually.

I waited in the parking lot for a few minutes; Samantha was always late. I didn't doubt that she'd be faster today since she wanted to know what was going on with me. I was going to have to figure that out for myself first.

Surprisingly, Samantha beat me. I took a nice cleansing breath, trying to get myself into a state of Zen before dealing with the barrage of questions I was about to face.

I waved in the direction of her car as I headed towards our favorite spot. Samantha drove a brand-new Ford Taurus, compliments of her Disneyland Dad. Her parents had divorced last year, and it was sadly an all too familiar story. Her workaholic dad started sleeping with his young secretary and got caught. When her mom filed for divorce, he started counteracting his bouts of guilt by spending copious amounts of money on Samantha, his only child.

She exited her car, and together we headed to our picnic

bench. Since meeting back in elementary school, this had been our meeting spot since it was approximately halfway between our houses. "Our" picnic table was located under a beautiful oak tree that provided just the right shade and sunlight.

If the picnic table could transcribe everything it had been privy to, it would detail love, loss, heartache, frustration, happiness, and all the emotions one feels while growing up. Recently, Samantha had developed trouble sleeping because of the stress of the divorce. On those nights, we brought blankets to the table to watch the stars twinkle and talk. I was a fan of getting at least 8-10 hours of sleep every night, but I was a bigger fan of Samantha, and for her, I was willing to make that sacrifice.

We sat down, and I held my shake out to Samantha, already feeling the effects of the sugary drink. She grabbed it and sipped slowly, and I could tell that she was dying to know what was going on.

"I've had quite the day," I said to her after a minute.

She raised her eyebrows, imploring me to start talking.

"Do you want me to start at the beginning?" I asked.

"Well, I've been sitting here wracking my brain. Something happened that has caused you to lose your mind. Start talking."

"Can I ask you a question first?"

She handed the shake back to me and nodded.

"Am I boring?"

She snorted, which she sometimes did when she laughed, causing her glasses to slide down her nose. "Is this a trick question? I feel like you're setting me up."

"No trick question," I finished my drink, stood up, and threw it in the trash can.

"You aren't boring," Samantha started. "You're predictable."

"Predictable," I said. "I'm not sure that is any better than boring."

"That is all a matter of opinion. Boring means you aren't willing to go outside of your comfort zone. Predictability means you know how a person is going to react. Why are you asking?" Samantha inquired. "What happened?"

"Ms. Goodman happened," I answered bitterly.

"I thought she was your favorite teacher," Samantha said.

I sat for a moment, thinking again. She was my favorite and I liked and respected her so much that I'd made it a point to work closely with her for four years of high school. "I do like her," I replied honestly. "I just didn't like what she said to me today."

"Are you going to drag this on forever, or will you spill details?" Samantha asked impatiently.

"Sorry. Honestly, the more I say it out loud, the more pathetic I feel for complaining about it." I said, "I wrote another story that I asked her to review. Today she sat me down and asked if she could be honest with me, and I agreed. She proceeded to tell me that my writing was very similar because it usually has little to no conflict and ends happily. I need to have less of a Disney existence and more of an adventurous life."

"Isn't Disney a multi-billion-dollar company because people like happy endings?" Samantha pondered.

I clapped my hands together, visibly startling my best friend, "Exactly my point. I knew you'd see it my way."

Samantha held her hand out, indicating a need to say more, "Let me finish before you speak. I love you, and your personality. I love that you are dependable and that you are a control freak, mainly because it saves me a lot on gas money since you always prefer to drive everywhere. Ouch, don't hit me." Samantha rubbed her arm, where I had given her a sister-like slug. She continued, "You could use some adventure in your life. I love you and Sean separately and collectively, but it's like you two are an old married couple. I feel like two years into college, you're going to be sitting in a recliner chair crocheting while he does crossword puzzles instead of going out and enjoying a night on the town."

"I don't think we'd be like that," I retorted as I pictured us doing that very thing and kind of liking the idea.

"Liar," Samantha said. "I can see right through you."

"Okay, okay, you got me," I admitted. "What do I do?"
"Find yourself an adventure, of course," she replied.

4

~Betty~ May 1969

Bug- Please come over when you're done with school today. I think I have perfected your flower cart. Since I created it, I feel like that officially makes me your first investor, but for now, I want that to stay between you and me.

    I would love to speak with you before telling your parents about the cart. I don't condone keeping secrets from them, but I have a proposition for you and would like us to discuss it first.

    I had to come here under the pretense of needing to borrow some butter so I could leave this for you. Please destroy all evidence of this letter, especially from your mother.

    Gramps

I picked the letter up from my pillow where my grandpa had placed it. It was funny that in my entire life, I had never had any correspondence left there, and in the last week, it had happened twice. I read it, and my heart pounded with excitement. I had a flower cart! I was one step closer to making my dream a reality.

I pulled the dress I'd worn to school off and threw on a loose-fitting peasant blouse and a pair of bell bottoms before rushing downstairs. I took out my long braid, so my hair fell in thick waves down my back. I couldn't wait to see my grandpa's creation.

I knocked loudly, barely able to contain my excitement. My grandpa answered after the second knock, and I could tell from his face that he was just as excited as I was.

Before my grandmother died, I felt like my grandpa was an enigma. He was so friendly, yet he rarely spoke, as was common for the men on both sides of my family. My grandmother had been very verbose, and I often wondered if he was just used to rarely getting a word in. Once he moved in next door, I started to visit daily at first to check on him and his grief, and later, because I wanted to spend time with him. His pain was so apparent after my grandmother's death that I worried he would die of heartbreak. They were childhood friends and husband and wife from a young age. Their marriage was the kind I hoped to have one day- one that wasn't perfect, but one that you could tell mattered more than anything to both of them.

We started by walking together every day, and slowly, my grandfather began to open up to me until it became normal for us to speak to each other daily. Now, as strange as it sounded, I felt like he was not only my grandfather but a friend and confidant. He even called me his special Bug, his Honeybee.

When he opened the door, I could sense my grandfather's excitement, and I knew he could also feel mine. "I can't wait to see it!" I exclaimed as I pushed through the door, hugging him.

"Don't hug me just yet, Bug," Grandpa said, though he didn't try to break my embrace. "You might want to see it first."

"I'm sure I'm going to love it," I replied as I pulled back and guided him in the direction of his garage. My body was tingling with a mix of nerves and anticipation. Bee's might happen sooner than I imagined it would.

I entered the garage, and my breath caught, "It's perfect,

Grandpa; just perfect!"

It was as if my grandfather had read my mind. He had taken what I had seen with the ice cream cart and modified it to suit my needs. The cart was a rich brown walnut that Grandpa sanded and stained, allowing the beautiful threads of the wood grain to show through. It had four wheels, a handle, and a middle section with multiple pockets on each side so a bouquet could rest there without tipping out while I pushed the cart.

"Why don't you give it a try?"

I walked tentatively over to the cart and let my hand run over the smooth surface of the wood. I traced the curve of the handle before giving it a gentle push. It moved freely and easily with its four wheels, and even when full of merchandise, I didn't expect it to be too heavy for me to maneuver. I beamed at my grandfather as I pushed it around his garage.

"Bouquet?" I asked, gesturing to my imaginary merchandise.

He smiled and nodded, playing along with me. "I would love one, but it wouldn't be right to purchase flowers from you, imagined or not, before you have a sign." He walked over to the cart, flipping over a piece of wood attached to the front. He had engraved in beautiful lettering on the sign, "Bee's Flowers."

I was not a crier, but it was so perfect it was hard not to tear up. "I love it, Grandpa! Thank you."

I went in for another hug, "Is it groovy enough for you, Bug?" Grandpa asked with a chuckle.

I laughed in return, "It is the grooviest. I didn't know you were up on all the lingo. What did you want to talk to me about? Are you hitchhiking across the US with Missy? Is she the one teaching you these words?"

"I think my potential hitchhiking days are behind me, unfortunately," Grandpa said, "but some of this does have to do with Missy. Why don't we go sit inside and talk?"

I nodded, now confused. I, of course, had been joking about the discussion having to do with my best friend. Missy and I had been inseparable since childhood. Our parents had been close since moving to Denver, and we ended up attending school together, sealing the friendship. When my grandfather moved in, he fit right in with our family/friend dynamic that we'd established between our families, including Missy's grandmother, Theresa, who my grandfather saw regularly.

We sat down at the table, and my grandfather cleared his throat before starting. "I have money set aside for you for after I die."

"Grandpa, what's going on? You're dying?" I was suddenly very nervous about where this conversation was going.

"Well, dear, we are all dying. I should have considered how bad that sounded. Let me try again. I have enjoyed getting to know you over these past few years, and our relationship is very precious to me. I have money put aside for you and all the other grandchildren for when I pass away, but I want to give it to you now. I want to be alive to see your dreams in action." He looked at me expectantly.

"Really?" I said, hopefully. "Are you sure?"

"I've seen how hard you've worked at school. I've seen you help your parents so they can both follow their dreams, and you've helped me through the loss of the love of my life," Grandpa started to tear up, and I had to look away, hoping not to embarrass him. He took a breath and continued. "Your mother mentioned that you have saved all your babysitting money to help you towards your flower shop dream. I want to help with that, but to be clear, I have two financial things we are going to discuss: investing in your business and giving you inheritance money early. The money that goes towards Bee's is money I am giving to you as an investor."

"Okay, deal," I said as I held out my hand to shake, so excited I could barely contain myself.

"Let's discuss the terms of this partnership first," Grandpa said, withdrawing his hand, "If you are going to be in business you need to know what you are getting into before you ever make things official."

I nodded, I appreciated that he was treating me like a

businesswoman.

"You will purchase the cart I made for you at cost plus labor. I'll also pay for your first order of flowers and materials, but I'll expect that money back. The inheritance money is only for things unrelated to business, but knowing you, you will use it for sensible things like living expenses. I'll be here for you, but I won't be giving you a freebie. You come from a long line of tougher women than society expects them to be, and I would expect nothing less from you."

I was practically speechless, which was rare for me. "Grandpa, thank you so much. It's a deal, all of it. I agree, and I want to work hard. I want to make all of you proud."

My grandpa stood up to hug me. I rested my head against his flannel shirt and focused on the moment, wanting it ingrained in my memory. He smelled faintly of tobacco and peanut butter and jelly sandwiches. "You already make me proud," he whispered.

I decided to change the subject before we got more emotional, "What does any of this have to do with Missy?"

"I was hoping that maybe you and Missy could find an apartment together at the end of the summer. From speaking with her grandmother, I know that you both talked about it at one point. We agree that you would take good care of each other."

"Just how often are you seeing Theresa?" I asked suspiciously, though I would approve of that relationship if my grandfather had decided to court again.

"Now, now, let's not jump the gun here," Grandpa said, "We see each other occasionally at the diner in the morning. We just both happen to like the pancakes and coffee there. Let's not start planning a wedding." He winked at me, and I smiled, winking back.

"Not yet anyway," I said under my breath. My grandpa chuckled.

"One last thing," he said. "I don't want your parents to think I'm overstepping any boundaries, so let's hold off on the money discussion. If they ask me about the cart, I'll be able to tell them honestly that you paid for it. Let's give your mother a little time to get over you not going to college. I'm sure that she's told you this already, but she didn't go to college and always wanted that for you. She knows how smart you are and doesn't want you to sell yourself short."

I beamed at my grandfather, "When you're dealing with flowers, there is no such thing as a disappointment as far as I'm concerned. People don't always bring me the same joy as plants do. It's just like her and her sewing and I know she'll understand someday."

My grandfather nodded in agreement and squeezed my shoulder. I gave him another quick hug. "I'll call Missy about the apartment. But first, I want to try my cart one more time."

5

~Rachel~ May 2007

"I love you," Amanda said as she looked into Antoine's eyes. She stared at his brown orbs, and they gazed back at her with such intensity she could see the flecks of turquoise in them.

"I love you, too," he said as he grabbed both of her hands and squeezed them, holding them tightly to his chest. "I can't wait to start our life together."

"To think we would have never met if your dog hadn't escaped that day," Amanda said as he stared lovingly at her and she at him.

"He sensed we needed each other," Antoine agreed. "Dogs sense things that we don't."

Excerpt from "Puppy Love," written by Rachel Bee-Wilson, age 16

I thought about the definition of adventure as I drove. Now that I was aware of my propensity for being predictable, I felt an urge to prove everyone wrong. Maybe I would try to find myself an adventure.

I listened to the upbeat music of Timbaland to help cheer

me up. I needed a little extra hype to get me out of my funk. I parked Old Blue in front of the house and walked to the front door. I paused before opening it, hoping to channel some of Grandma Betty's attitude before I faced my parents. I wasn't sure how the school reported ditchers, but I was sure they knew somehow. Also, I was stressed about my freak out on Sean earlier; I was positive he didn't know what to think about how I'd acted this afternoon.

I opened the door, ready to be done with drama for the day.

"I'm home," I said as I entered the entryway.

Stacia, my younger sister, was heading downstairs as I headed up. "You're busted. You better think of a good excuse now," she advised me quietly enough that my parents wouldn't hear her. I was glad that she consistently had my back despite our age gap, just like I had hers.

I walked into the kitchen and set my stuff down on the table.

"Where were you?" My dad quit stirring the chicken that he was pan-frying to face me. I was glad I hadn't been ditching to do something illegal or scandalous. I wasn't a good liar, especially when it came to my dad.

"I was upset, so I left at lunch and didn't return. Before you ground me, know that people are counting on me for the prom tomorrow, and I've never done anything like this. I went to Red Rocks to think, and Bee's to see Grandma, and then to the park to meet Samantha. I wasn't doing anything wrong. I just had a rough day."

My dad stared at me. "Did something happen with Sean?" He turned back around to tend to the chicken.

"Why would you think that Sean played any part in what happened?" I asked. "Aren't I allowed to have bad days that have nothing to do with my boyfriend?"

"Whoa there," my dad turned the stove-top to low and came behind my chair, placing a hand on my shoulder as if to help center me.

CORLETDAWN

I took a cleansing breath. "I'm sorry, I feel a little sensitive about relationships now. I had something pointed out to me today, and I feel disheartened. I've worked so hard, and though I'm excited about my future, I feel like I may need to live it up a little before I start my adult life."

My mom entered the kitchen. "I was in the hallway putting laundry away. I don't need an update; I already heard what happened," she said as she sat down at the kitchen table. "I understand your desire for more; I just don't think you should rethink your entire life plan based on one bad afternoon."

My dad looked at me with slightly more empathy, "What are you thinking?"

"I'm not sure yet," I said honestly. "I know I still want to go to college. That hasn't changed. Maybe I need to change my plans for the summer? I don't know what I need, to be honest. This morning I didn't know that I needed anything different!"

My dad placed the spatula on the counter before reaching into his pants pocket. "Does your grandmother know about this?"

"Yeah, why?" I asked.

"Because she just sent a text message, she wants to come over and talk to us."

I felt my heartbeat increase with anticipation. It was anyone's guess what my grandma was planning. She was a force to be reckoned with, and when she had an idea, there wasn't typically anything that could stand in her way.

My dad slowly plunked out a reply to her, still never having mastered the skill of texting. "She'll be here shortly; I wonder what crazy idea she's brewing up."

My mom nodded in agreement, "My guess is she isn't coming here to suggest anything. She's coming here to tell us something."

I appreciated that my grandma was known for her sass and stubbornness. It was the reason she'd been successful since she was 18 years old, single-handedly driving the success of Bee's Flowers. She established Bee's in 1969, during a period where there'd been war, protests, and the peace movement. Grandma Betty knew what she wanted in a time of turmoil and never settled for anything less.

Stacia came into the kitchen, "When are we eating? The chicken smells better than it usually does, so that must mean dad's cooking."

My mom looked at her with annoyance, "Is my cooking that bad?"

Stacia winked, in my direction, "No, mom, your cooking is the best."

"I saw you wink!" My mom exclaimed.

We were interrupted by a knock on the door. "I'll get it," Stacia said, leaving the room before dealing with the retaliation of the cooking comment.

We all greeted my grandma as she entered the kitchen and sat down. "Smells good. Greg must be cooking."

Stacia and I chuckled as my mom glared at us.

My dad ignored the cooking comments as he scooped the chicken onto plates. "Mom, are you eating with us?"

"I already ate, but thank you," My grandma answered, turning her gaze to me. "Did you tell them about your day today?"

I nodded. "I was telling them before you texted."

"What's going on?" Stacia asked nosily. "What did you do?"

"Nothing," I sighed, "I just had an interesting day, that's all. I found out I was boring and predictable, and now I can't quit being a baby about it."

"I could have told you that about yourself," Stacia said. "Why didn't you ask me?"

I looked at her with a shocked expression.

"Don't get me wrong," Stacia said quickly, "You're my sister, so I know that you can be fun in ways other people may not see right away. Amber and Luke always used to make you a leader when we played make-believe. There was always a control freak of a queen or president named Rachel."

"Well, okay. I guess leadership qualities are important." I replied, trying to find something positive in what she said.

"Yeah, the queen would like behead people who didn't follow her advice," Stacia said, obviously feeling her bravery increase with my lack of reaction.

I stared at her wide-eyed unsure how to reply.

"Stacia!" My mother exclaimed, "Your sister doesn't point out how obnoxious you can be; you should follow that example."

"We're sisters," Stacia replied, "We're supposed to have a little turmoil, geez."

I rolled my eyes at my sister, though I agreed with her. Goading amongst sisters was par-for-the-course. "So," I continued, "after discovering that my favorite teacher thought I was boring and wrote too many happy endings, I freaked out on Sean and Parker. Then I panicked and ditched school, and now I feel like questioning my life choices. I think I need an adventure in the future."

Grandma Betty's face lit up, "I was hoping that you were thinking about the possibility of something like that. Adventure is why I'm here. I prefer to talk to your parents first separately. We may have a few options, but I want their blessing."

I looked at my parents. Even though I was a senior and almost 18, dinnertime was always when we sat together and talked. I didn't want to leave the table unless they were okay with it. My dad nodded at Stacia, and I and we picked up our plates and headed into the living room to eat in front of the television.

We turned on MTV and started eating, later switching it quickly when my dad entered so he couldn't see that we were watching the Real World. It was our guilty pleasure when we were alone, but my parents weren't too fond of Stacia watching it at her age.

"Can you join us now, Rach?"

I followed my dad back into the kitchen, where I joined them at the table.

"I'm not sure if I've ever told you the story of how I started

Bee's Flowers," my grandma began.

I'd heard it my entire life, so I was surprised she would ask. "Of course, I know the story," I replied.

"Well," my grandma continued, "as with almost everything, there is more to the story than you know, but that is neither here nor there right now. Did you know that my grandfather gave me some money to help fund Bee's?"

I nodded.

"Did you know that he built my first cart and was my first investor?"

I shook my head; I hadn't heard this part of the tale.

"He has always been more than a grandfather to me. We've had a special relationship since he moved in next door. He believed in me and my dream, even though it wasn't what my parents wanted for me. He helped me believe in myself, and I've never forgotten how important it was to have that guidance from him. Though he doesn't remember me as well now, he knows that I was someone special to him, and I'm glad that you all still get to have him in your lives."

I, of course, always sensed that they had a special relationship. Every time we visited my great-great-grandpa, you could tell Grandma Betty was special to him. I had never grasped the importance of his involvement in the success of Bee's Flowers, and I was looking forward to hearing more of the story.

"My parents were not fond of my plan to go straight into the flower business. My mom wanted me to go to college since she didn't go herself. My grandfather helped me slowly and quietly at first and then more openly. He gave me inheritance money so I could start my life, stating he preferred to see me enjoy it rather than waiting until he passed away. I have an opportunity for you today. I've talked to your parents, and they agree with my proposal."

I felt a flutter of nerves, unsure of what was about to be suggested.

"Your grandpa and I decided a long time ago to do something similar. We've set aside some money for after graduation for both of you girls that we want you to use to become established. We also have inheritance funds. However, we want it to go towards something you can enjoy while we are alive and still able to reap the benefits of watching you enjoying it. You'll also get some money after we croak, so don't worry."

"Grandma!" I sputtered, almost choking on the sip of water I'd just taken.

"What? I want to be upfront and honest with you. I know you tend to worry sometimes, and I wanted to alleviate that worry," Grandma Betty winked at me in a Stacia-like manner. Stacia had inherited a lot of Grandma Betty's upfront sass, while mine was usually tapped down and controlled.

"Mom," my dad said, "Why don't you tell her your proposal."

"I have two envelopes," my grandma said, reaching into her purse. "One is an adventure that will yield some thrill but won't put you too far outside your comfort zone. One is an adventure that will provide you with as much excitement as possible. Upon opening the envelope marked number two, the contents will instantly transform you from Rachel to Raquel, adventurer, and thrill seeker. The choice is yours to make, but you have two minutes to make it." My grandma thrust the envelopes in my direction and glanced at her watch, sticking by the two-minute deadline.

Option #1- boring- was written on the first one. The second read: *Option #2- Raquel loves non-stop adventure and thrills.* I glanced at the two envelopes and tried to think about the best choice. I wanted some experience but was I ready to become Raquel, traveler, and thrill-seeker extraordinaire?

I gingerly touched envelope number 1. Then as if Raquel had taken over not only my brain but my body, I snatched up the second envelope. "Let's do this!"

My grandma stood up and let out a youthful squeal of delight. "Yes! I knew you could do it. Now open the damn thing."

I opened the envelope, and inside was plain white card stock. On the front, in all capital letters, it said *YOU ARE GOING*

TO........... There was an arrow pointing to the back of the card.

I flipped the paper over and gasped with surprise, excitement, and nerves.

"I'm going to Europe!" I exclaimed.

6

~Betty~ May 1969

Miss Melissa Younger and Miss Elizabeth Bee-

We are pleased to inform you that we have accepted your rental application for the two-bedroom, one-bathroom apartment lease. While we look forward to adding you to our neighborhood, please be aware of a few rules that you will need to follow. This is for the safety of yourself, your neighbors, and the community.

Absolutely no pets will be allowed. Failure to adhere to this rule will result in a fine of $100 and follow-up apartment checks. If violated more than once, it will result in removal from the premises and termination of the lease.

All guests must leave the residence by 9:30 pm sharp. There will be absolutely no overnight guests, no exceptions. Failure to comply will result in possible termination of lease and removal from premises.

No loud music. Loud music will result in possible removal from the premises.

Any resident caught using illegal substances will be subject to removal from the premises with no refund of deposit.

We value the property and ask that you value and respect it as well. You can help us do this through your actions and appearances. Please adhere to proper dress when in common areas.

Thank you, and welcome to the neighborhood,

Helen Hartford, Manager, Mountain Side Residences

Missy couldn't stop giggling. "So, to sum it up, failure to act like a boring person will result in termination of the lease and be removed from the property and fines. What is this? It's almost 1970, for goodness's sake. Are you sure the manager is one of your grandfather's old schoolmates? Were they friends or enemies?"

I agreed. I'd read it multiple times earlier and felt quite entertained by the vocabulary. My grandfather chuckled when I brought it over to his house, although I felt like he probably agreed with some of it. He and Helen attended school in a small community, and their parents expected them to be respectful so people could respect them in return. I felt like there was a lack of understanding of the changes we, as a generation, were trying to instill. I was okay with some rules, just not oppressive ones. Having to prove myself was just another reason to work harder at making Bee's Flowers successful. Still, I wasn't sure we could abide by all of Helen's requirements.

My grandfather's discussion with me made me more motivated to work hard. I decided that I wanted to venture out on my own. If I'd decided to attend college, I wouldn't be doing so and living at home. I would miss my parents and my proximity to my grandfather, but I was ready.

Missy agreed to share an apartment without hesitation; her grandmother had also planted the roommate seed in her head. She was still planning to hitchhike to California this summer, but Missy's parents were willing to pay the rent, whether she was there or not. I think they were financially supporting her to guarantee Missy's return from her adventure, hoping that they wouldn't lose their daughter to a "nomadic bohemian lifestyle."

The one hard requirement was that she had to return to Colorado in time to start nursing school in the fall. Her grandmother was ecstatic that she would be following in her footsteps. The fact that Missy was in nursing school, coupled with my grandfather's reference, had gotten us the apartment near downtown Denver at a reasonable rate.

Helen had respect for nurses, which she'd made clear when she interviewed us, mentioning something about being a sickly child. The manager had also made it known that if she were to decide based solely on me, she would have denied our application to live there. I nodded in agreement, not able to do anything else yet to prove to her that I would be successful. I didn't know why people felt that my dream of a flower shop was unattainable and crazy. I would have to be extra cautious and try to stay on Helen's good side. I didn't want to let any of my hard-earned money go towards her ridiculous fines, nor did I want to be removed from the premises.

My teachers had also voiced confusion when they found out I hadn't applied to any colleges. One even went so far as to mention that I was "wasting my smarts on plants."

I couldn't believe I still had to defend my dream to anyone. Flowers made me happy. Didn't they do that for everyone else? Instead of letting it discourage me, I let it fuel me, making me more determined to succeed. If they didn't think I could do this, I would work harder to make sure it happened.

Graduation was in a week, and the senior class was buzzing with excitement. We had much to do with our remaining time, including finals, prom, and graduation practice. Some of us that had grown up in the neighborhood were attending the dance together as one large group. I was looking forward to going, but I wasn't looking forward to dealing with recent changes to my friendship with Frank.

Frank and I'd grown up together, and I enjoyed having him as a friend. He was always someone I felt like I could talk to. Growing up, we spent many summer nights wandering around the neighborhood, exploring, and playing games with other neighborhood kids. We tended to act like siblings since we were both only children. Unfortunately, Frank had been making it uncomfortable lately by hinting that he wanted a girlfriend. I hoped that he wasn't directing the hint toward me, but the more he pushed, the more I wanted to back away. He was a neat guy but not my type.

It was even more uncomfortable because Missy liked him, and I wished more than anything that they would date so I could have my friend, Frank, back. My plan for prom was to do all I could to push them together so he would get his wish of a girlfriend with Missy.

She was the type of woman that any man would be lucky to date. She was brilliant and progressive beyond her years. She was verbal in speaking out about war and the need for more peace and love. She had two brothers, and I knew she was afraid they would end up in Vietnam at some point. She was always doing things for other people, and I felt lucky to call her one of my best friends.

My parent's blessing couldn't have come at a better time. With prom coming up, everyone was going to need flowers. My grandfather helped me brainstorm ideas to get the word out about Bee's Flowers. I informed my classmates that I would make a corsage, boutonniere, or flower adornment for less than they could get anywhere else. The orders had been pouring in, and I enlisted Missy to help me with the flowers while we discussed our plans for prom, graduation, and transitioning to our apartment.

In return for her help, I agreed to help Missy by making flower headbands for some classmates to wear at prom or adorn their graduation caps. We were a little nervous that the school administration might not fully appreciate the floral sentiments.

School administrators had been extra sensitive in the past few weeks after what happened at Berkeley. Residents, including students and hippies, upset about a vacant lot that continued to sit empty, had started planting trees and flowers, wanting to make it more beautiful and hospitable. Governor

Ronald Reagan had ordered the National Guard to stand post after that, a confrontation had ensued. In an act of rebellion, protesters had begun planting flowers in empty spaces. "Let a Thousand Parks Bloom" signs were placed all over the area to signal hope and growth. I loved that through planting, they were trying to create beauty while also sending a political message.

"It's going to be groovy living with you, even if Helen will be watching us like a hawk," Missy said as she cut the flower stem, just like I had shown her, and started to fashion it into a corsage with some ribbon.

"Agreed. Helen will watch our every move," I stated as I arranged my floral decoration.

"I can't believe we're already here," Missy declared. "I feel like we were just running around climbing trees and playing jacks, and now we're at an age when we're having to make adult decisions."

I felt the same way. It was crazy to think that the culmination of my school career was ending. I'd never minded attending class, and I felt saddened at the thought of never sitting in another classroom with my peers. I wouldn't be writing more essays or raising my hand to ask or answer a question. Knowing that felt surreal. I hoped my parents would eventually understand that I didn't want to go to college because I thought I was done learning or disliked school. I didn't see the point in spending money on educating myself when I already knew what I wanted to do. If there was anything I knew, it was flowers. I didn't know much about the business side, but I knew I could learn.

I'd briefly thought about getting a business degree. However, my impatience and the fact that it was still very male-dominated made it less appealing. I wasn't worried that I wouldn't make it, but I was worried about men who felt I wasn't as capable being a woman in the business world. By the time my fellow schoolmates finished college, I had hoped to have already been so successful that I had a storefront and no student debt. I couldn't wait to get out there and win the skeptics over with my determination, knowledge, and persistence.

I put my flowers aside for a moment, starting a record so Missy and I could arrange our flowers with some background noise. The melodic guitar for "All Along the Watchtower" filled the room. We talked about how we would love to see Jimi Hendrix in concert someday, possibly even at Red Rocks, as we made the first official Bee's Flowers arrangements.

7

~Rachel~ May 2007

The place I most want to visit in my lifetime is London. They have amazing free museums with a lot of art and history. There are also a lot of book-related places like Baker Street (Sherlock Holmes) and the pub where Edgar Allen Poe wrote. I would also be interested in seeing the old buildings, especially a castle, and learning the stories behind them.

    Rachel Bee-Wilson, age twelve, essay for history

E urope. I was going to Europe. After opening the envelope, I thanked my grandma profusely before calling my grandpa to acknowledge his part in making this happen. He, I learned, hadn't come tonight because he was meeting with a close friend of his, a travel agent, for dinner to work out all the details of my trip.

Out of sheer curiosity, I asked my grandma if I could open the other envelope.

"Sure," she said with a smug smile.

I wondered if inside, I would find a trip somewhere in

Colorado. I peeled back the glued seal. Inside was the same card. I opened it and had to read it a few times before looking at my grandma.

"What?" She asked, shrugging her shoulders coyly but failing to look innocent.

"So, no matter what, you wanted me to go to Europe?" I asked.

"I could have sent you to the boring parts or just one country," she retorted. "I wanted to gauge your commitment level before we made our decisions. The plan was that the type of trip you end up on would be determined by which envelope you chose."

"Well, I'm excited for you," my mother declared as she got to work cleaning up dinner.

Prom was tomorrow, and I wasn't looking forward to telling my friends that I was going to Europe instead of doing the things we'd planned for the summer. Yikes. Hopefully, it would be taken in stride.

I would receive a call in the next few days with the travel details so I could plan accordingly. I currently didn't even know how long I would be gone. The hope was that I would go after graduation and return a few weeks before the end of summer. This would allow me time to settle into the dorms and adjust before school started.

"I'm going to see if Stacia wants to do a facial or help me with my self-tanner," I said as I rose from the table. I kissed Grandma Betty on her cheek and thanked her again. "Tell Grandpa thanks again as well."

I headed upstairs and dropped my backpack inside my room before walking into Stacia's bedroom. She was sitting at her desk, working on homework. I flopped myself dramatically onto her bed.

Stacia swiveled around in her chair. "You seem stressed. Do you want to have a dance party? We could ask grandma if she's still here. That is when all your stress seems gone."

I sat up on her bed. "Really? Dance parties are when I seem

the happiest?"

"Well, yeah. It is the only time I see you let loose. You don't care about anything else when you get in your zone. I love watching it; you don't act like Queen Rachel when you're dancing."

"Well, Queen Rachel can't dance right now. Queen Rachel is branching out and-" I mimicked a drum roll on her bed, "-Heading to Europe! I'll try to have some dance parties there to assist with my issues."

It was my sister's turn to look at me wide-eyed.

"What do you mean?" she asked, looking at me in disbelief.

"Grandma and Grandpa are sending me on an adventure. I rea-"

Stacia interrupted me, "It's our last summer together, and you're leaving me?"

I gulped, a knot forming in my throat. I, stupidly, had not thought about the possibility that my sister would be upset about me leaving, reducing the amount of time we spent together during my last summer at home. I nodded, "I'll write to you. Don't be upset, Stace; I need to do this for my--"

"Please get out of my room," Stacia said sadly.

"Stacia," I replied, desperation in my voice. I hated it when we weren't getting along with each other. "Is it too late to work this out with a dance party?"

"No, thank you. Please, I want to be alone right now." She swiveled back around. She was dismissing me.

I nodded, standing to exit. I paused before leaving her room. "I love you; you know I do. I'm trying to do something unexpected and exciting. I have the rest of my life to be a grown-up. I'll always be your big sister, and I'm sorry if you feel like I'm leaving you behind." With that, I exited, closing her door behind me.

I had been eight years old when Stacia was born. My parents tried unsuccessfully to give me a sibling for many years, and I'm reasonably sure they had given up all hope of my mom becoming pregnant when she found out they were expecting. I was excited at the prospect of a built-in playmate but a little weary of having to share my parents, having been an only child for eight years. A fair share of my friends had siblings, but they were all closer in age. For the most part, the more I thought about it, the more a sibling seemed appealing. I somehow, in my excitement, didn't account for the fact that when she was born, she would be a tiny, helpless being with all the typical baby mannerisms.

I vividly remember the day they brought her home from the hospital. I had visions of pulling my sister out of the car and giving her a hug, which she would enthusiastically return before we painted our nails the same color and put on matching outfits before listening to music.

My Grandma Betty had stayed with me while my parents were in the hospital. She kept trying to give me more realistic expectations, but I saw the potential through glowing eyes. I didn't understand what she was implying when she acknowledged my dreams yet said that I would need to wait a long time to fulfill them as my sister grew older.

When my parents pulled up, the van snow dusted, I'd run to greet them at the front door. Anastasia had looked so frail, bundled in her car seat with a snowsuit and blankets. All you could see was her little doll-like face peeking out. I remember my dreams of a sister, a confidant, and a best friend slowly slipping away as I wondered how this little wisp of a creature could fulfill any of the fantasies I had for the two of us. Now, all that Grandma Betty had been trying to tell me made sense.

For my parent's sake, I decided to try to give her the benefit of the doubt. I plastered a fake smile that first night as they placed her first in my arms and then in the bassinet in their room. By the next morning, all bets were off. It had become clearer minute-by-minute that baby Stacia was 100% incapable of being any of the things I needed and wanted. She cried continuously. What made it worse was that I could hear every little wail from my bedroom down the hall, even after covering my ears with multiple pillows and blankets.

I discovered that the days were just as horrible as night. When she wasn't crying, she slept regularly. She smelled like poop and sour milk throw up and took all my parent's attention away from me. Everything revolved around her from the day she came home from the hospital, and her timeline became what we based all our activities around.

Then one day, she started to grow on me, and I have the photographic evidence to prove it. Stacia was about three months old, and the Colorado winter was transitioning to spring. Spring in Colorado can be sunny and beautiful or snowy and wet. It happened to be a particularly lovely, sunny weekend, and my parents had driven us to a park for a picnic. They needed me to hold her while they made sandwiches, and that's when it happened: Stacia looked up at me with utter adoration.

A smile erupted across her face as she looped her tiny hand around my pinkie. I looked into her big, gray eyes and became putty in her little hands. I knew at that moment that the best friend, confidant, and playmate would someday work out. Until then, I would be her big sister, her protector. My mom had snapped a picture at that moment, catching a look of bliss on both of our faces. From that day on, my thoughts and feelings about having a sister drifted in a positive direction. Of course, she loved my parents, but you could tell that I held a special place in her world.

The mornings, when I would hear her babbling in her crib before my parents could get her out, were the best. She would look at me with her sleep-crusted eyes and matted-down hair and raise her arms to me, the smile on her face making her eyes even brighter. She would allow me to lift her out of her crib and snuggle up close to me as I fed her a morning bottle, making me feel like the most important thing in her world.

When she started walking, it was me she would wobble towards when we were all on our knees, arms extended with toys or snacks, trying to bribe her. "Come here, Stacia," we would all chant as she tottered towards us, collapsing in my arms most of the time.

When she got older, it was me she would want to place a band-aid on all the boo-boos. "Sissy do it," she would say, her little s's coming out as more of a" th," so it sounded like "Thithy."

When she started kindergarten, it was me she wanted to help pick out her first outfit. She wanted to wear jeans and a plaid shirt, an outfit very similar to what I had planned to wear for my first day of seventh grade. When she got in trouble on day two of kindergarten for sassing the teacher, it was me she cried to after my parents scolded her.

Because of our 8-year age difference, we never experienced the pain or the pleasure of attending the same school or having the same friend group. Stacia did have the benefit of me experiencing things first and attempting to guide her in doing it better. The truth was, Stacia was very independent and a little sassy and didn't need my guidance. Still, I was always there to offer it up anyway.

When it had become apparent to Stacia that I wanted to have friends my age, Stacia started venturing around the neighborhood until she found playmates. She quickly made two best friends in the area, Amber, and Luke, who were still her best friends. She was always with them, getting into minor mischief, riding around on their bikes, and having adventures comparable to some of the great capers in classic eighty's movies.

I loved coming home and hearing about their adventures and doing my part as a big sister to encourage fun and discourage anything too crazy. Seeing her smile while she was with those two diminished the guilt I felt as the oldest sibling, wanting to have her own life, separate from her little sister.

I would have to make up for my leaving this summer somehow. Hopefully, as she got older, she would understand that when you came to a crossroads, sometimes you had to do things for yourself regardless of how it affected others.

8

~*Betty~ May 1969*

Class of 1969

We proudly announce the high school graduation of Elizabeth Kathleen Bee.

You are cordially invited to our residence on May 30th from 1:00 to 3:00 pm for a luncheon to join us in celebration. Please RSVP at your earliest convenience.

Prom was over, and I was honestly relieved. The night had gone relatively smoothly, but after getting all the flower orders ready, I was exhausted before the dance even started. All the girls: Missy, myself, and Jan got ready together, Jan opting for a more traditional prom look while Missy and I deviated a little bit. We briefly contemplated going barefoot, but I squashed that idea, afraid our principal would have a fit. As it stood, I wasn't sure if he'd be okay with how bohemian we looked. We were hoping that he would grace us with some leniency since it was our senior year.

He was a great principal, just behind the times. He was

close to retiring, and most of us felt like his views on things hadn't changed much in our four years of high school. I hoped whoever replaced him was more progressive and okay with the direction we needed to head as a society, especially in Denver. I'd seen him use a ruler to measure skirt lengths while most of us were dying inside to wear pants to school without comment.

We planned on meeting up with the boys for dinner. I hoped that we would end up with an odd number so no one felt like they had to pair up. Things had been less awkward with Frank lately, and I hoped that continued. In years past, we all attended the dance with whomever we were going steady with now or coupled up for convenience. That requirement didn't exist this year, possibly because pairing up seemed like a small thing to stress about with so much going on in our world. Or perhaps, in our senior year, we didn't care about anything but attending and having fun.

Most of the dresses we were shown when we went shopping consisted of brightly colored floor-length numbers with collared necks and flowered lace, which flowed from the neck to the bodice with a bow at the empire waist. The shop associates informed us that big bouffant hairstyles and white gloves would be very popular prom looks this year.

I picked a dress I liked, a navy-blue floor length with white lace overlay, and my mom sewed it. The original dress was traditional, so my mom added some special touches like flowers instead of a bow at the waist. It turned out both beautiful and unique, and I loved that no one at the dance would be wearing the same thing as me.

I decided to avoid the white gloves and bouffant because they seemed too formal for the look I wanted. Instead, I wore my hair down with flowers arranged as a headband so they would only be visible peeking out of the top part of my hair. Jan had gotten a traditional orange dress with a collared neck and orange bow at the bodice. She spent hours at the salon before coming to my house and arrived with a head full of strawberry blond hair in a large bouffant. White gloves hung perfectly pressed with her dress.

"I'm not sure I will be able to get my dress over my head," Jan admitted when I complimented her dress and hairstyle. "Hopefully, I'll be able to slip into it somehow."

Missy decided to wear a floral sundress and interweave flowers in her hair. She looked very bohemian, and the only way she could have probably shocked anyone more would have been by wearing bell bottoms and a vest like they were wearing in California. Colorado was progressive, but nowhere near as much as California.

Dinner went well. Thankfully there were four women and three men, so no one was stuck awkwardly coupled up. Since all of us were from the neighborhood, there was never a dull moment as we had lots of stories to share. Steve's Diner was always a favorite and, therefore, the most fitting place for us to go for one of the last meals we would have together before facing adulthood. In a few weeks, the expectation was that we would transition from young adults focusing mainly on school our whole lives to adults who had to think for themselves and make decisions that would impact the rest of our lives.

We talked about the old days in the neighborhood, which we mostly spent outside. We talked about playing kick the can and baseball in the park near our house and riding our bikes to Steve's for milkshakes during the summer. We talked about building snowmen in the fresh powdery snow and how when it was too cold to be outside, we would gather in someone's house to listen to the radio or watch television together. We laughed about the time we decided to play spin-the-bottle, where most of us had our first awkward kisses.

"I'm sad it won't ever be the same," Jan stated during a quiet moment. We all nodded, agreeing with her sentiment.

"I'm thankful for the memories, though," Frank said as he raised his malt to all of us. We copied Frank and raised our frozen creations, clinking them together, smiling, and feeling thankful for the fun times.

It hadn't gotten awkward until we walked into prom.

Principal Hartford tried to give Missy a hard time about her "hippie look," and it took some gentle persuasion on my end to get him to drop it. Once we had proved that we weren't under the influence of any mind-altering substances, like marijuana, he relented and allowed us to enter.

"Nothing will get us down," I said as we entered the gym, which the prom committee covered in starry night decor. We found a table where we could all sit together. We got our pictures taken by a professional photographer, mixing up the couples, so everyone had some photos with a member of the opposite sex.

I was surprised when Frank came up to me since he and Missy were flirting during most of the dinner. He held out his hand and bowed. "Dance?" He asked.

I considered saying no, but it didn't seem to be a romantic gesture, just a friendly one. I grasped his hand, and he led me over to the dance floor. We started to sway in time to the music.

"You'll always be one of my favorite friends," Frank said after the song concluded, and he led me back to the table.

"You too," I replied

"Missy looks stunning tonight," He said to me as we neared the group. She was approaching the table with cups of punch in tow.

I pushed him towards her. "Quick, go ask her to dance. Jerry Collins is heading in her direction."

Frank hurried towards her, and I could see her face light up at his question, obviously excited. They grasped hands and headed towards the dance floor.

I enjoyed the time with my classmates until I eventually became so tired that I could hardly keep my eyes open. Instead of ending the party too early for the group, I said my goodbyes and decided to walk the half-mile home.

I walked the familiar path from the school to my parent's house, looking at the landmarks I knew like the back of my hand. It felt strange that my days walking this route was down to a number I could count with my two hands. I thought back to being in elementary school and junior high, wanting so badly to be in high school, and now that pivotal point in my life was over.

As I walked, I reminisced. I'd breathed in the warm Colorado air and thought about what was in store for myself and my friends. We had the world, and the future, at our fingertips.

~

"Elizabeth Kathleen Bee!" I woke up abruptly, hearing a shriek from my mother and a frantic knocking on my door.

"What?" I asked groggily as she threw my bedroom door open.

"Graduation is in a few hours, and you need to get to school!" She informed me.

I sat up straight in bed, panicked. Thankfully I'd planned last night and fallen asleep with my hair wrapped around soup cans so I could wake up to some loose waves in my hair. Even with my hair needing less work, I was still going to have to hurry. How was it possible that I'd never even been a minute late in my entire school career, and now on the day that marked the end of it, my alarm clock didn't work?

I quickly unrolled my hair, shook out the waves, threw on my dress, and grabbed the hanger that housed my cap and gown. I shoveled down some oatmeal and drove frantically to the school.

I arrived with a few minutes to spare by the skin of my teeth. Frank and Missy were already there, holding hands and beaming at each other. I joined them and waited for the signal to walk onto the field.

My strategy from prom last weekend had worked, and from the sound of it, they would be going on as many dates as possible before Missy left on her trip next week. Seeing them together, I wondered if I'd possibly misread Frank's advances, and I hoped this would renew my strained friendship with him. Thankfully, I could tell from the look on both of their faces that I was the last thing on their minds.

"It's time," Missy said, squeezing my hand with

excitement as they gathered us into two lines before we marched onto the field. We sat patiently, trying to listen to the commencement speeches but failing as our minds wandered to the parties that would occur tonight, the future, and the finality of it all sinking in.

Soon, they made the graduation announcement for us, the class of 1969. Missy and I shrieked, hugging each other before throwing our caps in the air. We didn't rush off immediately, staying on the field to take pictures and hug friends and family members. We made plans for the evening before leaving to attend the family graduation events.

My graduation lunch was lovely, with many members of my mom's large family and my father's small one coming to wish me well and celebrate together. I got to see cousins I hadn't seen in a long time and catch up on life with the elderly relatives. I only received criticism about my business from a particularly grumpy aunt, which didn't dishearten me much since she complained about everyone and everything anyway.

Missy came over with her grandmother towards the end of the party, and I couldn't help but notice my grandfather and her grandmother sitting in the corner, visiting with each other.

"My grandmother is being extremely quiet on what's going on with them. It would be so groovy if we were related, though!" Missy said as she ate a piece of my mom's famous apple crisp pie.

"He won't tell me anything either," I said, stealing a bite of her dessert for myself.

"We could be related!" Missy exclaimed as she moved her plate out of my reach, "Maybe then, your mom will finally share her pie recipe with me!"

"I doubt it," I replied, "She hasn't shared it with me yet."

After all my guests left it was time for Missy and me to head to a graduation party. My mother had lectured us, as she always did, about the importance of behaving like ladies and not partaking in any alcohol or drugs.

We nodded in agreement, even though Missy and I'd

made a pact to try a beer for the first time tonight. We were both 18 and could legally have a drink, so we were going to. Frank even offered to drive us to and from the party, so we got around safely.

I hoped my mother would be fast asleep by the time I got home. I had one week left at my parent's house, and I wanted it to go smoothly. If she woke up, I just hoped that she would understand that my classmates and I needed to come together in this time of transition and celebrate life and our accomplishments. Who knew what the future would hold for any of us: Success? War? Death? Life? Peace?

9

~Rachel~ May 2007

Prom 2007

> *Theme: celestial or enchanted evening*
> *Colors: deep blues, yellows, gold, anything with sparkle*
> *Props: a gazebo for pictures or forest backdrop (borrow from the theater?), hanging crescent moon as alternate picture background, lots of twinkling lights, anything with stars, tulle to drape from fixtures, fog machine for mist*
> *A written proposal from Rachel Bee-Wilson to Janet Ying, president of the student council, age 17*

My alarm went off early, and I felt both excitement and trepidation. Once a Bee woman made her mind up about something, it was hard to convince her otherwise. I was committed to going, but I hated that Stacia was sad, and I hadn't told Sean what was going on yet. Last night I apologized via text, blaming it on prom committee jitters. His reply was simple.

It's okay, I love you.

I sent a text to Parker as well. *Dude*, he'd written, *I was excited to see you act irrationally. It's better not to hold that shit in.* It had made me smile, picturing how I looked grinding the gears while attempting to peel out of the parking lot.

Samantha was ecstatic that I was going on an adventure. She'd been on a "guilt trip" to Europe with her father last year, and on the phone last night she had helped me write a list of some of the places she recommended I go and the things I should do there.

~Raquel's Adventure Seeking Opportunities~

UK- London- see Piccadilly Circus at night when it's lit up, ride in a classic London taxi, have high tea, take a tour on a double-decker bus with a cruise on the Thames, and eat curry at every opportunity

Spain- Madrid- see a live flamenco show, visit a monastery, take a sunset sailboat cruise

Italy- Rome- eat pizza with a knife and fork, drink rich Italian wine, ride a scooter without crashing

Czech- Prague- take a picture next to the John Lennon Wall, walk across St. Charles Bridge, and tour a castle

I didn't know where I would end up yet, or if I would have a say in it, but every country I researched sounded terrific. I was getting progressively excited about traveling, just not about telling anyone else about it. Last night after Stacia coldly made me leave her room, I'd gone downstairs to talk to my parents. They voiced understanding that I wanted to travel but seemed disappointed that we would have less time together during my last summer living at home. I promised that the family would be a priority when I returned from my trip, no matter how long I was gone. Plus, unless Sean and I moved in together right after freshman year, it wasn't like I wouldn't be back.

I hoped Sean would be willing to stay with me despite my decision and not get too upset. I knew if he put me in the same position, I'd be sad and confused. Still, I didn't think I'd walk away, especially if it were a decision that could ultimately make him a better partner.

After going downstairs for breakfast, I said hi to my parents and Stacia, and it became clear that my sister was still giving me the silent treatment. My mom was preparing to go to our cabin in Grand Lake soon to open it for the summer. Stacia delved fully into helping prep, which she never volunteered for normally. I knew that she was trying to avoid me. I used all my usual tactics to get her forgiveness. I even offered to take her to my hair and nail appointments and pay for her pampering. Nothing worked.

We were going to prom in a large group, and we'd collectively decided to go all out with a fancy dinner and a stretch limo. Parker and Sean were both up for Prom King, and though they were trying to play it off, I knew they were both excited.

Samantha and I made our appointments simultaneously, and we were going to finish getting ready at my house. Everyone was meeting there for all the obligatory pre-prom pictures.

"What did Sean say about Europe?" Samantha asked as she selected a magenta-colored nail polish that matched the halter-style dress with the rhinestone brooch adornment she had chosen for the dance. I picked a clear polish at first, and it immediately dawned on me that that this act seemed too Rachel-like. My gown, also a halter style with a jeweled clasp, was a run-of-the-mill simple black dress. Now I felt the need to sass it up a bit, like my European-traveling alter ego Raquel would. I picked hot pink nail polish instead.

"Um, I haven't told him yet," I admitted.

Samantha's jaw opened in surprise, "Wait a minute, I must've misheard you. It sounded like you said that you haven't told Sean yet."

"In my defense, all my plans changed less than 24 hours ago," I replied. Though I did have time to tell him last night on the phone or in person, I just couldn't.

I loved Sean; I did. I didn't know how to deal with

disappointing him. He was the sweetest guy, and if I were going to have a Disney-like existence with anyone, it would be him. I wanted that, didn't I?

I tried to put it all out of my head as we got pampered, discussing Europe plans, riding the train of avoidance as long as humanly possible. I wasn't naive enough to think that would completely work in my favor, but I needed some time between the disappointments.

I decided I would pull him aside after the dance. I didn't want our senior prom hindered by a change in the plans we'd had for so long. Even if I was the one who'd decided to shake things up, Sean didn't deserve to have his prom night ruined, especially since there was a chance he would win prom king.

Although it had taken several hours, Samantha and I now felt like we were prom beautiful. I'd never been too interested in pampering as it involved me sitting still for way too long and spending money I would rather use for practical things. On normal days I prided myself on my ability to tame my thick, wavy hair and apply mascara in less than 10 minutes.

My anticipation for tonight kept building; I couldn't wait to see the student body dressed up and having fun. The prom theme this year was celestial nights, my idea, and I'd been texting the prom committee members all morning. Thankfully as a senior, I could delegate, and doing so meant that I had to trust them to do everything correctly. I tried to remember that one of my goals was to relinquish some of these control issues. I was just ready for the group to show up so we could take pictures and get on with our night.

"What's up, party people?" It was like a scene out of a 1990s prom movie. We were outside waiting for the guys when we heard the faint sounds of music. The limousine came into view with Parker popping out of the top. "This is Why I'm Hot" by Mims played at full volume. Sean had one of the side windows rolled down, and he was performing his go-to dance move, which consisted of him waving one hand repeatedly up and down in the air. Samantha and I danced our way over to the limo.

Everyone looked elegant in their prom attire. Parker and his boyfriend, Trey, were wearing matching tuxes. Parker added some skater flare by wearing a Thrasher beanie over his perfectly styled dreadlocks. He was the only person I could imagine pulling that look off while still looking stylish and sophisticated.

Our parents took many pictures, individually and as a group. Grandma Betty mostly behaved herself, thankfully, and neither she nor my parents mentioned the trip.

Samantha's dad, Dale, proved his guilty dad status when he handed over his credit card and insisted on paying for everyone's dinner. The guys looked at him with excitement, knowing how expensive the restaurant would be, still Rachel knew that they would all make sure Samantha was okay with that before taking him up on his offer.

As we pulled out of our cul-de-sac, Samantha insisted on letting him pay. She reminded us that her mother had still not recovered from the turmoil of the secretary scandal and divorce. "If you feel guilty, send my mom a bouquet from Bee's. It's her favorite place and cheaper than dinner."

On the way to dinner, we let Parker DJ as we all danced in our seats, hanging out the windows at stoplights. The only problem was that we couldn't hear each other over the din of the music.

Sean beamed at me; before mouthing, "You look beautiful."

Every couple seemed to be enjoying each other, even Clint and Samantha, who kept leaning into each other and flirting. Clint agreed to go to prom with Samantha even though they'd broken up almost a year ago. They started as friends, and after dating for a few weeks, they realized they were better off remaining that way. They stayed cordial and even liked to play matchmaker for each other. I joked with them that they would end up married someday.

During an abrupt end to a song, Clint put a damper on the night. "What do you mean she hasn't told Sean that she's leaving all summer?" he asked loudly, not expecting the song to end.

All eyes in the limo turned in my direction. I felt like my heart would explode, and a thousand butterflies skittered around in my abdomen. I opened my mouth to explain when the next song started, making it impossible for Sean to hear me. Everyone averted their eyes, but I could tell they were dying to watch and hear what would transpire.

The song that had interrupted my explanation was "You Give Love a Bad Name," of course, and I ignored the overwhelming urge to bury my head in my hands.

Samantha looked at me apologetically, having scooted away from Clint as punishment for his indiscretion. "I'm sorry," he mouthed.

I tried to grab Sean's hand, but he moved it under his leg, impossible to grasp. I placed my hand back into my lap and stared straight ahead, hoping to fix this as soon as possible.

We pulled up to the restaurant, and everyone shuffled excitedly out of the limo, except for Sean and me. I put my arm on his, gesturing for him to stay behind. I needed to talk to him.

"We'll meet up with you in a few," I said to Samantha as Sean leaned against the limo, arms crossed in defense. It would be better for everyone if we took a few minutes.

"I'm going to Europe for part of the summer," I blurted out.

"What?" Sean said with uncertainty.

"I'm leaving as soon as we graduate for at least a month."

"Wow," he replied, "I'm not sure what to say right now." He paced around the limo for a few minutes, head down in thought. "Can we come back to this tomorrow? Tonight, is our senior prom, and one of our last big events with all of us together. I'm going to need time to wrap my head around this."

I nodded, happy that he hadn't gotten upset and broken up with me immediately. Still, I was nervous about how he would feel tomorrow. I grabbed his hand as we headed inside, but with the loose way he held it in return I could tell that he was still mad.

Dinner was delicious. I wished I was wearing pants so I could unbutton them as all the guys were joking about doing because they were so full.

We arrived at the dance as it was already in full swing. I tried to lower my expectations for perfection, not wanting to walk into the prom as hyper-critical Rachel but more like nonchalant Raquel. I entered the gym and gasped. The committee members had done such a great job with the decorations.

The lights in the gym had been dimmed, illuminated by strings of white lights twinkling like stars. Amongst the tiny glimmers were larger star-shaped lanterns with cutouts in the sides, so light shone through in different shapes and designs. A mist machine was producing just the right amount of ambiance, making it look romantically foggy. A gazebo stood in the corner of the gym with a photographer taking pictures inside it.

I excused myself from the group to thank the prom committee members and returned to my friends, just in time for a slow song, the newest from The Frey. I wasn't sure at first if Sean was feeling up to dancing with me, but he held his hand out and guided us to the center of the gym. I put my hands on his shoulders, and we started to sway in time to the music. He pulled me closer, and I rested my head on his shoulder. "I'm sorry," I whispered into his ear.

"I can't pretend to know what's going on," he said. "I'm sad, but I get it. I want you to be happy."

I blinked away a few tears that slipped out, and they fell onto his tuxedo jacket. We continued to sway and hold each other like it was the last time we'd ever be that happy and oblivious, and maybe it would be. Only time would tell what was in store for us. We joined the rest of the group, and we danced our hearts out to all the songs. Belting out the words to the ones we knew at the top of our lungs.

Soon it was time for the prom queen and king announcement. Sean, Parker, and a wrestler, Joseph Niccolus, were in the running. I was usually a nice person, and it took a lot for someone to rub me the wrong way, but Joseph was an asshole. Plain and simple. He'd only gotten a nomination because he had dirt, real or fabricated, on so many people.

He was notorious for leaving negative comments on people's social media to make himself feel better. People were usually too frightened of what he would do in retaliation if they called him out on his bad behavior. I hoped that if karma accounted for anything, he would never move out of his mom's basement and do nothing but troll people for happiness. I knew it was harsh, but I'd seen him hurt too many people, including me, to make himself feel better.

We gathered near the stage to be supportive, and we cheered as Sean and Parker made their way up. I shot daggers at the back of Joe's head as he walked onstage, knowing that I couldn't glare openly at him. If he saw me staring, he would consider it a win. I decided to be a good sport still and clapped for him.

Parker had quite the cheer section since he was a fashion icon at our school. Our principal came up and spoke briefly. He thanked the prom committee and encouraged us to attend an after-Prom party where there wouldn't be drinking, which earned him a few boos from the back of the gym.

"Well, I must say," Principal Andrews began, "In all of our school's history, we've never had a tie for Prom king. Your two kings tonight are Sean and Parker." The auditorium went crazy. I was excited that our classmates recognized them and that Joseph, the troll, had not been picked. Karma- one, Joseph- zero.

"Calm down," Principal Andrews roared into the microphone after the clapping continued, "I would love to have a chance to announce the Prom queen." He paused dramatically. "Your queen for the Class of 2007 is Drew Duncan."

The auditorium erupted in cheers again. Drew was one of the sweetest people in our class; she participated in multiple clubs to make our school a better place. She was a cheerleader, she competed on the debate team, she volunteered for numerous charities, and of course, she was drop-dead gorgeous. She had a fantastic personality, and of all the people who could have been Prom queen, she deserved it.

Sean, Parker, and Drew stepped forward, and Principal Andrews placed crowns on their heads. "Time for the Royalty dance. You'll have to figure out how that will work."

They started playing "No One" By Alicia Keys, and all three of them wrapped their arms around each other and swayed to the music. After a few minutes of the three dancing, they started to grab other people surrounding them. Soon, their little dance circle had turned into a giant glob of people hugging and swaying.

I looked on stage as we were all dancing and reveling in our moment of togetherness and saw Joe still up there, looking at us with disgust. I started to feel bad for a moment before realizing that I didn't care. Trolls exist to suck the joy out of happy moments, to crush those that are enjoying themselves, and enjoying life, and I wasn't going to give him that power.

I smiled and gave him a little wave, which just caused his scowl to deepen. I wasn't one of those people who thought the world was full of smiles and rainbows. Still, I didn't quite understand people whose only happiness came from others unhappiness. I decided that giving him any more of my time would further satisfy his troll desire. Instead, I gave my attention back to the people who deserved it, my friends and classmates, on what was one of our last nights all together.

10

~*Betty~ June 1969*

Miss Elizabeth Bee-

We are pleased to let you know that in accordance with the City of Denver Municipal Code, your request for a business license for Bee's Flowers is approved. Please make sure to display the license at your place of business. You may reference the enclosed envelope for more information.

Mrs. Courtney Cleaver, County Secretary

"Betty," my mom called from down the hall, "your grandpa is here. He can help you finish packing while your father loads the boxes."

The time from graduation to moving day had flown by. Yesterday, Missy and Frank had come over together to figure out the logistics of today's move. Missy was leaving soon, and we decided it would be outta sight if we could move in quickly and have a few days together to get organized before she embarked on her adventure.

Graduation seemed like a distant memory, even though

it had only been a week. Thankfully with the move, I'd been too preoccupied to focus much on the void not having school would possibly leave. It felt like we were on summer vacation, and I was going somewhere temporary, like summer camp. I knew that eventually, that feeling would wear off, especially once summer ended.

I was in just as much denial that I wouldn't be living at home any longer. Sleeping last night in my bed felt normal until I remembered it would be the last time. As a child, I'd pictured not leaving until I was married or leaving for college.

I was sad that I wouldn't see my family every day. I would miss hearing about my mother's latest seamstress victory or struggle and smelling my father's scent after working in the shop all day. Knowing I would see less of them reaffirmed the need to pick my battles with them carefully and appreciate them more. I didn't want to think about one of the most significant voids, which was going to be left by not seeing my grandfather as freely. He was so dear to me, and I'd come to depend on him for so much.

Over the last week, I began going through my room and packing only the things I would need to take with me. My parents would let me leave anything I wanted in my room in case something fell through with the apartment, Helen got stricter with the rules, or I just wanted to come to visit them overnight.

I packed a few nostalgic mementos with me in case I got homesick. One of them was a quilt, given to my parents when I was born. I'd always had it displayed in my room. It was beautiful with patchwork flowers and honeybees. It was, of course, fitting for me to take it. It also smelled like home, which would be comforting.

There was a knock on the door, and my grandfather entered. He was carrying two steaming mugs. He made the best tea with a dash of milk and honey.

"Thanks, Grandpa."

"It looks pretty empty here, Honey-Bee." He surveyed the room, sitting on my desk chair.

"I know," I said as I continued packing my books. "It's surreal."

"I'm going to miss your company, Bug," he said affectionately.

"I'm going to miss your company, Grandpa," I said, moving forward to squeeze his hand.

"I feel like we've had a few serious talks lately," he said, squeezing mine in return, "but I need you to know that you mean so much to me. Your support was instrumental in me finding some peace over the death of my June. Since we are business partners and all, we may need to have some business meetings, And I hope to still see you for family dinners."

"I'm only thirty minutes away," I commented. "We can still see each other a lot."

"Yes, we will," he squeezed my hand. "Now, put me to work."

We finished packing in less than an hour, and the truck was loaded, ready to head to the apartment. I did one final walkthrough of my parent's house. I knew that I would still spend plenty of time there, but it wouldn't be the same, and it would no longer be my home.

Missy and Frank met us at the apartment to unload. My parents had surprised me a few days ago with a new bed that my father and grandfather had made. They crafted it from the same beautiful wood as my cart, and there were engraved flowers on the headboard. It made me feel grown-up heading into my apartment with furniture.

Missy's grandmother also donated items, giving us a couch and some chairs in her basement for our living area. Our parents had collectively given us kitchen utensils, dishes, pots, and pans, so we wouldn't have to purchase much. Neither of us cared about having a lot of things in the apartment; we were just happy to have places to sleep, sit, and the ability to cook.

With all of us there we got all the furniture inside quickly, and the only thing remaining was my flower cart. It suddenly looked larger than I remembered causing instant panic. Where was I going to put it?

"Missy," I said, pulling her to the side, "where will we put the cart?"

"Wow, that is radical!" Missy said before addressing the question.

"I know. He did a great job, and I don't want to leave it outside."

"We're on the first floor," Missy said. "We can keep it in the living room."

"That wouldn't bother you?" I asked, trepidation all over my face.

"I think it's far out that you have the cart and are going down your path. I support you; you're one of my best friends. You've always supported my adventures, and I'll always do whatever I can to support yours."

I pulled her into a giant hug, "I'm so lucky to have you in my life."

We got the cart out, and with a few turns of a screwdriver, my grandfather got it reassembled. Thankfully it was narrow enough to fit through the doorway. Honestly, had it not been, I would have found a way to make that doorway bigger without Helen finding out. Nothing was going to stop me from my dream before it even had a chance to begin.

It would be tighter quarters with the cart inside, but it was a sacrifice I was willing to make, and I appreciated the fact that Missy would deal with it as well. I was planning on starting to sell my flowers in the next week. First, I wanted to settle into the apartment before researching places within walking distance where I could get the most business. Now that the city had approved my license, I was more motivated than ever.

My parents, Grandpa, and I collapsed onto the furniture in the living room, the exhaustion from the move finally catching up with us. Missy and Frank left, going on another date with their limited time together.

"Your mom and I have never had to move anywhere," my dad said, "We've only moved other people."

"I'm never leaving our house," my mom replied, "so you won't ever have to."

After a brief rest, my mom stood up and motioned for me to join her in the kitchen, "You may as well take advantage of help while you have it."

I gathered my strength, got up, and followed her. She was already unpacking kitchen utensils.

"I can't believe my baby is all grown up," my mom said so quietly I almost didn't hear her. "I'm going to miss you so much."

"Aw, mom," I said, gently setting the silverware she was frantically sorting aside. I pulled her in for a hug. "I'm going to miss you so much. I'll always be your baby. It will seem strange, but I'm a phone call or a short drive away. You will probably see me so much that you'll be sick of me. Imagine if I were going away for school, then we would have limited time."

My mom pulled back from our hug, tears misting her eyes, "I feel like you were just a little girl, running around with all the neighborhood kids, skinning your knees, playing in the dirt, being rowdy. Even then, you were so much like me, independent and headstrong. It used to frustrate me how alike we were, but now I am incredibly proud. I'm lucky to have you as my daughter."

I tried to put on a brave face, knowing that it would be a rough night if I faltered now. I wouldn't look very dedicated if I spent the first night on my own at my parent's house.

"I love that I'm like you, Mom. You don't know how much I appreciate that you gave me a fierce streak. Without both of your guidance, faith in me, and love, I would have been okay with doing what I felt others wanted me to do and just existed. I appreciate that you're giving me the chance to do more than that. Even though you don't love the thought of me not going to college, you have supported me, and that is more than I could have hoped. I have a chance to be more, and I'm stubborn enough that, mark my words, Bee's Flowers will be a success."

My mom pulled me in for another hug, "You are enough like me that I have no doubt you will be successful."

"I read in the paper a few days ago that they've been talking about flower power since Berkeley. Maybe, now is a good time to go into the flower business."

My mom smiled, separating from me and returning to her boxes, "If anyone can spread the word about the power of flowers, it would be you. You've always been a little garden nymph. That reminds me, I almost forgot, Bee tradition and all."

My mother reached into her dress pocket and pulled out a bumblebee pin. "As you know, it is a tradition that each Bee member gets a talisman from their parents when they enter adulthood. I picked the honeybee because of our namesake and because the bee symbolizes community, personal power, and the sun. These are all things that you will need in your business."

I grabbed the delicate pin before beaming at her, pinning it to my shirt. "I love it, and I'll wear it for good luck," I said, kissing her cheek.

"I'm glad you like it, dear. Now, what are those men of ours doing?"

I peeked into the quiet living room, knowing that the silence indicated that both men were napping. My grandfather was lounging on the davenport, snoring peacefully, and my father was on the chair, doing the same.

I went back into the kitchen to report their activities and enjoy the process of my mother helping me in becoming a woman.

Part Two

Protea

Daring
Courage
Diversity
Transformation

11

~Rachel~ June 2007

Dear Stacia-

I'm sorry that my leaving has resulted in you acting like a turd to me. I hope to remedy some of this by writing to you every day. You're going to be so sick of getting postcards and letters from me, but I don't care. It's my job as your big sister to do things that irritate you, mostly to get back at you for annoying me. I'm sitting at my gate at Denver International, waiting to board my plane. I'm trying to ignore what you did to my luggage last night. I get that you're pissed, but my clothing didn't deserve what you did to it, ha ha.

I'm going to tell you something I haven't told anyone yet. I'm nervous. I'm scared that I'll be a new person when I return, and I don't want this to hurt anyone else. I may love adventures so much that I'll become a tulip farmer in Denmark, and you'll have to purchase wooden clogs to fit in when you come to visit me.

I love you, Anastasia, and I'm glad you get to have me as your sister. Just kidding, it has always been me that has been the lucky one. Please don't be mad at me.

Love always,

Rach

My mind and my body were currently at war with themselves. I was nervous about my flight. I'd never flown solo, and for my first time I would be traveling to a different continent. I was trying to hold it together, but I knew if I wanted to calmly embark on this journey, I might need to swallow one of the pills Samantha had made me put in my Ibuprofen bottle last night.

"You'll need to suck it up and take one of these," Samantha insisted as she grabbed the travel-sized bottle I was about to put into my purse.

"You know I don't like to take pills," I said, shaking my head as she plopped an unknown medication into the bottle.

"You're going to be a hot mess if you don't sleep, and you know it. The tour group activities start tomorrow, which doesn't leave a lot of room for forgiveness if you're tired and cranky. If you sleep on the tour bus, you'll miss everything, and the people you are touring with may dislike it if you snap at them!"

"We have several sightseeing days, but I agree, I don't want to miss anything. I know I'm not the most pleasant person to deal with without sleep," I admitted. "I'll think about it, but I'm only going to take them if I get too desperate."

I felt more than that now.

I looked around to make sure no one was watching me. I knew that it would look like I was taking Ibuprofen, but I felt guilty, being the rule follower that I was. I was taking an unknown medication before getting on a plane. No one was looking at me, so I slipped the mystery pill into my mouth and washed it down with a sip of water. I hoped whatever it was wouldn't work right away.

I got comfortable in my chair, picked up a book, and tried to calm down when I heard a scuffle. I was in the process of putting my book down when a heavy body crushed me. "Ahhhhhhhhh," I shrieked in surprise, causing those around me to turn and look at what the commotion was.

"I'm so sorry," the person attempting to get off my lap said. He jumped up, brushed himself off, and glared at his friends behind him before turning back to me. "My ass of a friend over there thought it would be funny to trip me."

Three other men, all looking to be around my age, appeared behind him. One of them looked guilty. "How was I supposed to know that this would be the one time you would fall." He grabbed the dripping cup from the ground near my chair. "Sorry, miss, but he should have been able to stay on his feet." He turned and walked towards the trash can, leaving me in shock. Was that supposed to be an apology?

I felt wetness soaking through my shirt. It was embarrassing enough to have someone fall on me in front of an audience. It was mortifying to realize that my shirt was no longer white. It was wet, sticky, and brown.

"Wow," was all I could manage. "I'm going to go get myself a napkin."

"Please allow me." Before I could stop him, the man from my lap turned and went in the same direction as the tripper, hopefully to talk to him about the proper way to apologize.

A few of the people around looked at me with sympathy. I took a cleansing breath and plastered a smile on my face even though I didn't feel okay inside. I had gone from being nervous about traveling to being irritated. I would have understood if it had been a mistake, but it hadn't been.

The tripper and the tripped came back, both with napkins. "I'm sorry," the man with poor apologizing qualities said, holding a napkin out to me. "I realize that I just sounded kind of like an ass, and, well, I apologize. These guys bust my balls all the time, and--"

"You should be sorry," I said, huffing as I grabbed the napkin from his hand. Was I supposed to feel any better? How did his friends busting his balls make this less mortifying for me?

As I grabbed the napkin from him, I couldn't help but notice that he was handsome, extremely handsome. I wasn't really in the habit of shamelessly checking out members of the opposite sex since I had a boyfriend, but he looked very similar to my all-time celebrity crush, Mekhi Phifer.

"This is an airport, not a place for horseplay," I said haughtily.

He glanced down for a brief second and had his skin not been a rich black, I'm sure I would have seen a blush. I tried not to feel bad for scolding him. I didn't want to sound like a nag, but I now had to buy a new shirt due to him and his friends' antics.

"I'm truly sorry."

"Well, I appreciate the real apology," I said, trying to maintain a slight level of sass, summoning my inner Grandma Betty. "I'm going to go buy a new shirt now."

He winced, as did his friend, the one who had crashed into my lap. "Hold tight. I'm assuming you're a small?"

"I'm fine," I replied, scowling. "You've done enough. I can buy my own shirt."

"I insist," the handsome one said as they headed towards an airport kiosk, leaving me, again, wet, cold, and annoyed.

The other two from the group plopped down into empty seats nearby, trying to look as innocent as possible as the drama unfolded. I glared in their direction, hoping that they felt terrible for what had occurred. One cringed and tried for a smile, and one avoided eye contact with me all together. I hoped that they wouldn't be on my flight even though we were all sitting at the same gate. Maybe they were going to Los Angeles permanently, not on a layover, like me.

They returned soon with a bright pink Colorado shirt. It wasn't my style, but this one wasn't covered with soda splatters. "Do you want us to watch your stuff," one man asked. I didn't answer. Instead, I picked up my backpack and headed to the bathroom.

By the time I'd changed and used a paper towel to clean myself and my shirt as best as possible, the plane had already started boarding. I hoped that this adrenaline would wear off soon so I could relax on the flight. I felt the opposite of relaxed.

I got into my seat and buckled my seatbelt, then I took the safety card out and began to review it. I heard laughter coming from the aisle and saw that the group of hooligans was now on the plane. I rolled my eyes, beyond irritated but hoping that they were sitting far away from me. I didn't want to fixate on their presence the entire flight. I needed to relax and eventually fall asleep.

Thankfully the sounds of laughter drifted to the back of the plane, and I settled in, ready for the flight to leave and this pill, whatever it was, to work. I put my headphones on and waited. As each second ticked by, I became less relaxed and more awake.

Had Samantha given me expired medication? Was I reacting the opposite of how I was supposed to be? Was I so focused on the occurrence at the gate that I couldn't relax enough for the pill to work? What was my deal?

Soon the plane landed in L.A. for a quick layover before the several-hour flight to London. Feeling worse than I initially had, I ran to a kiosk to grab a sandwich and water. Maybe eating or drinking something would help me feel better. I wolfed my food down and drank an entire bottle of water in the seating area of the kiosk.

After eating, I still felt like I had enough energy to run a marathon. I fished my phone out of my backpack and dialed Sam's phone number.

"What's up, adventurer?" Sam asked.

"What pill did you give me?" I said quietly into the phone, again not wanting people around me to hear.

"Why?" Samantha asked.

"Because since taking it I feel more awake than I've ever felt in my life and I'm freaking out a little bit," I hissed into the phone.

"Chill, I just gave you Benadryl," Samantha said nonchalantly as my brain homed in on what the problem was.

"Samantha," I hissed, causing a few patrons to look at me. I lowered my voice, "Don't you remember Girl Scout camp?

My Benadryl incident? It works on me the opposite of how it should!"

"Oh yeah," Samantha said quietly.

"I was so twitchy the scout leader made me run the obstacle course two extra times just to get me to shut up."

"Don't panic," Samantha said, hearing the terror in my voice. "Why don't you just get some sleep medicine from the airport."

"It sounds good in theory," I said to Sam, "But I am about to put myself on an almost 10-hour flight, and if I take something that makes me freak out more, I'll be in serious trouble."

"I'm sorry," Sam said, and I could tell that she was. Of course, she would have never intentionally done something like this to me.

I ran to the bathroom and was washing my hands when I heard my name called overhead informing me to get to my gate as the doors would be closing in five minutes. What. The. Hell. I usually never lost track of time.

I grabbed my backpack and ran to my now empty gate. I flashed the attendant an apologetic look as I handed over my ticket. I went from never being late to almost missing my flight to Europe. My heart raced as I rushed to my seat. I quickly sat down and turned to grab my seatbelt, looking right into the eyes of the tripper, the handsome one, who happened to be sitting in the seat next to mine.

"Hello, princess," he said with a grin.

12

~Betty~ June 1969

Betty-

It will be hard for me to hide my smile today because I see my daughter, my pride and joy, on her first day as a business owner. I look forward to watching you on your road to becoming a success. I know that you have heard bits and pieces of your mom's and my journey to Denver to follow our dreams, but one thing we haven't talked about enough is that along with highs come lows. Owning your own business comes with good and bad days. I want you to know that we will be there to celebrate with you on the best ones and during your worst times, we will be there to help make sure you don't give up on yourself.

We love and believe in you,
Dad

"Is this too much?" I asked, twirling around for my parents and grandfather.

They had driven the thirty minutes to see me on my maiden voyage. Bee's Flowers was officially open for business. I was brimming with nervous energy, which I think was apparent because I was adorned head-to-toe in flowers.

I was wearing a floppy orange hat with a rim that I hoped would protect me from the sun, with flowers I picked up yesterday interwoven into the ribbon on the brim. I was wearing sunflower bell bottoms, a bright orange shirt with my bee pin, and a brown fringe vest. Around my neck was a flowered pendant, and I was wearing a pair of loafers. Before she left, Missy showed me how some of the girls would paint their faces, and I had drawn a daisy on my cheek.

My elders looked at me in silence. I decided I should twirl once more so they could get the full effect.

"You are going to do your job in pants?" My mother asked, breaking the silence.

"Mom," I said, stopping mid-twirl. "It is 1969, and it is perfectly normal for a woman to be wearing pants."

"I think what your mother is trying to say," my father said softly, "is that people your age may be okay with buying flowers from you. But people of our generation and older may feel it is more appropriate to dress professionally."

"I'm selling flowers, not life insurance," I said, now doubting my wardrobe choice and whether it had been a good idea to have them come to see me before I left. I needed to start this process feeling confident.

My grandfather spoke, "I'll admit, I tend to look at a professional and make quick judgments about them based on what they are wearing and how they are wearing it. If you have a nice, tailored suit on, but it is wrinkled, I may think less of you professionally. Honeybee, do you feel confident wearing this?"

It was as if he'd read my mind. I felt fierce in this outfit, and I felt like I was representing my flowers as well. I wanted to appeal to all people: rich, poor, professional, or not. I just wanted to sell flowers, and I hoped that the clothing I was or wasn't wearing wouldn't matter in this instance.

I'd researched places in the area that tended to be crowded on the weekend and had decided on a park nearby where kids played, families had picnics, and couples strolled. I could be very persuasive but with some help from my family and friends had worked on different pitches for families, couples, and professionals.

I'd gone back and forth on the merchandise to start with on the cart and decided on simple bouquets, single stem flowers, and flower crowns. The hairpieces that we'd made for prom had been the talk of the school afterward. Many classmates voiced interest in them, and hopefully, interested parties would be seeking me out this summer.

Missy left two weeks ago, and she'd gotten word to her grandmother that they were in Arizona. They were traveling as a group now in vans, which was great as it minimized the amount of time they'd need to hitchhike and would be safer.

Our principal, learning of Missy's travel plans, pulled her aside. He talked to her about the potential for being hurt by hooligans who might not be able to refrain from hurting a pretty young girl. He'd implied it would be her fault if someone found her irresistible enough to harm her. Though I was sure she would find ways to be safe, I felt better knowing she was traveling smarter.

I was glad Missy was enjoying herself, but it was lonely in the apartment without her there. The complex was so quiet at night that it resembled a mausoleum, which I was confident resulted from Helen's letters. So many things already felt frightening. The world was in a state of unease, and it was a shame to feel this way, even at home. The state of the world was still one of the things motivating me to bring some cheer to people with brightly colored petals and green stems.

Standing in front of my family, I understood what my parents said, but I wanted to be a part of society's progress. It may seem like such a small thing, but something as simple as wearing bell-bottom pants and painting a flower on my face felt like fighting oppression.

"You aren't changing, are you?" My mother asked with a sigh as she hugged me goodbye.

"No," I said, planting a kiss on her cheek. "Remember when you said that you loved that I was feisty?"

"Feisty is an understatement," my dad answered with a wink.

"You've got this, Bug," Grandpa said, hugging me. "Make some money today."

They helped me maneuver the cart out of the door before leaving with good wishes. As I passed the office, I could see Helen peeking out her window with a sour expression. I waved at her, hoping to break her down one pleasant interaction at a time.

I flipped the sign over that said Bee's Flowers on it, and my heart rattled with excitement. This was going to be great! I got some curious stares as I walked down the sidewalk.

"Flowers for sale," I said, giving each person direct eye contact, a tactic I'd learned from my mother with her seamstress business.

"Eye contact determines whether or not someone believes you are capable of what you are offering them. You should be able to tell what color eyes every person you enter into a business agreement has."

"Flowers for sale," I said. Green eyes, I noted to myself as I passed a woman on the sidewalk. She gave me a pursed-lip smile and walked on.

I got to the park, trying not to feel defeated. I just assumed everyone was as excited as I was about flowers. How could I have made it from my house to the park without even one interested person? I decided to do a lap around the lake in the hopes that I would be visible and interested parties would be able to see me clearly from every vantage point.

I was on my second lap around the lake, and a few hours into sales attempts, before I had my first customer stop. Of course, it was a little girl of about seven who I was sure didn't have more than ten cents.

"Daisies!" she exclaimed. "I love daisies, and you have daisies on your cart, and you have a daisy on your cheek. Is that a daisy on your pants?"

I was about to answer her when she corrected herself, "Sunflower, those are sunflowers on your pants. I love flowers; how much are they?"

I told her the price for a single stem, a crown, and a bouquet.

"Bouquet, please," she pointed to the largest on display.

"Two dollars," I said as she reached into her pocket and pulled out a shiny quarter. I waited a moment to see if she had more money in other pockets. She stood next to me as she looked at me excitedly and expectantly.

My heart and head were conflicted. The flowers in the bouquet probably only cost a little more than 25 cents, but I'd been walking the park for two hours already, plus the time it took to prep them. The minimum wage was around $1.03 plus the cost of the flowers, so I was already behind what I needed to make.

She smiled again, and I could see that she had two missing front teeth. She looked so happy that I couldn't fathom letting her down. An idea struck me as I grabbed the bouquet out of the pocket it was resting in.

"Are you here by yourself?" I asked, stooping down to her height.

"My brother's over there," she pointed to the baseball diamond where a group of teenage boys was playing baseball. "He says I'm not old enough to play with them, so I'm on an adventure."

"How about we make a deal, I'll give you this container of flowers to sell to people for ten cents a flower, and I will give you this bouquet in exchange."

Her eyes lit up in excitement as she grabbed the container and ran towards the grassy area, which was starting to fill up with people and picnic baskets. Instead of walking another lap, I walked up and down the row, keeping the little girl and my flower container within view.

In less than thirty minutes, she was back with an empty container and more money than I'd expected she would get if they were ten cents apiece. I'd made my first three dollars in two hours!

"I couldn't remember what you said it costed, so I showed people what my money looked like, and that is what they gave me," she smiled her toothy grin again, looking excited.

"Wow," I said, "you did a great job! You earned this bouquet fair and square," I went to get it out of the pocket when I felt a pull on my vest.

"Can I take more flowers," the girl said. "That was fun, and there is a lady over there who wanted one, but I ran out."

"Are you sure your parents or brother don't mind you being with a stranger?" I asked.

"I'm Karen," the little girl said.

"I'm Betty," I replied.

"Now, we aren't strangers. I was bored, and this was fun. Please, can I have more flowers?" She looked at me expectantly again.

I was okay with her helping me, but I also didn't want my new business license taken away because I'd violated child labor laws. I'd consider the first round an even trade but making her continue to work would probably be frowned upon by the city.

"How about you show me the people who want flowers, and when we have gotten rid of those, we'll make you a flower crown together. You can play and point the flower cart out to people if they ask you about your crown. Does that sound like a deal?"

"Deal," Karen, with the missing-toothed grin, replied.

13

~Rachel~ June 2007

Dear Sean-

    I'm writing to say that I'll be thinking about you often while on this trip. I know this isn't how we talked about spending the summer, and for that, I apologize. I'm sorry we won't be together for my birthday as we previously planned, Parker mentioned you had something special in mind, and I hate that I spoiled your plans.

    I appreciate you supporting me in this adventure; I have some things I need to learn about myself. Please don't take offense to that. I hope that you can look at this as something that could strengthen us in the future, not hinder our progress.

    I'll call you if I can, and it isn't too expensive. Otherwise, we can write to each other. I meant to bring it up when we said goodbye, but it felt awkward.

    I love you, Sean.
    Rachel

"**P**rincess, huh," I scowled as I sat down next to the obnoxious man from the gate. I may not be fond of confrontation, but I didn't appreciate his comment. I looked down at the babyish shirt I had on. The one I was wearing because of his antics, "I'm 100% queen."

"Touché," he said as I buckled my seatbelt, trying to ignore how closely I would have to sit to this awful man.

I pulled a magazine out before sliding my hiking backpack under the seat in front of me. I knew that I wouldn't sleep anytime soon, and I would feel awake for hours if this were anything like the scout incident. I tried to ignore that I would have to survive tomorrow without proper rest.

I waited until we were in the air before putting my head back on the seat and closing my eyes. With every passing minute, the plane got quieter, everyone seeming to be aware of the growing time difference with every mile we traveled.

I tried to quiet my brain, to trick it into forgetting the Benadryl. Unfortunately, it was as if my mind was stuck "on" when I wanted it turned "off." With each minute I wasn't sleeping, I became more panicked. As I mindlessly thumbed through my magazine, my mind went back to yesterday. The goodbyes I had been the most nervous about had not gone well.

Crash! Boom!

I'd just decided to take a break from packing and was in the kitchen, making myself a sandwich, when I heard a crash upstairs. Unsure of what could have caused such a loud noise, my mind immediately envisioned the worst-case scenario. I dropped the turkey container on the counter and headed toward the stairs, taking them two at a time, imagining what I would do if I found one of my family members sick or injured on the floor. I quickly tried to brush off the cobwebs from my first-aid class in case I needed to utilize my skills.

I reached the top of the stairs at Olympic level speed and followed the noises to my bedroom, where I found the source of the distress, Stacia, the 10-year-old terror. It became apparent quickly that the sound I heard was her slamming my hiking backpack to the floor, throwing what had been my nicely packed clothing all over my bedroom.

"What are you doing?" I asked as I grabbed her by her shoulders and walked her out of my room, keeping her squirming body at arm's length to prevent further damage to my belongings or me.

"I don't want you to go! You promised me the summer! You are leaving me and that isn't what was supposed to happen!" Stacia exclaimed angrily, trying not to cry.

"I know," I said as I advanced towards her, arms no longer keeping her away but now extended out, trying to pull her in for a hug. I still wanted to smooth things over before I left, hoping to take away the hurt my little sister was experiencing because of me.

Stacia stubbornly clamped her lips together and pushed my arms away, clearly intent on continuing to punish me for my decision.

"Anastasia," I said.

"You're nothing but a... but a... a butt nugget!" Stacia threw my direction. She angrily stormed past me on her way through the hallway and down the stairs. I winced as I heard the slam of the front door.

I felt a hand on my shoulder and turned around. Our parents joined me in the hallway.

I rolled my eyes. "Well, she's not getting any more used to this, is she?"

My mom looked back at me, "I'm sorry. We're all a little upset, and we'll miss you. She's your younger sister, and you have to understand this from her point of view."

"I know," I said, feeling sorry for Stacia but suddenly annoyed that I had to repack all my stuff. Before entering my room, I decided I had to have the last word.

I turned to face my parents, "It's also unrealistic of her to think I will live here until she's 18-years-old and I'm 26! My leaving someday was inevitable."

My mother threw me a mom glare sharp enough to pierce my soul before heading down the stairs to check on Stacia. My dad followed me inside my bedroom and surveyed the mess.

"Yikes," he said as he uprighted the pack and started to scoop up my clothing. I cringed as he grabbed a handful of my panties. It was just my luck that that would have been the first article of clothing within his reach. His face reddened as he realized what he was holding. I gave him a nervous laugh, trying to make it less awkward but, in turn, making it more so. He maintained his composure as he tossed the panties in the backpack. He sat down on my bed and patted the space next to him. I plopped down beside him, and he embraced me in a side-hug, letting me know everything would be okay.

"Earth to the princess," I was jerked from my memory by the annoying voice next to me. "We should talk. Obviously, we're the only two people awake right now."

"Just because I'm not sleeping doesn't mean I want to speak to you," I said, aggressively turning the pages of my magazine. "What don't you understand about not calling me princess?"

"Ouch," he replied. "I forgot. Look, I think we got off on the wrong foot." He held out his hand. "I'm Chad."

I ignored him, continuing to leaf through, not reading anything, but trying to distract myself. He cleared his throat a few times with no response from me. Suddenly I felt my magazine leaving my grasp. He had grabbed it right out of my hands, the nerve of this guy!

"What are you doing?!" I hissed, trying to maintain a quiet tone of voice.

He held the magazine out. "I'm sorry I grabbed that from you, I'm aware that was another impolite thing in the series of rude things occurring between us. I know that I don't know you, but you were assaulting that magazine, and I wanted to make sure that you're okay."

"I'm fine, thank you very much," I snatched the magazine back.

"The half-shredded magazine may think differently. Seriously, can we please start fresh?"

"Not unless you have a magic spell to make me fall asleep," I said under my breath.

"What did you say?" he asked.

"Never mind," I huffed. I sat back in my seat, thumbing through the magazine, which did appear a little roughed up. Now that Mr. Obnoxious had pointed it out, I would have to be more conscious of the aggression and speed of my page-turning.

"Can we try this one more time with a fresh start?" he asked quietly, repeating his earlier request. "I'm facing the next several hours awake, and I don't want to to do so solo." He stuck his hand out in front of me; in another attempt to introduce himself, "Once again, I'm Chad."

I hesitated before begrudgingly shaking his hand. "I'm Rachel."

"So, Rachel, are you an anti-plane sleeper as well?"

"Not opposed to sleeping on a plane," I answered. Despite our first encounter, I supposed I could work on my attitude and attempt a normal conversation with this man. "My best friend drugged me."

Chad looked at me in horror. "What do you mean? Like in the past, or now?"

My statement clearly sounded worse than the reality.

"She gave me pills to calm me down so I could sleep on the flight. She forgot that I react the opposite to Benadryl than a normal person does. It may not seem like it, but I have enough energy to run 10 miles up and down the aisles."

Chad looked from me to the magazine before smiling. "That would be interesting to witness. At least I know that all that aggression was medication-related, and I feel a little safer now."

"Ha, ha. It was also partially you."

"Ouch," he replied. "I feel like I need to explain."

"Well, you've got the time to do it." I put my magazine down.

"The guys I'm with are friends from high school. We just graduated and decided to go on a trip before going our separate ways. We come from different walks of life, you could say. You happened to catch me in one of my not-so-fine moments trying to get payback for something."

"I noticed," I said, keeping my response short. I was willing to have a brief conversation with this man, but I wasn't sure how far I wanted to delve into life stories now.

"Why are you here?"

"I needed some adventure in my life. I'm too boring," I replied. Chad laughed deep and loud causing someone a few rows back to shush us.

He swiveled around to see who the culprit had been before turning around. "It's not like it's a library."

"People like their sleep," I whispered.

As if the airplane itself was telling us to be silent, the in-flight movie started playing, and we both accepted earphones so we could watch. Juno was the feature and why they decided to offer a comedy during an overnight flight was beyond me. As the scenes progressed, I felt less guilty as my seatmate was also chuckling quietly. Watching the movie made me forget yesterday's disappointments until some of the scenes reminded me of Sean and my last interactions.

I had woken up yesterday, not looking forward to saying goodbye to anyone, especially Sean. We met for dinner—the charge in the air was apparent, and I hadn't been able to determine whether it was positive or negative energy I was sensing. Things were changing, and there was no stopping it now.

"What's on your mind?" I asked as we waited for our meals.

"I'm not sure what happens from here," Sean answered honestly. "I feel like I knew where all of this was leading, and now I'm unsure."

I paused as I thought about what he said. "I know that I love you, Sean. Isn't that enough for a fairy tale ending?"

He reached forward and grabbed both of my hands. "Maybe the main character needs to have a fairy tale adventure before she gets her happy ending."

I squeezed his hands tightly. Even though I knew this needed to happen, it still hurt. A few tears dropped onto my arms, and I'd let go with one hand to wipe them off my cheeks.

"I'm sorry, Sean. I didn't even know I needed this, and now that I have this opportunity, I can't imagine not going. I want us to end up together; I love you."

Sean smiled sadly, "I love you too, Rach. I want you to be able to experience whatever you need to, and if that drives us down the same path, then so be it. If not, I understand."

I tried to calm the burning in my heart. "Are you breaking up with me?"

"Not at all," he clarified. "I'm just saying let's not put pressure on this. Let's stay Sean and Rachel, but the less pressurized version. If we can weather over a month of distance, when you get back, we can start fresh. Sean and Rachel, no pressure, version 2.0."

I smiled, happy that he wasn't giving up but sad that instead of the forward progression we'd planned, I was forcing us backward.

"I can live with that," I said as I gripped his hands. "I appreciate you being willing to stick this out."

Our goodbye had been quicker than I'd imagined, and I think we were trying not to prolong the inevitable. We hugged and kissed, and instead of it being one of longing, a kiss that made me drop all my plans to follow our previous dream, it was unremarkable. I appreciated that there wasn't a drawn-out goodbye, but it seemed to be lacking the emotion that I felt soul mates would have when they were parting ways.

I was left on the plane, contemplating what that final interaction said about the future. I was interrupted from my thoughts by a silent shake next to me, Chad silently laughing at a funny scene in the movie. I decided to focus on what was happening now and the adventure I was facing. I turned my attention back to Juno and her pregnant antics.

14

~Betty~ June 1969

Dear Betty-

California is amazing. We finally got to our destination! I can't imagine being anywhere but here, sitting on the warm sand, listening to others play music in front of the campfire and the sounds of waves in the background. I wish you were with us.

You would love it here and all they are trying to do for peace and women. I keep hearing about flower power, and I think fondly of you every time. They would love the message and concept of a flower cart here. Maybe you and your cart should take a road trip.

I hope Bee's Flowers brings you joy, happiness, and success. I also hope that Helen is leaving you alone.

Peace and Love,

Missy

I was one week into the start of Bee's Flowers, and I felt like I was gaining knowledge daily. There was a huge learning curve, but I could be successful if I continued to learn from my mistakes. My parents, unfortunately, were correct. What I wore did make a difference in who would buy flowers from me. It had come as a disappointment. Why did some people still have the inability to see past something superficial?

After working at the park the first few days, I'd decided to branch out and capitalize on dinnertime so that I could target couples on dates. I wore an outfit with bright colors and flowers. I approached an older couple holding hands, asking them to purchase a bouquet.

"At least this hippie has a job," the man said before rudely shooing me away like my very existence was polluting his path.

I decided that I would have to find a way to express myself while catering to all customers. It was a hard pill to swallow, but I knew I needed to first build a name for myself. One day I would have a storefront and wear whatever I wanted, and I wouldn't refuse anyone's services based on their clothing choices.

I learned quickly that couples on dates were excellent business prospects and trying to make the sale in front of the women was helpful. I'd always been great at debate and speech in school, proving beneficial to my business. The other thing that had been advantageous to my company was Karen.

Karen had come to the park almost every day and was proving to boost my flower sales. I found that if I made her a flower crown in the morning to wear, she would bring customers in my direction. Something about her was irresistible to people, and I wished that she was old enough for me to pay her in more than a flower crown every day.

I felt terrible that her brother didn't allow her to play baseball with him and his friends, but part of me got it. She was much younger than him, and he seemed like a caring, attentive brother when he came by the flower cart to take her home. He took baseball seriously, and from a bystander's point of view, he didn't want Karen to be injured playing with the older children. Still, the way she would watch them during their games, starting on the bleachers or making her way to the dugout like she was hoping she would be stepping up to the pitch as the next player, was heartbreaking to me.

Karen would flit like a fairy between the park, the baseball diamonds, and the cart, and I had started packing extra snacks or drinks to give to her. She talked a lot, but always about easy things, like gardening and riding bikes. It felt strange to look forward to the company of a child, but I was happy to see her on the days she came.

At night, I would pack as many flowers as possible into my refrigerator or the coldest parts of the house. I'd learned to offer a lower price on the stems that started to wilt to minimize the loss of products. I was a little overzealous on the first few days of ordering and had to throw some flowers away, which had broken my heart and pocketbook.

I'd seen Helen outside and offered to make a bouquet for her every few days that she could keep in some of the common areas for a reasonable price. She murmured something about allergies before she wandered off, obviously wanting to be around me as little as possible. I was simply happy that she wasn't complaining about me yet.

I'd made a little bit of money. Since my overhead cost wasn't horrible, I knew that if I continued to be smart with my time, decisions, and spending, the potential was there to continue to be profitable. I was trying to be smart at home, turning lights off, keeping the temperature down, cooking individual portions and making my meals stretch. It helped to have relatives who'd grown up during the Great Depression who had taught me how to be thrifty.

I was a little lonely without Missy, my parents, and my grandfather nearby. I missed seeing Frank, but I didn't know how appropriate it would be to have him at my house without Missy present. The plus side of loneliness was that it motivated me to work often and harder.

After my morning rounds at the park, I'd been using the leftover flowers to make romantic-looking bouquets. I decided to dress up a little more tonight and put on a navy dress, my bee pin, and navy flats, hoping it would be more suitable for the crowd. I placed a daisy behind my ear, feeling that this tiny gesture alone spoke to my independence so I could dress the part with some sass.

I loaded the cart and headed to an area about half a mile away, which happened to be near restaurants and a movie theater.

"You look lovely this evening," I stated to the first couple I encountered, gesturing to the lady. "Would you like to buy some flowers for this delightful woman?" I looked into both of their eyes as they stopped to look at the merchandise — green and blue.

I assisted them in picking a beautiful bouquet with roses, a few daisies, and some greenery.

They paid me and even gave me a tip. "Your flowers are beautiful," the woman complimented me. "Have you ever thought of taking your cart to events?"

Maybe this was another avenue to pursue? Park in the morning, restaurants at night, and events as often as possible. I'd have to talk to my family to find out if they had ideas on where to track activities, possibly in the newspaper?

Another couple appeared, and I tried the same approach. This couple wasn't holding hands, but it was clear that they were both dressed up and on a date.

"You are looking lovely this evening," I said, trying the line from before as I moved my cart in their direction. "Would you like to buy this beautiful lady some flowers?" I got close enough to make eye contact and looked at her eye color, brown. I looked into her date's eyes and was surprised to find that they were two different colors, one blue and one brown.

"Your eyes are different colors," I said, jolted out of my usual flower speech.

He looked at me, surprised. "Most people don't notice that."

"My parents taught me to make good eye contact and shake with a firm hand. Both are better for business."

His date interrupted me, looking at me with distaste. "If

you aren't going to get me flowers, we need to get to dinner. I haven't eaten all day, and I'm starving." She stared at him expectantly.

"Tell us about your bouquets," he said after a moment. His facial expression made it seem like he was put off by her brashness.

"Just pick one for me already," The woman said before I had a chance to say anything about my flowers, how they were all grown locally and how I'd arranged them myself.

I opened my mouth to answer when she interrupted me again, "Daaaaavid."

He looked at me apologetically, "I think we'll head to dinner and come back for flowers afterward, so we don't have to carry them with us."

"I'll be around," I said as I pushed my cart towards another prospect. I felt sorry for David as his date didn't seem like a pleasant person.

I didn't expect to see them back at all, but a few hours later, our paths crossed again. He walked up with a smile, and she looked as sour as she had when I'd first encountered them.

"I'd like to buy some flowers," he turned to his date. "I'm sorry, Susan. I've tried talking to you a few times about this tonight, but I don't know how else to let you down. I am buying flowers, but they aren't for you."

"David," she said with a pout. "I thought we were having a great time."

"Susan, I don't want to hurt your feelings, I've been trying to tell you this for the last hour, but I haven't gotten a word in edgewise. Let's say I don't think we are a good match. I'm sorry."

I sat there uncomfortably, unsure what was going on and why I was involved, but given how Susan had acted towards her date and me, I didn't blame him.

"What's your favorite bouquet?" David asked after Susan sulked a short distance away, lurking on the periphery, staying close in case he changed his mind.

I picked the brightest of the bunch. I loved how beautiful

and classic a red rose could be, but I had always found the most beauty in the flowers people didn't usually pick first; carnations, sunflowers, daisies, and all the other flowers that weren't usually people's first choice.

He paid, and I gave him the bouquet, and he handed it right back to me. "I know this is a bit unconventional, but I'm intrigued by you. I'm so sorry that you had to witness everything that just happened, but I promise it was inevitable before I encountered you. Would you be willing to give me one chance?"

I was speechless, which was not usually the case. I saw Susan walk away with her hands balled into fists. I agreed that this was not ideal, but he was handsome and didn't seem to appreciate how his date had acted. It wasn't as if he was asking for my hand in marriage.

"Just one date," I said as I accepted the flowers with a smile.

15

~*Rachel*~ *June 2007*

Dear Mom and Dad-

    I want to start by thanking you for your unconditional support. I know that it can't be easy thinking of your oldest baby traveling Europe all by her lonesome. Mom, I can picture your worried expression right now, and you need to knock it off, or this will be a very rough month for you. Dad, you have no reason to worry, either. I remember those self-defense moves you tried to teach me.

    Just know that I am cautious and paranoid by nature, and that will serve me well. I would say that I will approach everything with the caution of my grandma, but let's be honest, she would probably get in more trouble than any of us.

    I love you both, and I can't wait to tell you all about my adventures when I get back.

    Rachel

    P.S. If Stacia still seems mad at me, please put in a good word. I hate fighting with her.

Once the movie ended, we sat in uncomfortable silence. I picked up the magazine and started to leaf through it, hoping that since hours had passed, the pills would begin to wear off, and I would be able to sleep.

"You said you're traveling because you're boring. What's the whole story?" Chad whispered after a while.

I put the magazine down. "That's a pretty broad question. What do you want to know?" Though I felt less annoyed by him after watching a movie together, I still wasn't sure how much to share. Our initial interaction, medicine, and lack of sleep made me feel vulnerable. I was fearful that though my brain may have every intention of filtering material before it traveled to my mouth, it was moving so quickly that there may not be time to stop the downward spiral of words once I started to unleash them.

"Whatever you want to tell me," he said, leaning over the seat divider so we could talk with lowered voices.

"I also just graduated," I started. "I had my life all planned out and then decided that I needed a little change. My grandparents helped send me out here for a while, so I can figure myself out before starting college next fall."

"That's great that you have that support."

"Yeah, I'm pretty lucky," I said. I folded my magazine in half to place it back into my backpack. I felt like if we were going to talk, I should at least give him my undivided attention. I unzipped a front pocket. The magazine wouldn't fit which was strange because I hadn't placed anything in there. I pulled the object out and, after unfolding them, saw that it was a giant pair of control top panties, displayed for anyone around to view in all their glory.

"Oh. My. God!" I squealed as I bunched them up and crammed them back into my backpack.

Chad looked at me in surprise, "No judgment here. I'd assume they are comfortable."

"Let me explain," I said. "My grandma is responsible for

this because she likes to mess with me."

Chad looked at me in doubt.

"It all started at my graduation party," I started, flashing back to that day.

~

My family had attended my graduation ceremony and had come to my house after for appetizers and presents. My closest friends and I had staggered our party times so that we could attend a portion of each other's celebrations. All went seamlessly until I started to open my gifts.

My grandma handed me a beautifully wrapped present about the size of a television. I already felt like they spoiled me with the month-long vacation, and I couldn't imagine getting something else. I opened the box with the inscription: To Rachel/Raquel, With Love, Grandma, and Grandpa.

Inside was a ton of tissue paper. It took minutes to comb through, finally reaching the gift, a pair of control top granny panties. It had been impossible not to show everyone what was in the box. As I held them out for everyone to see, I felt my cheeks redden as Samantha giggled, Parker scoffed, and Sean looked horrified.

"Grandma! Grandpa!" I exclaimed.

My grandpa looked at me, "I had no part in this one."

"What?" my grandma asked innocently, "A talisman is our tradition." She fingered the honeybee pin on her shirt, indicating that she still held hers close.

I knew about the tradition that each Bee woman got an item for their transition to womanhood that was supposed to ground them and make them remember their roots. I had never in my wildest dreams imagined that my article would be a gigantic pair of granny panties.

"This is your talisman so you can remember if life goes awry. All you need to do is pull your undies up and remember that life is short. You need to feel the wind in your hair, get lost on the streets of a little town in Italy and not panic. You need to eat good food and drink some good wine until you are drunk, literally and figuratively--"

"Mother," my dad interrupted.

"What," she said innocently, again. "The drinking age in Europe is lower than ours. Is there anything wrong with the child letting her hair loose and living a little?"

My parents looked at her, unsure how to react. Grandma Betty shrugged, and I looked at them all, beyond mortified, giant panties still in hand. I watched my friends as they all tried to remain stoic. Parker had broken the tension, letting out one of his amazing throaty, contagious laughs. We all followed suit, and I tossed the panties aside. I planned to wait until later to discreetly discard and then forget about them, but that hadn't happened.

~

"No way," Chad said, trying to stifle his laughter so someone sleeping on the airplane wouldn't silence us again.

"She had my parents or sister do this," I said, burying my face in my hands for a moment. "Please tell me your family is wacky and crazy."

Chad's face instantly changed. "I don't have any family left."

I blanched. "What happened? Never mind, it's none of my business. I'm so sorry."

"Car accident," he said quietly. "I lost my parents a few months ago."

I looked at him with sympathy and horror, the second reaction I hoped he couldn't see. I couldn't imagine losing my parents at any age, but especially not right before you tried to enter the world: when you needed your parent's guidance and experience. "I don't know what to say. You must miss them."

Chad looked at me. "More than I can put into words. Thank you for not saying you're sorry for my loss. I know people

104

mean well and that it's something we're conditioned to say, and I feel like it's all I've heard for the last few months."

Oddly enough, that had been the first thing I wanted to say, but I'd just said the first thing real thing I felt instead.

"The saddest part is I felt like I was just getting to know them," he said, obviously needing someone to talk to about this. "I wasn't the best example of a son. My friends and I were always getting into trouble. Believe it or not, this is the toned-down version of all of us. I decided to join the Air Force and finished high school strong, trying to live up to my full potential. They were so proud of me and the changes I was making. They didn't even get to see me graduate."

I took a deep breath. Talking about grief like this made me uncomfortable; it was so raw and real. Knowing that a stranger felt like disclosing this to me made me feel even more vulnerable. I wasn't used to these types of conversations, but I knew that was part of me branching out.

"I know this sounds like me just trying to make you feel better, but I'm sure they were proud of you," I said, looking into his eyes, something my grandma had always encouraged. His eyes were a beautiful deep amber. I tried to ignore them, thinking about Sean and how humiliated the airport incident made me feel earlier. I'd seen a few sides of Chad already. Just because he was showing a sensitive side now may not mean anything.

"Thank you," he whispered, "I don't know if I can talk about this anymore today."

I nodded, knowing I couldn't even fathom how hard it would be to relive a tragedy like that every day. "Are your friends joining the Air Force too?"

"Landon joined with me. He's the one you met up close and personal earlier. He doesn't have the greatest home life, so it made the most sense for him as well. We're both looking forward to having a different type of family. Trent and Caleb are going to Colorado University in the fall. They're both lucky enough to have not only intelligence but wealthy parents that support them. Where are you going to school?"

"Colorado State University in Fort Collins," I informed him. "English major. I want to teach children about books. I've always loved reading, and if I can help get kids excited about it too, I would be happy."

"I love Fort Collins," Chad declared. "It's a fun town, and you'll have a blast there."

By the time we got notification of our final descent hours later, Chad and I had talked non-stop. We'd talked about growing up in Denver, the places we liked to frequent, and how, at some point, we probably knew some of the same people and hung out in some of the same places.

We talked about our vacation path. I was starting and ending in London, traveling only by Euro-rail and staying in hostels. My trip was scheduled for a glorious twenty-four days. According to Chad, they were going for a few weeks and "flying by the seat of their pants."

As the plane started to wake up and flight attendants prepared us for landing, I felt a twinge of disappointment. I enjoyed talking to him, and there was a moment I'd almost asked his relationship status. It hadn't been a flirty conversation, plus I had a serious boyfriend. I'm sure people connected on flights all the time without becoming romantic. Right?

The plane lowered, and when the person in our row next to the window opened the blind, I was awestruck. I couldn't wait to see the beauty of this old country, to explore a world that had such a history that was so different from what I was used to in America.

We landed, and row by row, people emptied off the plane. Chad was behind me, and I felt a little odd at our departure. We had talked so easily once we'd let our guard down, and I hoped that maybe someday I'd get to see the airplane version of Chad again. We hadn't really said goodbye, just packed up our things and waited patiently to get off the airplane.

I started walking in the direction of customs. I heard my name being shouted behind me, "Rachel, hold on a second." I saw

Chad running in my direction, leaving his friends to join me.

"It was nice talking to you," he said. "Thanks for giving me a second chance. I didn't know how badly some of that needed to come out, and I appreciate you listening to me. Can I hug you?"

I nodded, glad that we would have a better goodbye than before. We hugged, and I tried to ignore the tingles in my stomach. I tried to justify it by remembering that I usually didn't embrace strangers I had great conversations with who looked like Mekhi Pfeifer. He handed me a slip of paper and smiled before turning around and running back to his friends.

(303)555-1255- Call me, the slip of paper read.

# 16

~*Betty~ June 1969*

Dear Betty Bee Flower Lady-

Your flowers are pretty, just like you. When I see them, it makes me happy. Sometimes, things make me sad at home, and I'm glad I have you and your flowers. Your bouquets make people smile, making the world more beautiful. Thanks for all the snacks.
Love Karen
P.S. My brother helped me write this because he said my handwriting was sloppy.

I didn't know what I'd been thinking. Now didn't seem like the right time to start dating someone. My brain was assaulting me with multiple ways this would end in disaster.

I, in a panic, had made two lists, one with reasons not to go on a date with David and one with why I should. Reasons to stay home included: the need to concentrate on my business, the fact that he'd broken up with Susan in front of me, and the fact that he intrigued me meant he would also distract me. Reasons to attend the date were: the fact that his eyes were different colors, he was handsome and charming, and he hadn't liked how Susan was acting and dealt with it accordingly and fairly.

My list didn't prove helpful. My brain continued to argue

with itself. It was my grandfather who convinced me to give it a try.

"You know Betty Bee, being successful and working hard is important, but if you aren't taking the time to live, it will all be in vain. You don't want to get to my age and realize that you worked more than you enjoyed."

"But I enjoy my work," I countered before adding, "I enjoy it most of the time."

I loved my job, but the same issues that had been there from the beginning were still there:

- People who didn't respect me or respected me less based on my clothing choices.
- People were trying to argue about my price.
- Mother nature.

Weather in Colorado was usually decent, with the sun shining at some point in the day most of the year. There were generally scattered rainstorms in the afternoons during summer, and I'd gotten better at timing my day. I'd sell individual flowers, flower headbands, and some bouquets in the park in the morning. I'd head home to make romantic bouquets during the rain in the afternoon and head to patrol the restaurants at night. I was probably putting in a good ten-twelve-hour days, which was exhausting, but when I walked home with some profit at the end of the day, it felt worthwhile.

I thought about what my grandfather had said when David called asking me to dinner. I had hesitated only a fraction of a second, hearing him laugh at my hesitation, saying: "I'm sure you're nervous after seeing my interaction with Susan. Our mothers work together, and they set up the date. I assure you I try to stay away from women who have temper tantrums. Please don't judge me on that experience."

"I was trying not to," I said honestly, "but I appreciate you clarifying that. I would disappoint you pretty quickly if you expected me to behave like your date did."

He'd laughed again, and the warmth behind it had sealed the deal for me. "I'll go to dinner with you."

It wasn't as if I'd never dated. I'd been on many dates but hadn't gotten serious enough with anybody to go steady. It's just dinner, I kept reminding myself. It isn't like this is the person I will marry.

We'd decided David would pick me up at my apartment, and we were going to a movie or dinner. I was nervously arranging some flowers for tomorrow when I heard a knock. I ran to the bathroom and checked my appearance before answering the door. I'd worn my hair down in loose waves, a lovely dress that my mom had sewn for me recently, and my bee pin, which I'd been wearing daily. I felt like it brought me luck.

I opened the door and smiled shyly, speechless. What was wrong with me?

David looked handsome in a light blue pair of bell bottoms and a cream shirt. He carried a house plant with a macramé holder, which he thrust in my direction.

"For me?" I asked, taking it from him.

"Well, I wanted to get you flowers, but then I thought maybe you dealt with flowers so much that you would prefer something else. I assumed you liked all things green, so I got you this."

I smiled, we didn't have any plants, and until I received this one, I hadn't realized it was something I missed from my parents' house. I was the designated green thumb, and I made a mental note to check to see if the plants at my parents' house were still alive.

"Thank you," I said, inviting him in so I could put the plant down.

He politely stayed in the foyer, which got me out of the obligatory apartment tour. I appreciated it. Things like that should be reserved for after more than one date.

I returned, and he opened the door for me politely. For me, the verdict would have to be out on that one. I wasn't usually fond of male chivalry, but I would be willing to try it out for a little while to see what he had to offer. As a teenager, my mom had told me that dates were similar to job interviews and that it was okay to sit back and see what the prospect has to offer before making snap judgments.

"You look beautiful," he said as we walked out of the apartment.

"Thank you," I said, hoping he had more to offer than comments about beauty.

"I didn't ask you on a date because of your beauty," he said, reading my mind.

"Good," I said, "I'm not the kind of girl who wants to be

nothing more than a pretty face. I'm a person with thoughts and dreams and ideas."

"That," he said, stopping in his tracks to look at me. "That is why I wanted to get to know you better. That and the daisy."

"Daisy?" I asked.

"The daisy you had behind your ear. The night we met it was as if you dressed for business but had to show some fire."

My heart fluttered. If David was trying to get a second date, he was saying all the right things, and we were only minutes into this one.

"Well, I am full of fire," I said as he guided me towards his car.

"Is that a promise?" He asked before opening the car door for me.

I got into his Volkswagen Beetle. "It's a fact," I said with a smile.

He smiled in return and drove away from the apartment complex.

"Where are we headed?" I asked.

"I still thought a movie would be great," he replied.

"I would love that. We don't have a television set, and though I don't think I'd have time to sit and watch it often, I miss being able to relax like that."

"Have you seen True Grit yet?" he asked.

"No, I've heard good things about it, though." I wasn't usually a fan of westerns, having been forced to watch them with my father, but I'd heard that this one was worth seeing.

"Rumor has it that there is a girl with a fiery spirit for the main character," David said with a little chuckle.

"We'll have to see about that." I was glad that he didn't seem put off by a woman's independent spirit.

"Tell me about you," David said. "I know that you're confident, driven, autonomous. Is Bee's Flowers your business?"

"Yes," I beamed, excited to admit that. "My parents wanted me to go to college, but I needed to do this. With the state of the world right now, I couldn't imagine doing something I wasn't passionate about for the rest of my life. People our age are dying, and for what?"

He looked at me solemnly. "My parents made sure I enrolled in college; they are still afraid I could go to Vietnam. My father and grandfather were both in the service, so I would consider it an honor, but I can't say that this war is something I believe in."

I felt so stupid. Here I was talking about not going to college to follow my passion, and he was telling me about going to college as a necessity. I was glad he was driving so he couldn't see my face, "I'm sorry; I feel like my comment was insensitive."

"It is the way it is. You didn't decide that this was the way it would be. You don't need to apologize." We sat in silence for a few minutes before he added, "Honestly I would have opted learn a trade instead of college. I've always been great with machinery: cars, boats, you name it. My mom is extra sensitive to all of this because my sister passed away as a baby. I don't remember it because I was young, but it has made my parents fearful of losing one of us again. I have another sister who just turned eleven. She's fierce, kind of like you. Do you have siblings?"

"I don't. My parents grew up in very large homes, and I think they were okay with just having me. I'm so sorry about your sister."

"How about we make a deal the rest of the night, no sad talk. I'm hoping you will reconsider your one date policy, but until then, we will have to focus on happy things."

I nodded in agreement before clarifying, "I'm agreeing to happy talk. We'll see where we stand at the end of the date."

The movie was good, and the main character was a fierce young woman, who I found endearing. Midway through the film, we grasped hands, and the electric pulse I felt told me that I would be going on more than one date with this man. Holding hands was so simple but so lovely at the same time. After the movie, neither of us was ready to go home, so we decided to go to a diner close by and get something to eat.

I was enjoying myself, and our conversation was seamless. We liked a lot of the same things: music, books, and outdoor activities. David was friendly and laughed often. I had to try not to stare at his differently colored eyes too much, they were so striking.

We both ordered cheese Frenchies, fries, and chocolate malts. We hadn't talked in advance about what we were ordering, so it made the date even more perfect that we had the same go-to meal. After we ate, we still weren't ready to part ways and decided to go on a walk.

We walked, hands intertwined, not talking, just enjoying the night and each other's company. Suddenly, David came to a halt. The abruptness startled me. He faced me, "I hope it's okay that I kiss you. I know this is our first date, but-"

I planted my lips to his- electric. The rest of the walk became interspersed with walking and kissing, lots of kissing. When he dropped me off, I was breathless with sore lips and a smile. I walked through the door and plopped onto the couch, pulsing with feelings.

I was going to have to be careful because David was going to be a big distraction.

17

~Rachel~ June/July 2007

London-

> To: Stacialovessoccerandpigs@yahoo.com
> From: RachelBee2007@yahoo.com
>
> Stacia-
> Greetings from London. It's so cool here! The city is full of people with amazing thick accents. Sometimes I wish I had a way to subtitle what they were saying, but since I can't, there is a lot of smiling and nodding on my part. The pictures you see depicting London with taxi cabs, phone booths, and double-decker buses are accurate; they are everywhere.
>
> How have the first few days of summer gone? I hope you are doing some fun things with Luke and Amber. Mom mentioned in her email that you guys got season passes to Elitches, which should make for a great summer. Maybe I could join you once or twice when I get home?
>
> I love and miss you!

Your big sissy,
Rachel

Dear Samantha-
I had an exciting first day in London. I, of course, didn't sleep at all on my flight here. Don't worry; I've forgiven you for the Benadryl mishap. My seatmate stayed awake, and we talked all night. I hated him at first but would now consider him a friend. It is a long story and better told in person.

After I landed, I was able to take a classic taxi (per your recommendation) straight to the double-decker bus tour. My bus had the red, blue, and white of the United Kingdom flag on it- SCORE. I went to the very top to get a full view of London and managed to stay awake. The excitement of being in a new country helped me to rally the entire three-and-a-half-hour tour.

Our guide, Kevin, was excellent and knowledgeable, telling us all the facts along our route. We saw St. Paul's Cathedral, London Bridge, Big Ben, Piccadilly Circus, and finished with a river cruise on the Thames.

My favorite was the hustle and bustle of Piccadilly Circus and the sounds of the street artists singing and playing instruments for money. I loved the high peaked white towers of St. Paul's cathedral and the blue hue of London Bridge. I wish you were here with me because it would be fun to experience this with my best friend.

My birthday is in three days. I'll spend it being all sophisticated in Paris!
Love you, miss you!
Rach

Paris-

Dear Grandma and Grandpa-
WOW! Thank you so much for reserving the first-class cabin for this leg of the trip! I felt so grown-up and sophisticated in my train car. Grandma, you would be proud to know that as each day ticks by, I feel more like Raquel, traveler of the world, adventure seeker, breaker of rules, rebel, and non-conformist. Grandpa, don't

be worried about the previous comment. I'm being cautious and have felt safe everywhere I've gone.

I'm sorry to make this so short, but I'm going to enjoy my beautiful French pastries and coffee while I write more letters and enjoy the view of the countryside.

Thanks again. I love you.

Rachel

To: Sk8erBoyStylin'@aol.com
From: RachelBee2007@yahoo.com

Parker-

I don't care if you must sell all your designer clothes to buy a plane ticket, you must get to Paris sometime in your life. The view, the romance, the food; all of it is exquisite, and you would fit in here so well. Everyone is sophisticated and stylish, just like you. People put so much focus on the Eiffel Tower, but this city has so much more to offer.

My parents surprised me with Moulin Rouge tickets last night for my birthday, and the costumes, the singing, and the dancing were breathtaking. I had a blast by myself, which was so new and liberating.

I hope all is going well. I miss you guys!

Love,

Rach

P.S. How is the boyfriend situation?

Mom, Dad, Stacia-

Thanks for the tickets to the show. It was terrific, and I feel like our next dance party should feature a kick line. You can practice in my absence, and I will practice as well.

Today, I went to the Louvre, and the artwork took my breath away. The pictures I took will have to speak to its beauty. I can't stop snapping photos of the scenery, sculptures, paintings, and old architecture here. I've taken thousands of pictures on the digital camera that I can't wait to share with you.

I miss you all. I can't believe I'm 18 now, an official adult.
Love,
Rachel

Versailles-

Sean- I went to Versailles today, only a twenty-minute train ride from Paris. I'm sorry I missed out on your birthday surprise. Parker told me you'd been feeling bummed because you had something special in mind. I never meant to wreck plans, that was never my intention. Honestly, I needed to do something like this and I'm not sorry I'm on this trip. If that hurts you, I apologize.

This place is so majestic. Today I toured Versailles Palace. I can't begin to describe it; Louis XIV wanted this place to be impressive, and he succeeded. I felt like royalty just walking around. The Hall of Mirrors had the most fantastic gold adornments and windows everywhere, overlooking the grounds. Look it up online and then imagine something much more impressive. When we own a house someday, it will probably need some chandeliers.

The gardens, which I just stared at for what felt like hours, had winding green shrubs in regal patterns and tulips in the grassy areas. Maybe we could try to landscape like this?

Learning about history from a textbook or research is different from experiencing it firsthand and seeing history unfold in front of you. I miss you, and I hope you are playing a lot of baseball and enjoying the summer with your friends,

I love you, Seany-Poo!
Rach xoxoxoxo

Samantha-
Did you know that bed bugs are a thing? I heard two people talking about it at my hostel this morning. I will be thoroughly inspecting the mattresses in every place I stay from here on out. I may have left all my clothing in the dryer for a long time yesterday in case I'd already procured some unwanted travel buddies.

Despite the bug fright, I'm learning how to travel better. I quickly learned how vital that multi plug-in adapter that you got me has been. I've learned how to hold my purse to lessen getting pickpocketed. I've learned to take pictures calmly and precisely, so I don't appear to be a crazy tourist. I've gotten better at asking people in the hostels for recommendations that are off the beaten path.

I took a bike tour of Versailles yesterday, as was recommended by Michele at the hostel, and it was one of the most memorable things I've done so far.

Have you talked to Sean at all? I've written to him a few times but haven't heard back. I'm not worried quite yet, but I wanted to check.

Love ya,
Raquel
P.S. I'll explain later

Amsterdam-

To:Stacialovessoccerandpigs@yahoo.com
From: RachelBee2007@yahoo.com

Stacia-
I'm not sure that you're old enough to read "The Diary of Anne Frank" yet, but I recommend you read it as soon as mom and dad allow it. I went to the Ann Frank house today, and it was heartbreaking. When you think that your world could exist in a space that small when you are at an age when you need to be out in the world, experiencing all that life has to offer you is unimaginable to me. I know you are still upset about this summer but please remember that life is short.

I took a luxury river cruise that started at the house and continued down the canals of Amsterdam. The view was great, but it was hard to enjoy knowing that we still had this obstacle between us. Life can change instantly, and I need you to forgive me no matter what it takes.

I love you, sissy.
Rachel
P.S. I've gotten you a cool pig-related trinket in every spot I've visited.

P.P.S. Please write me back, I spend a lot of time on trains, and though it is beautiful and I have books to read, I miss talking to you all.

Parker-
Okay, I know I said you'd love Paris, but I feel like Amsterdam is SO YOU! I'm sure my grandparents have heard about what happens in Amsterdam, but I'm not entirely sure they KNOW what happens in Amsterdam. Some people come here so that they can spiral out of control. Thankfully I'm at a hostel with people who want to enjoy Amsterdam without the pressure of trying every drug possible.

I did go with some of the girls from the hostel to a hookah bar. I didn't partake, but the smoke in the air did make me a little loopy. Afterward, we went to a nightclub and danced for hours! It. Was. Amazing!

Tomorrow I'm going with some of my new friends on a day tour of the Dutch countryside so we can see the tulips! I may just bring you back a pair of wooden clogs!

Love ya!
Rachel

P.S. Is Sean okay? I've had a hard time getting ahold of him.
P.P.S. I got an email from you, but all I could see was the subject tagline. Something about me needing to know something. I'm not sure if you forgot to include anything or I had a spotty internet connection. Regardless, I've enclosed a slip of paper with my Vienna hostel address. I won't be there for a week and a half, which would give a letter enough time to get there if you want to write me.

Prague-

Mom, Dad, Grandma, Grandpa-
I hope you all enjoy this postcard since you all love the Beatles! The John Lennon Wall is so bright. Did you know they paint over it occasionally and start fresh? I have several pictures of what it looks like today and found this postcard that I thought you'd all

enjoy!

    XOXO Rachel

    To: Stacialovessoccerandpigs@yahoo.com
    From: RachelBee2007@yahoo.com

    Stacia-
    Thank you so so so much for writing me back! I agree that someday I'd love to recreate this trip with you. I'm becoming a reasonably seasoned traveler and know more about Europe, so I would feel more comfortable doing this next time with some experience.

    I'm glad to hear that you, Amber, and Luke have been to Elitches every day except one, though I'm sorry you didn't go because of possible food poisoning. As I've recommended in the past, avoid food from theme parks unless you have no other option.

    So far, Prague is one of the prettiest places I've been to. The architecture here is a slightly different style than the other countries. I walked the Charles Bridge, and I didn't realize how old it was until I saw the sculptures, which were so fragile I felt like most of them would crumble if I touched them. The Astronomic Clock is also a sight to be seen. You'll love the video I took of it.

    The food here is a little more exotic. They eat a lot of meat. I went to a restaurant near my hostel and ate so much I could have thrown up. They have beef tartar, which is raw, wiener schnitzel, and beer. I had a tiny mug of pilsner, which was okay because I am old enough to drink here. My favorite dish was svickova, a piece of beef with a creamy vegetable sauce. They also serve a lot of dumplings. Thankfully I've walked a lot, so I don't feel too bad about being glutinous. "When in Prague."

    I look forward to hearing from you,
    I love you! Your sister,
    Rachel

Vienna-

Family-

I want to tell you about Vienna, but this will be a short letter. Know that I'm okay, just sad.

I got here this morning and paid for a hop-on-hop-off tour to see all the sights quickly. The architecture reminded me slightly of Versailles, and Schonbrunn Palace was breathtaking. Saint Stephen's Cathedral was probably the prettiest cathedral I've seen so far, though they all are somewhat similar.

Tomorrow I'm taking a break from history and going to the zoo.

Sean and I have broken up. I know this comes as a surprise, but I'll explain it when I get home. Even though I'm sad, I will continue to work on myself while I'm out here.

Rachel

Parker-

I got your letter this afternoon; I know that though it was hard to tell me what was going on, I appreciate it. I love you and hope we can still be friends.

Rach

Sean-

I know what happened, please don't be mad at Parker, he told me everything.

First off, I never expected a marriage proposal, and I'm sorry if I ever made you feel like that was a requirement or expectation. I understand that you wanted to propose to me on my birthday and my trip made it so that wasn't possible. I wish you could have told me what was going on instead of pretending everything was okay.

I'm not sure if your frustration about your wrecked plans caused what happened next, but I feel like if you'd ever cared about me, what happened at the mixer would have never occurred

I never expected you to sit around and pine for me while I was gone, and I would have expected nothing less than you going to a mixer and meeting some people attending our school. Making out all night with Drew, who I happen to know, in plain sight of everyone, is unacceptable. If you'd wanted to break up with me, you should have done that first.

It is apparent to me that we need to end this. Based on the lack of communication since I got here, I've concluded that you feel the same. I'm glad that we figured this out now instead of years down the road. I'll always think of you as my first love, and I wish it ended in a way I could respect.

-Rachel

18

~*Betty~ August 1969*

Dear Elizabeth-

We dropped by, but you are probably out working. We are happy that you are going on an adventure with your friends. Please be careful, and don't accept anything from strangers. We will gladly stop by your apartment and check on your houseplants, but we will only do this temporarily, so please come back in two weeks as you've stated you would. A music festival with your friends sounds lovely, and we hope you have fun.

Love Mom and Dad

I pulled the note off the front door where my parents had folded it, leaving it for me to find. I was excited about our upcoming adventure.

A lot had happened with me and in the world in the last six weeks. I was over the moon to have found David so I could experience some of these things with him. A month ago, we'd cozied on my parent's couch with Mom, Dad, and Grandpa to watch men walk on the moon. It had been out of this world, literally.

I'd introduced David to my family shortly before the monumental event, and I could tell almost instantly they approved. My father and David were outside tinkering on my grandfather's car by the end of the day. My mom had been inviting us over for dinner every Sunday, and it was amazing how seamless it seemed to have him around.

Meeting him had been life changing. I was trying not to fall for him, but he made it very hard. He took everything I threw at him with patience and grace. I panicked after our second or third date, telling him if we were going to see each other, it would have to be one day every few weeks, so I didn't lose business.

"I'll take any time I can get with you, Elizabeth." His statement had immediately softened my heart. What was the point in putting my all into Bee's if I didn't celebrate the ups and downs with someone? For now, I was learning how to enjoy David and being a business owner.

Missy returned three weeks ago, traveled, and wiser. She had learned so much about herself and the potential for life. She'd learned how precious time was as she met men on her trip who were facing a tour in Vietnam. Some had already lost friends and had signed up voluntarily because they felt they had to.

Frank, Missy, David, and I have been together almost non-stop since her return. She helped me with flowers during the day, and just like Karen, she was very beneficial to my sales. Missy received word last week from a woman she met during her travels about a music festival that was going to occur in New York. She thought if we loaded Frank's VW bus with flowers, we could go there, hear some music, sell merchandise, and enjoy people who were feeling the message of peace like we were.

We all had this sense that things were changing quickly. The war was hanging over all our heads, and with our boyfriends being 18, we worried that someone else would make a decision that would cause their lives to change. I felt like escaping for some music and peace was needed. I decided that we would pack some flowers and take Bee's Flowers on the road.

My parents agreed to check over the apartment while we were gone, and we loaded the van up with the plan to drive straight through to Bethel, New York. With the sounds of KIMN radio playing the Colorado Hit Parade list in the background, we headed out of Denver. We would take turns navigating, driving, and resting in the back.

Keeping flowers fresh had posed a bit of a problem, and Missy and I had decided to make dried flower crowns since we could make them ahead of time without worrying about keeping them alive. My grandfather, ever the businessman, reached out to a friend he knew on the East Coast who had recommended a flower wholesaler, and we were going to swing in and pick up some fresh flowers on the way.

I wasn't sure what to think about the music festival. None of us knew what to expect but were excited, nonetheless. Once we hit New York, everyone around us was there to do the same thing: attend Woodstock.

"How big is this festival supposed to be?" Frank asked as we passed another bus, covered in flowers, full of people.

"I thought just a few hundred people," Missy said, "but you never really know until you get there."

We stopped for a quick burger before heading to the wholesalers and were outside eating when a van, crammed full of people, pulled up.

One of the men stopped to talk to us. "You headed to the festival?"

"Yeah," David said, "What's the word?"

"Well, man, if you don't get there today, there might not even be room to park," he answered. "We heard there could be thousands of people there."

"Far out!" Missy exclaimed. "Maybe we should eat these burgers on the road and grab the flowers. No more stops. The festival starts tomorrow, and I want to make sure we didn't go all this way for nothing!"

We thanked the man and clambered back into the van. We were coursing with palpable excitement. There could be thousands of people there, holy smokes!

We made it to our merchandise pick-up and loaded as much as comfortably fit in the car. It was becoming clear that I could fill the van three-fold and still not have enough flowers to try to sell to the number of people we would possibly be encountering.

People started to park their cars and walk, hands full of belongings.

Missy hopped out of the front seat. "I'll find out what's going on."

The rest of us sat in awe of the activity around us. There were people as far as we could see.

Missy wandered around for a few minutes before popping back in. She had gained a new scarf in her brief time away from a nice woman who said she had a beautiful spirit.

"I have news," she said excitedly. "The music is still supposed to start tomorrow. From where we're parked, we have about a two to three-mile walk to the stage. They didn't think this many people would show up. It sounds like Jimi Hendrix may be here." I looked at her, and we both squealed in delight.

It took me a minute to think about what to do with all the merchandise. A possible three-mile walk to and from the festival wasn't realistic. Even if we took turns, that would be a lot of walking. The dried crowns wouldn't be an issue; we could all carry a basket with some in them.

"How would you guys feel about selling the live merchandise now and then just selling flower crowns at the event tomorrow?" I asked, feeling like it would be the best way to make a profit and then enjoy the rest of the festival.

My friends all agreed to help me, and we used some cardboard and markers to write "Flower Power- $1." We all took as many flowers as we could carry with a plan to meet back at the car when our merchandise was gone.

I decided to plant myself down the road to try to sell

flowers to people just arriving. The vibe all around was palpable. Excitement lingered in the air, along with the hints of marijuana and cigarettes. I met too many people to count in my few hours selling flowers. I received hugs, words of advice, a little necklace with a peace medallion on it, and offerings of food and water. Not a single person walked by without saying "peace" and complimenting my flowers.

I sold my first load in about an hour and quickly got another one before it started to get dark. Most of the flowers in the van were gone, so I decided to stay there and sell them through the open door, so I would be right there when everyone finished. Once everyone returned, we could load up our sleeping bags and food and take any additional flowers with us on the way.

People were still arriving in droves, and though I did have to turn down some strange trades, like brown acid, overall, if someone wanted to trade for something useful, I took it. I would already make a substantial profit if I sold all the flowers we'd gotten on the way up, and I still had the flower crowns to sell.

Seeing all these people coming together for love and peace made me want to focus less on the money I would be making. Despite some of the misconceptions about hippies, it was still important to me to work hard and pave my way. Having my grandfather as an investor in everything I did at Bee's also made me want to work that much harder.

One by one, my friends returned with money in hand and empty baskets. I paid each of them for their time, even though they all tried to resist, and soon we were loaded and heading to the Woodstock Music and Art Fair. We walked with our brothers and sisters in peace and love towards whatever the next few days held.

19

~Rachel~ July 2007

To: RachelBee2007@yahoo.com
From: BaseballSean89@hotmail.com

Dear Rachel-

I'm sorry I hurt you, and I know that what I did was unforgivable. I was in love with you, and I'm not sure what got into me. Something changed when I found out you wouldn't be around on your birthday. I was planning to ask you to marry me. In hindsight, maybe it is good that I didn't. I was also upset that you were experiencing this whole big thing without me, but I shouldn't have done what I did.

I understand why you broke up with me. I was dishonest, and instead of facing reality and telling you, I avoided you despite your communication attempts with me.

I know it's a lot to ask for, but please don't be mad at Drew. She was there to comfort me, and she felt terrible about what happened.

I hope that we can still be friends no matter what, especially since we will all be going to the same school together in the fall.

Sorry. With love always,
Sean

P.S. Don't worry, Parker is just as mad at me as you are, and he hasn't talked to me for weeks.

Vienna-

I was trying to enjoy my time despite my sadness. I kept reminding myself that some people would never be able to travel like me, at no cost to myself, and with a lot of freedom. I thought about Chad traveling because of the loss of his parents and the life change ahead of him. I knew that the situation with Sean counted as a loss, and I needed to heal. Letting go of the perfect life I'd pictured with a wedding and "forever after" would take time.

After arriving in Vienna, I contemplated contacting Chad to find out where they were right now, yearning to talk to someone from back home who was currently in the same area of the world. But when I'd looked for that slip of paper, I was disappointed to see that something wet had smeared it, making the last four digits of the phone number unreadable.

For now, I would have to stew in my feelings. I kept flashing back to Homecoming with Sean and Drew dancing with Parker and beaming at each other. The sad thing was that I could see them together. Unfortunately, picturing them dating made me sick to my stomach. In the moments when I was most angry, I imagined ripping the cheap Prom crowns off their heads and smashing them. I hoped to tame some of the anger before seeing Sean again.

I knew I would have to hold off on telling Samantha if she didn't already know. She would not be able to contain her anger, which could be dangerous. Samantha may look meek, but mix Sam, a disaster, and a hint of passion, and nothing but fire comes out.

On my first day in Vienna, I'd shown up at the hostel excited for the last leg of my trip. From here I would have my last long stay in Budapest before stopping over in London for one night and heading home. I was excited to get back to the states in a week but sad that my trip was nearing the end.

Hank, barely looked up from the book he was reading when I'd appeared at the front entrance. He finally put the book down after a few other people walked in behind me. He led me through the shared space and the kitchen area. There were a few people my age in the common areas, and I'd smiled and waved.

Hank showed me the bathroom closest to the room I would be staying in with other guests. "Now, you just need to hear the rules," he said, obviously eager to get back to his book on mushroom foraging. I wasn't excited about hearing them because they had been so similar in all the hostels.

"No disrespect, no thieving, share and clean up after yourself," he rattled off with his thick accent and a simple nod, not waiting for a response before turning around and walking back to the front desk.

One of my roommates was in the room reading a book. I glanced at the cover, "Water for Elephants," which caused immediate excitement. Friendship was our destiny, I thought instantly.

"I'm reading that book too," I said, settling my hiking pack under my bed.

"It's amazing so far, but the ringmaster is a bit of a wanker," the girl replied in a thick Irish accent. She sat up, put the book aside, and reached out her hand. "I'm Sophie."

Sophie and I had gone to lunch and hit it off quickly. She lived in Ireland, loved to travel by herself, and reading. She reminded me of Samantha, which was comforting. She was with me when I read the letter from Parker, and she swooped right in to comfort me after I'd burst into tears.

"Anyone who is threatened by you experiencing things is a complete and utter arse," she handed me a tissue out of her purse. "You and I will have fun for the rest of your time here. What do you say?"

Sophie helped me plan what to do with my remaining time and by the end of the day, we'd gotten a group from the hostel to go with us to the zoo. It was a welcome distraction, seeing different animals from around the world with people also located all over.

On my last morning, Sophie woke me up with some great news. She was changing her Eurail pass to Budapest so we could hang out before my flight back to London. I knew that with Sophie keeping me distracted, I could make it through this heartbreak until I got back to the United States.

Budapest-

We arrived at our hostel around lunchtime and checked in. Budapest was beautiful, with magnificently crafted sculptures and many smiling faces. Even with the beauty of my surroundings, I was still sad. Thankfully, Sophie was planning lots of activities for us until I was back home where I would have the support of my friends and family and hopefully the desire to talk to Sean about what had happened.

After talking to some people in the common area, we decided to go sightseeing and then to a bathhouse which had come highly recommended.

"Let's see where fate takes us," Sophie said as we packed our day bags. I'd thankfully packed a swimsuit before leaving America, unsure if I'd have the occasion to use it.

"Let's see where fate takes us," I echoed.

We walked first up the Danube. We stopped to watch the boats go up and down the waterway before stopping at the Shoes on the Danube, a World War II Memorial. It was heartbreaking seeing the empty shoes, minus their owners, on the riverbank. We sat in silence, wiping tears off our faces before moving on. Next, we admired the beauty of the Hungarian Parliament building before ending up at Szechenyi Thermal Bath.

"Are we in the right spot?" I asked when we got to the bathhouse, "It looks like a palace!"

"We're in the right place," Sophie confirmed, looking down at the paper she had printed out with the address on it. "It's a beaut!"

We purchased a day ticket, changed into our suits, and walked around to see where we wanted to spend our time. Parts of the inside were castle-like, with the bath areas most depicted in movies. We ultimately opted for the outside pools so that Sophie could check out the boys. These pools were in a courtyard, surrounded by lamplights, so it resembled a town square.

Inside the pool were a lot of families and older people, and as we waded into the heated thermal water, we scanned for people our age. Since it was early in the day, I assumed we wouldn't have much luck. I closed my eyes, soaking and taking advantage of time alone to relax while Sophie set out trying to find a stag party to flirt with.

I was as close to a sleep/Zen state as one could accomplish in a pool without drowning when I heard, "Rachel?"

The voice sounded somewhat familiar, but Rachel is a common name. I closed my eyes again.

"Rachel?" the voice was closer. I opened my eyes and saw Chad heading in my direction.

"Chad," I said, dumbfounded. How was this possible?

He reached me and scooped me into a wet hug. "I was hoping I would see you again. You and your adventures have been on my mind. How has your trip been?"

I felt like crying but stopped the tears, refusing to let my situation with Sean diminish all the fantastic things I'd experienced. "My trip has been amazing," I said as Chad sat next to me on the pool's inside ledge. "How about yours?"

"Phenomenal! We've had the greatest time, but unfortunately, it's coming to an end. We leave tomorrow afternoon," Chad said, "I can't believe it's already over. So far, it's been fast and furious. We've been to London, Brussels, Rome, and Budapest. If you asked me what all we've seen and done, I wouldn't be able to tell you right now. I will have to use pictures to put it all together later. We hoped to spend our last night here with a Sparty, but apparently, we're here the wrong time of year."

"What's a Sparty?"

"It's a pool party that happens here at night with DJs, lasers, and lights. We wanted to go out with a bang!" I heard a voice chip in, Chad's friends heading in our direction,

"New plan," one of his friends said, "We ran into a bachelor, I mean stag party here, and we're going to a ruin bar. Who's up for a full night of dancing?"

Chad and his friends raised their hands, and Chad looked at me expectantly. "You in?"

A few minutes later, Sophie swam up to us, apparently having run into the same stag party. "Rachel, we're going to a ruin bar tonight!"

Chad and I grinned at each other before making introductions. Landon, Caleb, Trent, and Chad stayed with us until we were all prune-like and ready for the next adventure. By the time we left the pool, I felt like we all knew each other well enough to have a fun time tonight.

I was trying not to make snap judgments about Chad's friends, but it seemed like Landon was the group's caretaker, and Chad was the sensible one. Caleb and Trent liked to rally people together, ensuring everyone was having fun. I was glad that we'd gotten to know them before going to something called a ruin bar, which sounded like a place of torture to me.

We planned to meet in Hero Square later to take some pictures of the statues and eat dinner before heading out.

"Ok, what kind of bar are we going to because it sounds scary?" I asked Sophie as soon as we left.

"It's pretty much a pub in an old building. The one we're going to will have music all night, and from what I heard from the gents, there's a different DJ on each level. I can't wait! How come you didn't tell me about the cuties from the plane?"

"We didn't have the best first interaction," I said honestly.

"Chad seems to be into you," Sophie said, which caused my stomach to flutter for a second.

"He's definitely nice, easy to talk to, and beyond handsome, but it wouldn't be fair to him or me if I didn't take time to heal from my breakup."

She nodded in agreement. "Landon is the one for me. I think some snogging is in order tonight."

We took a quick nap before getting ready and heading to Hero Square. After walking around taking pictures, we headed to a restaurant where they forced me to try bone marrow; the verdict was unclear for me on how it tasted because I was too busy trying not to let it come back up based on the consistency alone. We headed to the bar, and our excitement levels rose with each step.

Chad hung back so we could walk together as Sophie and the others joined arms, singing hype songs to prepare for the night.

"I can't help but feel that something has happened since I saw you," Chad said. "You don't have to tell me if you don't want to, but I'm pretty intuitive. Is it all the adventure?"

"My boyfriend and I broke up. He was homecoming king, and he cheated on me with the homecoming queen. He had plans to propose to me on my birthday, my fourth day in Europe. Since I decided to come here, leaving him behind, he lost it, I guess. The worst part is he didn't tell me, and his best friend did. I broke up with him, and it's only been a few days since I found out."

"Ouch," he said, "I can't imagine how you're feeling."

"It hurts for sure," I answered. "It's funny that I thought that getting married young and settling down was what I wanted until this happened. It's partially that this trip has changed me and partially that I don't want to settle down. I want to see what the world has to offer me and then decide."

"It's strange the way things turn out," he agreed. "I've learned that you have to expect the unexpected in life, and if you have the desire and ability to roll with situations as they arise, you get through it less scarred."

"I'm rolling with it for sure," I said, "but I'm ready to have a few drinks and dance the night away for tonight. Dance parties are my jam."

"Mine too," Chad said with a swoon-worthy smile as we walked inside.

The inside was cold and dank, with old brick surrounding us. I couldn't imagine the history of events within these mossy walls. Sophie danced over to me, handing me a Urquell beer. I'd consumed a few drinks on my trip and had learned that I needed to take it slowly with lots of water in between. Beer in hand, I began to sway to the intricate beat of the music. My new friends were all doing the same, and soon the dance floor was packed full of people dancing and drinking.

I thought about Stacia and what she'd said to me about being the happiest when I was involved in a dance party. Looking at all the smiles around me reinforced dancing as an art form. It was inspiring to think that all these people from different walks of life could come together with their victories and tragedies and dance the night away with smiles.

Warm tears streamed down my face thinking about all of it, me releasing both happy and sad feelings. Chad looked at me and made a thumbs-up gesture. I returned the thumbs-up, wiped the tears off my cheeks, and decided to allow everything I was feeling to melt away.

We walked out of the ruin bar at 7 am, sweaty, slightly buzzed from the alcohol and the night's excitement. Sophie and Landon walked together; hands clasped. I wasn't surprised, I'd seen them making out several times throughout the night.

"Best. Night. Ever," I said. I couldn't stop smiling.

"Best night ever," Chad shouted into the atmosphere. Our friends all echoed with roars of their own.

We walked for a bit, discussing our favorite memories, riding the adrenaline as long as possible.

"Can you guys come to see us off later?" Landon asked, pulling Sophie into a hug.

"I have a better idea," I said, not ready to leave our new

friends. "We go straight to breakfast. Then we'll come to help you pack up and hang until the train leaves?"

Chad threw his arms in the air, "Best day ever!"

We filled our stomachs with greasy eggs and toast before heading to the hostel to help them pack. The realization that this was coming to an end became prevalent closer to their departure and the train station. I felt closer to these people after one night than some people I'd known since childhood.

"We need to exchange email addresses and stay in touch," Caleb said as he split a piece of paper into six sections. We wrote down our information and promised to correspond often, and too soon, it was time for them to go. There wasn't a later train to the airport, or I felt we would have prolonged the goodbye even longer.

We all hugged, smiles spread across our faces, reminiscing still. Chad was the last person I reached.

"I know that you're still fresh out of a major breakup, but I know how short life can be. I think that you are a queen, Rachel, and if the time and place ever work for us to try something, I'll be here."

I smiled and kissed him on the cheek. He returned the gesture, pulling back slowly. Suddenly, it was as if our lips needed to connect, we turned simultaneously, and his soft lips slowly caressed mine. He didn't try to invade my mouth, instead he gently massaged my lips with his as his hands tightened around my waist. The pull was so strong that it felt like we would never stop kissing.

This was the kind of goodbye kiss I'd hoped to get from Sean and didn't. My knees wobbled as my heart thumped out of control in my chest. He reached a hand up and caressed the side of my face, and I became putty on the spot.

"We have to go!" Landon exclaimed, sneaking one last smooch from Sophie before running towards the others. Chad gave me one final kiss, pulling away with a smile before sprinting to the train.

"See you later, Queen," he shouted from the platform as it pulled away from the station.

20

~Betty~ August 1969

Today we witnessed history in the making. Not too many people can say that they were in a place at a time that generations after ours will talk about, an event that will never be forgotten. Missy, Frank, David, and I are at the Woodstock Art Festival, proving to be so much more than that. There are thousands of people as far as the eye can see; young and old, rich, and poor, soul-searchers, and those that are content. Everyone is coming together with love. It seems like the matters of the world are right here yet dimmed by the sense of community and music. The changes we need will happen; how could it not?

Notation from Betty's Diary, August 1969

"There are people everywhere," I noted, stating the obvious. There were people in all directions, and the rate at which the mass was growing wasn't slowing down. After leaving the van, we started walking in the same direction as everyone else. After about a mile, soft music sounds appeared, the sound of guitars making everyone's pace increase until the music was full force in our ears, and we could see a stage. By the time we got there, the music had stopped, telling us that they were probably testing the equipment for the start of the festival tomorrow.

We'd all anticipated paying a hefty festival fee but found out it would now be a free concert. I decided then and there that I would make sure that the money I was planning to pay would go towards doing something beautiful for someone else, possibly Karen.

The sun was starting to disappear behind the horizon, and we quickly found a spot to put up our two small tents. After we set up our area, we decided to walk around, wanting to get a feel for the environment and the people. Everyone was friendly and approachable, quick to offer a kind greeting, a hug, or offerings of water, food, beer, and drugs.

I was usually not known to partake, but I took a tiny puff of marijuana as it passed me, not because anyone had pressured me to do it, but because it seemed like a safe place, and I felt comfortable.

Though I hadn't brought any of the flower crowns with us to explore, wanting to scope out the environment, Missy and I were both wearing one and received many comments about Flower Power. Others inquired where we'd gotten them, and I assured people I would be walking around with them for sale the next day. We went back to our camp and made some sandwiches. After seeing the sheer number of people in attendance we decided we'd have to be responsible with our food and water rationing. With the pot relaxing me just enough to block out the noise, we turned in early, each couple in their own tents, exhausted from the journey from Colorado to New York.

The next day was a blur of activity. People continued to come in droves, and though it was fantastic to be there, it was getting more crowded by the hour. The rain had come in, making it more hectic, causing the farm we were camping on to become muddy. We had yet to locate any shower facility, so we'd made a group decision to embrace the dirt and try to clean up as best we could with what we had.

We were starting to hear rumblings of people having to walk ten or more miles to get here and rumors that police would have to start turning people away soon. I assumed it had something to do with the free entrance and with each growing hour the space seemed to get tighter with more people entering the festival space.

By the time 5 pm came, we were all a muddy mess and ready for the music to begin. Richie Havens was the first act to go on. By that point in time, we'd sold all the flower crowns. We had nothing left to do but enjoy music and participate in all that Woodstock offered.

Together my friends and I danced, sang, ate, smoked, and enjoyed the atmosphere for hours. During the chaos of the post-rain mud dancing and the height of sleep deprivation, Sly and The Family Stone came on with the night sky, illuminated by the stars, and revived us all. David turned to me and spoke loudly above the music. "I want to marry you someday, Elizabeth Bee."

I sat there, speechless. Before Sly and his gang, the crowd had started to wind down; people heading back to their tents until the sounds of funk music began to fill the atmosphere, returning them to the stage. Was he just revitalized? Was the constant cloud of marijuana smoke tainting his judgment? Had he taken other drugs without me knowing about it? I didn't know his stance on marriage since we hadn't talked about this type of thing before. What should I say?

He seemed to be reading my mind, as he often did. "Don't worry; you don't need to say anything right now. I just couldn't let such a perfect night go by without telling you how I felt."

I was excited to hear David say that to me. I hadn't thought much about marriage with everything else that was always on my mind, but just knowing he felt like there was potential for us, no matter his state of mind, made me consider the future we may have.

I kissed him and pulled him close wanting to continue dancing the night away, feeling free and empowered. We were a generation that was going to make a difference with our desire to make love and not war while spreading the word of peace and flower power.

By the time Jimi Hendrix played the final cords of the last official song of Woodstock, we were ready to go. We were muddy, smelly, hungry, thirsty, and beyond tired. We packed our belongings with slight sadness that it was over, but with a sense of camaraderie with our generation, each other, music, and nature.

We weren't sure how it would work getting our car out. There was the potential to be stuck there for days as the crowd thinned out. "Let's just get there and sleep in the van until we feel rested," I suggested.

"I'll be happy if we manage to find the car," Frank said as we lugged our belongings, hopefully in the right direction.

Despite the lack of sleep and the haze of the festival, using familiar landmarks, we made it to the van. We used water left in the car to wipe away the last muddy remnants of the festival. Though the mud was gone, our memories stayed fresh. The cars in front of us hadn't moved, so we tiredly plopped our belongings into the van and curled up amongst them.

As I lay cozied next to people that now felt closer to family than I ever thought possible, I thought of the different people I'd encountered, the messages I'd heard, and all that I'd learned. I was glad Woodstock hadn't just been about the music. I'd seen so much I agreed with:

- Not sending our young men to fight in a war that didn't need to involve us.
- The need to see people equally.
- Standing up for social injustices.

I'd seen people embrace their nudity, some making love out in the open. Though that practice was not for me, I appreciated that they were embracing our most primal sense to be naked and multiply. I also enjoyed the way people pulled together for the camp's sake. By the end of the festival, we'd erected tents solely for food and water, medicine, and shelter we could take people to if they had a bad trip. I was glad that none of us tried acid and was particularly delighted I hadn't accepted any of the brown kind offered to me the first day. During the concert, they'd had to make an announcement that everyone should stay away from that as it was causing horrible hallucinations.

I'd encountered a group near us that I'd been intrigued with at first and eventually slightly frustrated with. They talked about our parent's generation killing themselves working hard and their desire not to work so they could explore wherever the wind took them. They spoke as if by existing, success would occur.

They all had nice clothing and enough drugs and food to hand out freely. I found out from Missy that they'd received money to come down to Woodstock from their parents, who would also support them in college. It didn't make sense to me that you would shun your parent's hard work but accept money from them freely. I felt lucky to appreciate the work ethic my parents and grandparents had instilled in me while still considering myself a hippie. I hoped to continue making myself and them proud.

David and I hadn't talked about his mention of marriage, and I knew that we'd eventually need to discuss what had happened, but I preferred to wait until we could have the conversation privately. Frank and Missy made such a great couple and even better friends, laughing and dancing the night away next to us. I hoped things would work out well for them, just like I hoped things would continue to work out well with David and me.

Even with the cost of the flowers from the supplier, the flower crowns, the flowers we gave away or traded, and paying my friends for their help, I'd come out on top with enough money to pay for my trip here and back. I'd also be able to pay my grandfather for his investment in my business. If I kept working this hard, soon, I would have enough money for a storefront. I loved being outside, but it could be difficult to deal with the temperamental Colorado weather.

As I drifted to sleep, I wondered what the future would hold, not just for ourselves and our friends but also for our generation.

Part Three

Lilac

Growth
New knowledge
Wisdom

21

~Rachel~ May 2008

To: StrictlySophieinDublin@gmail.com
From: RachelBee2007@yahoo.com

Sophie-
Oh, my goodness, I can't believe that you're coming! We're going to have the best two weeks ever! I can't wait to show you around! I've contacted the guys as well, and we are a go for getting together. Don't forget the weather here is challenging. Bring mostly summer clothes and maybe a sweatshirt and jeans just in case we go to the mountains. Call me as soon as your plane gets here, and we'll come inside to greet you.
Kiss kiss kiss,
Rach

"Just a minute," I shouted to the person currently knocking on my dorm door so aggressively that I feared it would splinter and break. I decided to answer it before throwing the last of my things into my duffel bag. I opened the door and was practically tackled to the ground by Stacia and Samantha.

"I missed you, freak," Stacia said as she squeezed me tightly. I now feared it would be my ribs splintering and breaking.

"Someone's been eating their Wheaties," I said as I peeled her back to look at her. "I can't believe that in two months, you're now almost taller than me."

Stacia beamed proudly. "Measure us, Samantha." She kicked her shoes off and gestured for me to do the same. We stood back-to-back, and Samantha used her hand to measure the gap between our head heights.

"You are only taller by this much," Samantha said to me, holding her fingers out a few inches.

"Well, just you wait," I said to Stacia, "I was the tallest girl in fifth grade, and I haven't grown since then. You may only be this tall forever."

"You're just bitter," Stacia said as she put her shoes back on.

"Don't I get a hug? Am I just a measuring tool to you?" Samantha asked with a laugh as she held her arms out. We embraced, and I commented that I couldn't get used to seeing her with contacts instead of glasses. So much could change in such a short period.

My first year at Colorado State University was in the books, and I was excited to get home for the summer. I tried to get down to see my family every few months, but I still felt the sting of their absence, even though they were only about 90 minutes away.

I thought back to last summer and all that had changed. I'd finished high school and traveled to Europe, where I'd found myself. Sean and I broke up, and I moved onto the college campus. I was an English major for one semester before deciding that it wasn't what I wanted to do and changed my major to Horticulture with a Floriculture concentration. I was studying flowers, just like my Grandma Betty.

It hit me like a ton of bricks one day. I loved to read, and I loved English, but having to approach it as a career was making me love it less and less. After returning to Denver post-Europe, I thought about how happy I'd been, working in my grandparent's flower shop multiple days a week to save money for the school year. I'd been excited to wake up each morning, and I could go from being in a bad mood to a good one by merely smelling a bouquet.

I'd gotten a part-time job at a flower shop close to campus when I started school and become close to the owner, Shirley.

She thought I had a talent for floral design and sent me to a few workshops in the area. I was more addicted to flowers now than ever.

I was no longer the Rachel of before, but I wasn't Raquel either. I'd settled into Rach, independent and unpredictable while remaining stable and cautious. I learned to do things that best suited me while not planning too far in advance, leaving room for new ideas and variables.

My grandma had been excited when she found out that I was changing my major, but she always checked with me to make sure it was what I wanted and that I wasn't varying for her sake. The fact that every time I got to play with flowers at work or school, I felt happy, cemented the decision for me.

It didn't hurt that since changing my major, I didn't run into Sean as much on campus. We'd met up shortly after I'd returned from my trip. The Rachel pre-Europe would have wanted to figure things out immediately, but I wanted to spend some time with my family first, so I did. I'd also wanted a chance to process my feelings to be fair to both of us and the situation.

Sean had been apologetic, stating that he should have just talked to me about everything. He admitted that he felt pressure to propose to me because he felt like that was what was supposed to occur. We tried resolution, briefly dating for a week before it became apparent that too much had changed between us. Less than a week after our attempted reconciliation, he and Drew promptly started a relationship.

I often saw them holding hands while walking on campus, and though it did sting a little, I always waved and smiled. I'd learned to appreciate what had happened between us over time, realizing that I enjoyed being single and now appreciated time with myself.

I'd written Ms. Goodman an email right after I switched majors, thanking her for giving me advice. I sometimes tried to picture where my life would be right now had she not had the courage to be honest with me. I may have been an eighteen-year-old fiancé with no variety in my life. She'd written a kind email back telling me never to give up my love of reading and books, stating that she was glad I was happy.

Samantha and Stacia would drive me and my belongings back to Denver since I couldn't fit it all into my station wagon. The plan was to start working at Bee's again, and in a week,

Sophie would be here. I was so excited that she was vacationing in Colorado, and I couldn't wait to see her and our friends again.

Surprisingly, all of us from that night in Budapest stayed in touch. We wrote group emails weekly, filling each other in on the good, the bad, and the ugly of life. Chad and Landon hadn't been able to write as much when they were in basic training, but the emails when they could write included a lot of juicy details about what they were going through. Landon had written about how Chad, who talked in his sleep, sometimes yelled things loudly in the middle of the night, in front of everyone, causing him to get the nickname "Postage Stamp" after he accused the sleeping soldiers of stealing his last stamp. Chad wrote about how Landon, trying to impress a girl, ate his breakfast too fast, which he promptly threw up on his cafeteria tray.

I had gotten used to talking to these people regularly. There was something so refreshing about our communication. We were constantly rehashing the fun night in Budapest and joking about our first interaction at the airport while keeping up with each other's lives.

Chad and Landon had initially gone to San Antonio, Texas, for basic training before transferring to Peterson Air Force Base in Colorado Springs, only an hour's drive from Denver. They had a weekend leave pass and had plans to stay with Caleb and Trent this weekend. Both were still at the University of Colorado with plans to return home for the summer. Caleb was majoring in business and Trent in accounting.

We talked about meeting up since most of us were in Colorado, but things never seemed to line up where it would work for all of us. I was excited and nervous about seeing Chad again. Since Sean, I had only gone on a few dates, and I wasn't looking to be in a serious relationship. This didn't stop me from thinking about Chad often, and it was impossible to look at pictures of him in his uniform without noticing how handsome he looked. When I recalled that goodbye kiss we'd experienced, my body couldn't help reacting.

Chad's emails had been extremely respectful, and when we corresponded outside of the group, there was never any pushing, despite his knowledge that Sean and I remained broken up.

My phone dinged, and I looked down. It was Parker: I get

to see you tonight, right?

I can't wait, I replied.

I thankfully got to see Parker often. Parker was good at letting Sean and I share custody of him, ensuring that he visited both of us when he made the trek up from Denver. He attended the Art Institute in Denver and majored in fashion merchandising, which fit him perfectly. He and Trey were still trying to make it work but with Trey attending Cal State Long Beach, living in different states was proving to be much harder for them. Their relationship status seemed to change weekly.

"Rachel," Stacia said as I put my phone away. "Come on, I want to get home!"

We loaded everything into my station wagon and Samantha's father's truck, and my sister climbed into Old Blue with me. She updated me on everything I missed in the last two months, including that she, Luke, and Amber all got detention for booby-trapping a door with water that was supposed to fall onto a friend's head but instead fell onto a teacher, soaking her to the bone. I was happy to hear they were still thick as thieves. It would be interesting to see what their dynamic would be like as they aged and sexual tension became an issue. I had a feeling that it was bound to happen at some point.

Stacia still had two weeks of school left, and I promised to drive her and her friends there in the morning. She claimed they were "so over" riding the bus. I didn't mind, I was looking forward to seeing my sister every day again. "I missed you, Stacia."

"I missed you too, Rach," she patted me on my leg before returning to her storytelling.

We pulled up to my parent's house, and though I had been there many times since moving into the dorms, it felt good to be there but a little odd at the same time. It was still my home without being my home. I assumed this was a normal part of growing up, figuring out how to piece together your old and new life.

I went to the back of the car and opened the hatch.

"Can we get stuff in a little bit?" Stacia asked, looking down at her phone, "Mom said she wants to say hi really fast. She's missed you."

"I can just grab a tiny load," I said, leaning into the car.

"Please, Rach," Stacia said, getting close to me, puckering

out her lip while batting her eyes, a trick I'd taught her as a child and instantly regretted when she started using it against me.

Samantha pulled up behind us and came to stand with us, not even asking what we were discussing; she also started batting her eyes and puckering her lips.

"Fine," I lowered the hatch, and we headed inside the house.

"I'm home," I hollered from the entryway.

"Down here," My mom called.

We walked downstairs, and I almost had a heart attack when people jumped out from various hiding spots. "Surprise!"

22

~Betty~ May 1970

My Lovely Mrs. Bee-Wilson,

I miss you terribly. I try to keep busy, playing cards with the guys and napping as much as possible. Honestly, I sometimes expect to wake up from a nap to find you by my side. Sometimes I catch a whiff of flowers, and I'm taken back to memories of you. It is horrible that the sound of gunshots startles me less and less, not that I'm not always cautious, but when you hear something multiple times a day, eventually it becomes more routine. The sound of gunshots should never be normal.

I wish I were there with you, learning how to be husband and wife in person instead of through letters, but knowing that you are there handling things, which you have always done better than me anyway, makes me rest easier. I hope that the fighting will stop soon, but until then, I will continue to fight for our country.

With love, your husband,
Mr. David Wilson

T he direction of our lives forever changed on December 1st, 1969. We had still been riding the excitement of Woodstock and the horror of the Charles Manson cult killings. The last few months of 1969 seemed like such a strange time.

To make the draft fairer than in the past, where middle-class white men were often not drafted, they decided to select soldiers using a lottery system based on the day of birth. If you were a man between the ages of 19 and 26 and your birthday was drawn, you had to report for duty, and they would determine eligibility.

We had all huddled in front of the television as they pulled the first blue capsule out of a glass container. David's birthday, September 14th, was the first to be called.

I stifled a cry, not wanting to scare David, who was now facing way more of a challenge than I. I hugged him to me, and the thought that the days we could hug each other freely were now potentially numbered destroyed me. I suddenly had to face the realization that he may leave and not return.

His mother's wail had been so visceral that I'd woken in the middle of the night for weeks, recalling the sound of pure terror coming from a human. I knew that his family had served in the past, and David was willing to help. But it didn't make the fact that he would most likely have to go any less horrifying.

"We can get through this," David said, trying to calm me down.

During the second lottery, "J," "G," and "D" were the first three letters called. My heart sank, knowing that his chances of going were even higher now. We hoped his college enrollment would help him.

We spent as much time together as possible, David coming with me at night to help peddle flowers, attending demonstrations against the draft, holding signs up high, and encouraging politicians to send their sons if they felt so strongly about fighting this war. We went on walks and hikes, we went to movies, and each night as we bade each other goodbye, we kissed like it could be the last time our lips touched.

I'd known that him going wasn't a complete death sentence, but it felt like one. He would live or die in Vietnam.

Frank had decided to enlist voluntarily, feeling like it was his duty to serve. After he signed, Missy came home hysterical. She tried everything to make him change his mind with promises of marriage, children, and travel. He calmly told her, "I'm putting myself on the chopping block, so maybe my younger brothers won't have to be in this situation in a few years."

Missy had no other choice but to support and love him until he left. They were also spending all their time together, and though I'd thought we couldn't possibly get any closer after Woodstock, having life and death dangled in front of us made us thick as thieves. I felt like Missy and Frank were the siblings I'd never had while growing up, and I felt like David was the man I wanted to be with forever.

I'd gone from not being interested in love to being surrounded by it, and all it took to get me there was David. His passion, love, and support were the ingredients I was missing. I couldn't believe that I'd found my soulmate and now may lose him.

January came and with it the news that David was going to Vietnam. He'd come to my house after reporting for his evaluation, and all it took was one look at his face for me to know. Despite trying to remain strong for him, I broke down sobbing, and that night he'd slept in my bed, us holding each other as if the world depended on it. If Helen had shown up at my door that night, inquiring why we broke the overnight opposite sex guest rule, I would have unleashed my sorrow with an animal-like wail of my own into the night.

Two days after David found out about the draft, I brought up what he had first mentioned at Woodstock. "Let's get married," I said, not being able to imagine him leaving without knowing my hopes and plans to be with him forever.

He'd looked at me questioningly, knowing me well

enough to know I wasn't like the girls of generations before me, existing to be proposed to and made into a wife. "I'm not sure what to say."

"Say that you'll marry me."

"Elizabeth Bee," he'd said, grabbing my hands, "I feel like you just proposed to me, and I wanted to be the one to do that. I'll marry you as long as you tell people from here on out that I asked you."

"You said it first back at Woodstock, so you officially brought it up first." I threw my arms around him, knowing that whether he was killed in action or died lying next to me as an old man, we were now promising to God, our family, and our country that we would face all of it together.

"I owe you a real proposal then," David replied.

"I'm not that kind of woman," I responded. "I just want us to be together."

We married in a small ceremony three weeks before David would be leaving, giving us a few weeks to enjoy each other's company and experience a taste of what marriage felt like before transitioning into the warped reality we were living in right now.

Our families were supportive of our decision to marry, understanding the desire to do so and the time constraints. We were happy with their support. We knew marriage was challenging and that we'd have to work that much harder at it because of our circumstances.

"Welcome to the family, son," My grandfather had said quietly a few minutes after we told him our plan. He hugged us both but not without me noticing the tears in his eyes.

When I asked my mom about it later, she informed me that he had witnessed his father leaving when he was young to fight in World War I, and he'd remembered how hard it had been for his mother.

"Your grandfather loves you so much," my mom said. "He knows that your hearts need to do this, but he doesn't want your life to be any harder than it has to be."

I appreciated that my grandfather wanted my life to be easy, but seeing David go off to war without binding us together would have broken my heart. If he died, I wanted to have a right to get the notification, and I wanted the right to see him if he became wounded and hospitalized. Most of all, I wanted to be part of the motivation he needed to stay safe.

There were rumors of young men continuing to hide in Canada, and though it was an option I openly mentioned to David, he felt it was his duty to serve as the men in his family had done before him. I'd been slightly irritated that I wasn't allowed to join him. If the government was forcing him, why couldn't I go as well?

"Mark my words," I said to him, "Women can fight for their country and will be allowed to do so someday."

We married in the small church my parents attended, Frank and Missy, our wedding attendants with our families as our witnesses. David wore a vest, shirt, and bells, and I wore a cream-colored floral sundress with a ring of flowers atop a circle of braids. We held the reception at my parent's house. It had been a grand day.

When David left in early February, I'd cried for weeks, Missy and I wallowing in our sorrow. Missy was heartbroken, she and Frank deciding they were going to wait and see what happened while Frank was gone. I think Frank didn't want to tie Missy down, but I knew that we'd all be communicating through letters.

I looked again at the letter I received this morning, three months after he'd left, and I missed his presence so much. A year ago, I didn't know David, and now I felt his absence with every heartbeat. I packed up the flower cart and put the letter into the handbag I kept with money for change, shears, and now David's love letters.

I wondered if I would see Karen today. Her father was also serving in Vietnam, causing Karen to be sullener than before. Her brother included her more than he had in the past, which was good, but you could tell their already questionable family dynamic was even worse now. I didn't have the heart to ask about her mother, but with the time Karen spent confiding in me, I felt like she was lonely at home.

I was about to walk out the door when nausea hit again. I ran to the bathroom and threw up. I rinsed my mouth and looked down at my pants, where a little bulge was starting to show. I was going to have to tell David and my family soon; we were expecting.

23

~Rachel~ May 2008

Rachel's Surprise Party Invite by Stacia Bee-Wilson

> *For some reason, my sister means something to each of you crazy peoples, and because of this, I would like to invite you to a super-secret surprise party for her.*
>
> *Reasons to keep this secret include:*
>
> *1. My sister has crazy detective skills, and it would be a miracle if we pulled it off*
>
> *2. She is less of a control freak than she used to be, so she may enjoy the party*
>
> *3. I want to meet all of you so you can see how cool I am despite having Rachel as my sister*
>
> *4. My parents are cool*
>
> *5. My grandparents will be there, also cool*

"What is going on?" I asked with surprise as I surveyed the people in the room, honing in first on Sophie, who had appeared from behind the recliner chair. She danced her way over to me, wrapping me in a hug. I saw Parker, Trey, Clint, Samantha, and a few girlfriends from CSU who lived near Denver before my eyes settled on Caleb, Trent, Landon, and Chad.

"What is going on?" I repeated, looking toward my parents as I hugged everyone around the room.

"It's your birthday surprise party!" Stacia exclaimed.

"My birthday is weeks away!" I replied.

"Well, we knew that if we planned it with you living here, you would figure it out, so we pulled some ninja stuff and arranged it," Stacia said proudly before adding under her breath, "even though you're a horrible person with bad breath."

"Thank you so much, sissy. I appreciate it," I said, grabbing her in for a hug and whispering in her ear, "You have the face of a potato, and I hate you."

Stacia laughed and pulled back. "We're ordering dinner here and then going moonlight bowling."

I'd never been surprised, ever. I was the person in the movies, and when reading books, that thought five steps ahead, usually guessing the ending and even sometimes the next line of dialog. Despite this, I loved surprises.

"Thanks, Stacia. I love you," I planted a big kiss on her cheek.

"Gross," she said. "Go hang out with your friends."

I went over to join Sophie, who was hanging out with Chad and the crew. "I'm so glad you're all here." I squeezed her arm.

"Who picked you up from the airport?" I asked, recalling that I was supposed to pick her up from Denver International Airport next week.

"We did," Chad chimed in, "We were coming from Colorado Springs anyway, so we just swept her up on the way."

I looked at Chad. Now that I'd worked out all the surprise details, I could assess the situation better. Both he and Landon looked bulkier than they did in their pictures. He smiled at me, and it was hard not to look at his lips without thinking about how amazing that kiss had been.

That kiss. The kiss I compared all kisses to. I'd used that kiss as one of the reasons not to pursue a second shot with Sean. I knew first kisses were new and exciting, but I honestly couldn't remember kissing that phenomenally with Sean, or anyone else, ever. I tried to put all the impure thoughts about his lips into the back of my mind so I could focus on being friends. We were friends. Just friends.

Chad and I exchanged pleasantries, catching up on life. The first anniversary of his parent's death occurred in late April, and it had been apparent in his emails that it was hard on him. I'd asked how I could help him, and he'd thanked me again for not replying like everyone typically did with the usual "Are you okay?"

"I look forward to your emails, more than you know. Hearing from everyone is nice, but I look forward to yours the most." He looked around to see who was listening to him. "Don't tell the others. They may think we're cheating on the group friendship."

I felt my heart rush as I held my pinkie out to interlock with his. "I promise." I knew that Sophie and Landon talked all the time privately, but it made me feel special having a "secret" with Chad.

Sophie was like a little pixie, zipping around and talking to everyone in the room. She and my grandma were currently locked in a very heated, possibly inappropriate conversation.

"You are a cheeky booger," my grandma exclaimed loudly. "Now, what's a wanker again?"

Stacia piped in, "Wanker? What is that?"

"Nothing," Sophie and I shouted together. I looked at my grandma, "Trouble, you are always causing trouble."

My grandma shrugged innocently, though her face told a different story. "What? She's teaching me things that they say over in Europe."

Chad interjected, thankfully changing the direction of the conversation, "I was talking to your grandma earlier. How come you never told me your grandparents went to Woodstock?"

Stacia and I froze, "You and Grandpa were at Woodstock?"

The whole room seemed to quiet as we waited to hear the answer.

"Well, yes," my grandma answered as if Woodstock was as big a deal as a trip to the grocery store. "Why do you think we have that print from Time Magazine in the basement? We, my best friend Missy, and her boyfriend, Frank, all went together. All of us are in a picture published in the magazine. That was Bee's Flower's first cross country event. Many of the flower crowns you see in the pictures were Bee's Flowers originals."

"You aren't naked in your picture, right?" Stacia asked, a look of sudden disgust crossing her face. "Cause I would probably be traumatized."

"You're just going to have to look closely at the picture next time you're over," Grandma Betty said, raising her eyebrows.

"Gross!" Stacia exclaimed.

"Pizza's here," My parents called from upstairs, and we all headed up to make some plates before heading out to bowling. I'd missed Justin's, my favorite local pizza place, and I piled slices of New York-style pizza on my plate, cheese oozing over the sides of each piece.

While everyone was finishing their food, my dad motioned me aside. "Do you want me to help you unload the car before we go bowling?"

He knew me too well, knowing that even though I'd let go of a lot of my control issues over the last year, I still liked to know that everything was mostly in its place. Before Europe, I would have unloaded the car and put everything away before I would have been able to function well. I felt much more balanced now.

We headed outside and opened Old Blue's hatch. "We're so glad you're home," my dad said as he squeezed me into a side hug before starting to load items into his arms. "So, are you and this Chad fellow dating?"

"Why would you ask that?" I questioned him, grabbing a load for myself.

"What's wrong with that? He's a nice man, and I've seen how he looks at you."

"What do you mean?" I asked nervously.

"He looks at you often, and you seem to do the same as well," my dad answered as we lingered by the car, trying to finish the conversation before we went back to join the guests. "I'm not saying you should or shouldn't pursue a relationship with the young man; I want to give you a little fatherly advice. It's been a year since you and Sean broke up. You're a different person, and I know you felt last year like you needed to prove that to everyone, but you don't. You deserve to follow your heart and your head."

I nodded; I knew he was correct. Part of me wanted to pursue something with Chad, and part of me enjoyed becoming who I wanted to become without the pressure from anyone else. It may be stupid and selfish, but I wasn't quite ready to give that up. If fate wanted Chad and me to be in a relationship, it would happen. But I did hate the thought of him getting snatched up by someone else permanently.

"Thanks, Dad. I appreciate the pep talk. I'm just trying to take it one day at a time and see what happens. I can't confirm or deny the looks; I'll have to plead the fifth."

We dropped the load off in my room, and I joined my friends again, enjoying catching up with everyone until my parents informed us that our bowling lane reservations were fast approaching. Stacia told me that she'd already picked who should drive together.

"Geez, bossy," I said to her as we headed outside.

She shrugged her shoulders. "I want to be dominant by the time I'm your age; it's a work in progress."

I laughed at her assertiveness.

"I was assigned to drive you," Chad said as he walked toward me. Stacia started walking away but turned around and waggled her eyebrows at me behind Chad's back. I made sure he wasn't looking before I shot her a glare.

There was plenty of room for us to ride with others, but instead of raising a stink, I nodded and followed Chad to his truck. I hopped in, and before I could focus on the possibility of it being awkward, his phone rang.

"Hello," he said, "Yeah, we're just leaving. I'm not sure if I'll be able to stop by until tomorrow." He laughed, his deep throaty laugh penetrating my heart. Was he flirting with someone?

"No, I don't want you to go through any trouble. Are you sure? Okay, okay, bye Honey," he hung up the phone.

Inside I was fuming. Chad had to be talking to a girlfriend. I was sure he'd produced that sexy laugh just for her hearing pleasure, AND he had called her honey at the end! I tried not to be upset. I didn't have any right to be angry when I couldn't determine whether I wanted us to date. I at least recognized it wasn't fair to want to stay unattached while expecting him to do the same.

I turned off my brain, not wanting to look, appear, or act crazy about this.

"Do you know where we're going?" Chad asked as he motioned to a GPS on the dashboard, fingers poised, ready to type in the address of the bowling alley.

I gave it to him, and we sat for a minute, waiting for the instructions to appear.

"So, tell me how you've been? Any more Sean/Drew sightings?" He started driving, navigating the streets per the robotic voice from the GPS's instructions.

"I saw them a few weeks before school got out. They looked happy, which doesn't make me as mad as it should," I admitted. "When I think back to our relationship, I don't think either of us knew how to be ourselves yet. If we'd stayed together, we would have eventually resented each other for that. I, at least, have a better idea of who I am now."

"I hear you. After I lost my parents, I decided not to waste time anymore, especially on small things that won't benefit me or others. I want to live each day being a good person, a good man."

"Well, well," I said with sarcasm. "I'm glad that you found me worthy enough to come to my birthday party."

"Way to make it about you," Chad said back with equal amounts of sarcasm.

"Um, because it is my birthday party and all about me."

"It's not your birthday yet," He snarked back, causing a flitter of excitement within me. Until I remembered the sound of his voice, talking to his honey.

My head and my heart were in a constant battle about how to proceed. I would have to work a little bit harder to keep my feelings on a friendship level when I was around him.

24

~Betty~ *May 1970*

Betty-

I hope that you're okay with me writing to you. I know we've been friends for a long time, and I need someone I can be perfectly honest with, and we've always had that kind of relationship.

I'm scared.

I don't even know how to explain how it feels to be here. The jungle is beautiful, yet dangers lurk everywhere- Viet Cong, snakes, insects, and plants. It is as if everything here wants to harm us. I sometimes picture what it would be like traveling here to see the beauty of this country and the people instead of being stuck in the middle of a pointless war, killing and being killed because that's what they tell us to do. I go through bouts of sadness and anger, wishing I could wake up from this nightmare.

I don't want what I'm saying to make you more frightened for David. Working on the helicopter, he's in a slightly more protected position. I see him sometimes, and he looks well.

How is Missy? I hope she will someday understand why I broke things off. I don't want her to feel like she must stay with me out of pity. I don't know if I'll ever come back and if I do, I know I won't be the same person.

I know I'm supposed to be a man and feel numb to death and gore, but how could anyone see and do what we've done and come out okay. I don't want to turn into a shell of a man, but that's what is happening.

Please write to me; I need something familiar in my life.
Your friend,
Frank

I hadn't known I was pregnant until David had already been in Vietnam for a month. My first indication was that the different scents and smells around the park, which I used to love, suddenly made me nauseous. The first time it had been so bad I needed to throw up had been in front of Karen.

She'd come over to say hi while I took a break, and I'd been talking to her about how much she'd grown in the last year. It seemed like she was no longer a little girl but a young woman in transition. Someone walked by with a hot dog, and the salty smell of the meat had forced me to bolt into the bushes to throw up.

Karen stared at me, wide-eyed. "You must be coming down with something. You just seemed normal!"

"I feel better," I said as I used cloth from the cart to wipe my face. "That was strange."

I had felt normal after getting sick, and when I continued to feel okay for a few days after that, I put it out of my mind thinking it had been food poisoning or a 24-hour bug. Then, I started noticing tenderness in my breasts. I didn't wear a bra anymore, which usually didn't affect anything, but I started having to wear one again for comfort.

After a few more bouts of vomiting, I decided to go to my doctor. I sat on the examination table, spinning my wedding band around my ring finger, an heirloom from David's grandmother, as I waited for the doctor to come and talk to me.

"You're expecting," he told me, and for a moment, I

couldn't comprehend what he was telling me — expecting what exactly?

"A baby," he said after I sat there for a minute, blank-faced and confused.

"But my husband's deployed," I replied, tears streaming down my face. On the one hand, I was beyond excited to have a little flower child that I could carry in a pack to sell flowers, one who would be an amazing person simply because they were part David and part me. On the other hand, I didn't know if David would make it home. Men were dying every day, and there was no guarantee that he wouldn't be one of those.

I hadn't talked after that, just sat on the exam table until a nurse in her pristine white dress and hat came in and told me I had to leave because another patient needed the room.

Today I was going to tell my grandfather. I realized that it seemed strange to tell him before my parents, friends, or husband. I just needed to tell someone whose reaction would be nothing but loving and supportive. I knew my grandfather had experienced a lot of joy and heartbreak in his life, and I knew he would understand.

I also wanted to talk to him about Frank. I was worried about him after the letter I'd gotten recently. I'd cried reading it, the fear, and the feeling of helplessness so apparent that I couldn't ignore it. I hoped my grandfather could provide some insight or talk to Theresa, Missy's grandmother, about my concerns. Missy had been sad and understandably hurt that Frank had ended the relationship. When I tried to talk to her about it, she claimed she had to hurry to the hospital and couldn't be late, and I hadn't brought it up again.

Nursing school had been great for Missy, but there were noticeable bumps in the road after she and Frank broke up. As soon as she got the letter from him, she went from spending nights at home reviewing material and studying with nurse friends to going to Boulder with some of her wilder acquaintances. Though I was glad she had support, I hoped that her studies wouldn't become impacted.

I'd only had one run-in with Helen a few days after David and I were married, and she'd come by one morning. "I noticed the young man that has been courting you did not leave last night, and we are going to need to hold an emergency discussion in the manager's office promptly."

I'd held my left ring finger out, flashing the wedding band. "My husband stayed last night, as he will stay every night for the next two weeks until he leaves for Vietnam."

Helen, who always seemed to have a negative response to everything, said, "As long as there are no noise complaints, I'll allow it. My daddy served in the armed service." She awkwardly did an about-face and left, leaving me surprised that there hadn't been an argument. David, standing behind the door, ready to jump in if necessary, had looked at me, shrugged, and then enveloped me in a hug. I was thankful that Helen had given us one less thing to worry about before David left. I'd dropped by a fake flower arrangement the next day, hoping that this wouldn't exacerbate any of the allergies she'd spoken of previously.

I knocked on my grandfather's door, and as usual, he answered immediately. I called this morning to let him know I was coming, mostly because he and Theresa had spent more time together, and I didn't want to interrupt that. I was pretty sure that they were more than just restaurant friends, but I planned to let him tell me in his own time.

"Hi Bug," he said as he opened the door. "Can I still use your nicknames even if you are a married woman?" He asked as he led me into the living room, where he'd already set two cups of tea.

"You can always call me Bug and Honeybee, Grandpa," I touched the bumblebee pin on my dress. "I enjoy both names."

"I made your tea the way you like it, a little honey, milk, and sugar," Grandpa told me as he scooted my cup to me.

I blew on the hot tea to cool it before taking a sip. "Sheer perfection," I said as I let the heat from the cup relax me.

"I have something to tell you," My grandfather said as he

took a sip of his tea and waited for my reaction.

"I have something to tell you too."

"I haven't told anyone," my grandfather said conspiratorially.

"I also haven't told anyone."

"You go first," Grandpa said.

"You brought it up first, plus you are the elder. Elders first."

Grandpa swatted my arm playfully. "Elder, I don't recall being called that face-to-face by anyone, ever."

"Okay, how about we both say our thing at the same time," Grandpa looked at me like this suggestion was crazy. "Humor me here, Grandpa."

"Okay, Honeybee, are we going to do a countdown?"

"Sure," I said, pushing my teacup to the side. "3,2,1. I'm pregnant."

"I'm getting married."

We both looked at each other with surprise.

"Pregnant?"

"Married?"

"Congratulations are in order," I said, standing up and pulling my grandfather up and in for a hug. "Um, who are you marrying?"

"Theresa," he said as he embraced me tightly.

"I knew it," I said.

"My little Bug will have a baby bug," Grandpa pulled back, and I could see that he was emotional, probably about both of our situations.

"My grandpa will get married," I said, tears also gathering in my eyes.

"When do we start telling people?" Grandpa sat back down, swiping at his eyes before grabbing his tea.

"Well," I said, also reaching for my cup, "I'm guessing you have to tell people before the wedding date, and I have to tell people before this belly gets any bigger, though I could hide it in sundresses for several more months."

"How far along are you?"

"Well, if the doctor did his math correctly, I'm about three months along. I want to tell David, but I don't want him to worry about possibly not coming home to two people."

"He needs to know," Grandpa said quietly. "It may be hard for him, but it could also give him something more to live for."

I started to cry softly, "I don't want to tell him in a letter. I wish I could talk to him."

"I know Bug, and the alternative would be him coming home to a child he didn't know about who is over a year old. Most men would see that as a betrayal."

"I know; I keep hoping that the war will end soon, and I won't have to worry about any of this."

"Oh honey," he said, scooting his chair closer. "We all wish it were different right now, but wishing isn't going to change it, unfortunately. We need to hope for the best, not just for David, but all our young men out there."

"I'm worried about Frank," I remembered suddenly. I pulled the letter out of my pocket, where I'd placed it for safekeeping to show to Grandpa. "I know Missy and Frank aren't dating anymore, but I thought Theresa might be able to help. I know Theresa enjoyed Frank's company while he was with Missy."

Grandpa put it in his pocket. "I'll make sure to pass it along to her. I know that there is a lot of turmoil right now. We aren't guaranteed to have a tranquil existence, unfortunately. In my elder years, as you called them, I've learned that we need to love and support the people around us and live each day like it may be our last."

I nodded. "I just want us to all walk away from this happy and okay."

"So do I, Bug, so do I. Now, what do you say we start spreading our good news? Let's go tell your parents."

25

~*Rachel*~ *May 2008*

Vast-

    written by Rachel Bee-Wilson, age 18, English Composition

    She looked to the sky, to the stars, to the sun, to the air, to the atmosphere. Where she used to feel suppressed and smothered, she now felt the infinite space, the expanse around her.

    She had herself, and where that used to leave her lacking, she now felt bathed in endless possibilities.

    She looked at those that told her she couldn't make it alone, and it no longer mattered. She knew the power and strength that was perched just below the surface.

    She enjoyed the solitude that came with independence, and instead of seeking acceptance from others, she pulled it from her core.

    She was becoming.

We got to the bowling alley just as everyone else was pulling up. My parents were the last to arrive, with Amber and Luke now in the car. I guess there wouldn't have been extra room as I'd initially thought.

My parents had reserved a few lanes so we could all play next to each other. The lights inside were minimal, and the lanes were illuminated by black lights with bright lasers, adding to the ambiance. I went to where Sophie and Samantha were already sitting, fast friends.

"They don't serve fish and chips very many places here," Samantha informed Sophie.

"We can find some," I told Sophie as I plopped down next to them. "But I bet you'll be very disappointed."

"I guess you'll have to teach me all about American food," Sophie replied. "I've had food from all over, but I may go through fish and chip withdrawal."

My parents came over and pointed out the lanes that were ours. "Don't worry," my mom assured us, "We'll pick the farthest lane away from you and play with Stacia and her friends. We don't want to cramp your style."

"My style is that I missed you guys. Let's randomly pick teams so we can all enjoy visiting. We can switch again before the next game."

Stacia, listening carefully, came over to me, beaming. "That will be much more fun. You have matured more nearing your nineteenth year of life." Quietly, so only I could hear, she said, "And you are way less of a control freak."

I smacked her jokingly on the arm. "I'm not nineteen yet. Any more comments like that, and I'll make you bowl with mom and dad."

Stacia ignored me, taking charge by dividing everyone into three groups and sending them all to their assigned lanes to play.

My number landed me with Sophie, Landon, my sister, her friend, Luke, and my dad. We were in the middle lane, which was nice because I could see what the people in the other lanes were doing and still talk to everyone.

Sophie and Landon were flirting, which wasn't a surprise after our night in Budapest and how they spoke to each other in emails. Stacia kept looking at them in abject horror, which was funny. Luke kept giving her sideways glances, and I wondered if he had a little crush on her. She kept bossing him around, so maybe he was just irritated about that. I made a mental note to get information out of my parents on them this summer.

"You're going down!" I heard from the other lane. I looked, and Chad was joking with my college friend, Andrea. She was giggling, and as much as I loved her, I hoped she wasn't going to pull her typical helpless female act to try to get Chad's attention.

I grabbed a bowling ball. I needed to ignore the flirting. I shouldn't care. Why was I so concerned? It wasn't my right to be jealous, but it would be his honey's.

I took my turn, getting a few pins on my first and second attempts, nothing to brag about. "I'm just getting warmed up," I stated as I walked back to my seat.

Since she was a guest, Sophie went next, and I took her seat next to Landon. "How do you like the Air Force now that you're out of basic?"

"I'm enjoying it. It's given me a different respect for hard work, honestly. It's also turned my bullshit meter way up. I'm not talking to my parents right now, but that isn't bad. They need to work on getting healthier before we fix things."

"I can't imagine that's an easy situation. I hope they can try to get clean for themselves, and of course, for you."

Landon stood up and hugged me. "Thanks. You can't choose your family. I'm lucky to have some great friends, though."

"BAM!" Chad shouted, "Strike!"

"Yeah," I said, my mood suddenly shifting, "Some great obnoxious friends. Does Chad also chew with his mouth open? That would be the icing on the annoying cake."

He looked at me curiously. "He does. What's the deal with you guys anyway? Chad is radio silent when I ask him. We all saw that steamy kiss in Budapest, and you can't say there aren't feelings there."

"We don't have a deal. We talk in the group email and

occasionally on our own. My heart tells me I want him, and my head tells me I'm not ready. I can't seem to stop the conflict, you know? Plus, I wouldn't want to pursue anyone who already has a girlfriend."

"Chad's single. What are you talking about?"

I looked at Landon in surprise, "He was talking to someone on the phone when we were in the car, and he called her honey. He seemed awfully flirty during the conversation."

"Honey," he said with a chuckle. "His cousin is named Honey. She lives in Denver, and we're visiting her tomorrow. Yeah, I think he was pretty pumped to see you while you were both single but don't tell him I told you that."

I looked at Landon, my heart racing with relief and excitement. "Oh, oops."

Sophie came over to us. "I almost hit every pin, even with jet lag."

"Champion," Landon said as he raised her arm over her head in a show of victory before sweeping her up in a giant hug, smooching her loudly on the cheek, further disgusting my sister.

We finished our game. Sophie won our lane and we all switched teams around again. By the time the party was over, I felt like I'd had a chance to talk to everyone.

Chad and I were in the same lane for the second game. I tried to focus on the friendship. I felt better knowing that he didn't have a girlfriend. Every interaction was flirty, but it could just be friends having fun. At this point, I was a hot mess when it came to him.

It had been easy last year when I was coming off a relationship. It was easy to see him as a friend when we were all emailing each other back and forth. It was easy to put off our ability to have a relationship while he was states away in the service with limited amounts of free time and freedom.

After the game, my bossy sister informed us that we were to ride back to my house in the same car. I followed Chad to his truck, feeling nervous again. I reflected on our first encounter and how obnoxious he was. I hadn't seen that side of him since then, thank goodness.

But, the Chad that sat on the plane and talked to me all night, the Chad that walked with me to the ruin bar in Budapest, the Chad that kissed me silly before running to catch a train; all of those Chads distracted me.

We sat with nothing but the sounds from the radio until we were partway to my house. "I heard you thought I had a honey, the girlfriend kind, not the cousin kind," Chad said jokingly.

That Landon, he was trying to stir the pot! "Yeah, well, yeah." I stuttered.

"I know I initially said this to you after a long night and a recent breakup, but I'll say it as often as I need to. I like you, and I've liked you since my actions caused Landon to land in your lap. You instantly reacted to me being a pompous ass and didn't ever stop. I can handle being your friend, but I will always want more if we're in each other's lives. Please do me a favor and tell me when you're ready for that or the time comes that you don't ever see us being more. I think you are a Queen, and that will never change. You just let me know if you're ever ready for me to be your King."

I gulped, "Holy shit."

"Holy shit?"

"Did I say that out loud?" I asked. I was flustered, flustered with a capital F.

Chad laughed. "Yeah, you did."

"Okay," I said, taking a few breaths, hoping he wouldn't sense how what he'd said was affecting me. "When I think about us together, it makes me incredibly happy. My issue is that I promised myself I'd get through some life experiences, like college and moving away from home before I gave up my independence to be with someone. I really like you too, Chad. I think I have ever since I got off that plane to London."

"Where does this leave us?" He asked, inching his hand towards me. His pinky brushed mine, and we locked fingers.

Just having my skin in contact with him made me feel like

I was back in middle school. It felt new and exciting, but I knew I wasn't ready to sacrifice myself. I knew that if I got back into my old patterns, we would never be what we could be in the future.

"I want us to try something someday, Chad," I admitted. Was I stupid for not jumping on this opportunity? My heart screamed yes, and my head assured me no. "I was in a relationship for so long, and I feel like I'm still learning how to be a whole person. With Sean, I was young and thought that I needed a fairy tale existence. I now know that being me, completely me, is the best gift I can give my next boyfriend."

"I respect that," Chad said. "Honestly, I know I'm still grieving the loss of my parents, and I probably need to go to counseling again. Let's be honest with each other in the future. If you ever meet someone else that makes you feel more than you think you would feel with me, please tell me. I have one request."

"What is it?"

"Someday I want to see you in that horrendous pink Colorado shirt again."

"I still have it," 'I said, laughing.

"I was so bummed you didn't call me before seeing you in Budapest," Chad admitted.

I laughed again, recalling what had happened to that slip of paper. "I spilled something on that my first day in London, and it smudged the last four digits of your phone number. I thought about contacting you, too; I didn't have the correct information."

We got to my parent's house, and he turned off the ignition. I could sense the sexual tension in the air, and it was so thick I was surprised the windows didn't instantly fog.

"I don't want anyone else, Chad. I'm only looking to get to know myself first."

"Friends sometimes kiss, though, correct?" Chad asked, looking at me, again resembling my celebrity crush Mekhi Phifer. He was so freaking hot.

"Hell yes, they do," I replied as I turned and smashed my lips into his. It was just like I'd remembered. Electricity coursed through me from the top of my head to the bottom of my feet. This was what kissing should be like. Musicians wrote love songs based on kisses like this.

I knew we'd have to walk into my parent's house in a few minutes and, later tonight, part ways. We would continue to write to each other and continue being friends, and when the time was right, we could be Queen and King together. I hoped it all worked out as smoothly as it sounded in my head.

26

~Betty~ June 1970

My Beautiful Wife and Baby Bee-

As I read your letter, I'm weeping for joy right now (and not even trying to hide it from the guys around me). I'll admit it took me a few minutes to realize what you meant with the picture, but it was very amusing- a bee in your bonnet.

I'm only sad that I can't be there to hold your hair when you are ill in the morning and rub your sore feet. I didn't think you could be any more beautiful, but you looked radiant in the picture you sent.

I will continue to fight and stay safe. You are always on my mind, and now I have another person to look out for. I am trying to think of the good in all of this. If I get out in my two years, the baby will be just over a year old, and as they age, they won't be able to remember I wasn't there.

I understand your worry about Frank, and I can't imagine what some of these troops have witnessed. I've seen men go into a combat zone and come back looking like creatures from Night of the Living Dead with blank expressions and no trace of their former selves. It is so sad.

I wish I could be there for your grandfather's wedding! Your and Missy's wish came true. Now you can call her cousin. Please continue to send me pictures. I want to see how you look as you are progressing.

I love you, my beautiful wife — kisses to you and the bee in your bonnet.

David

I was starting to feel better; the nausea and vomiting was happening less and less. I had gone from feeling exhausted to having some energy, which was good because I was working non-stop. I didn't want to have to work another fall or winter outdoors. I'd done it, but it hadn't been easy, and this next fall/winter, I'd have a baby. I could imagine a baby in a shop with me but not outside.

After discussing it with my grandfather, I'd told my parents we were expecting, realizing that I needed extra support after talking to him.

My mother started crying instantly, and I was afraid at first that it was out of disappointment because I was only 19. But then she drew me in, asking if she could touch my belly. My father smiled from ear to ear, talking about having a little buddy to work in the shop with him.

"Even if it's a girl?" my mother asked.

"A girl would have even more of a reason to learn how to fix things since her grandpa won't be around forever," he replied, excitement radiating on his face.

I waited for my grandfather to spill his news after mine, but he calmly shook his head at me, indicating that it wasn't the right time. I appreciated that he'd let me have my exciting moment.

My mom made plans with me to host a dinner so that we could inform David's parents. I was in contact with them often, but I knew that it would be helpful to have my family there for some extra support, especially if their reaction were emotional, as I was very sensitive these days.

It was my abnormal outbursts that had clued Missy into my condition.

I began crying again after a floral bouquet wasn't looking right. Instead of continuing to work with the stems, like pre-pregnancy me would have done, I'd gotten frustrated and thrown the bouquet down on the table, spraying bits of plant everywhere, sobbing uncontrollably.

Missy looked at me from the stove, where she was cooking some spaghetti for us. "You haven't seemed like yourself lately. I need to ask if there's something you want to tell me?"

"I'm pregnant, and it's turning me into a wreck!" I wailed.

"I knew it!" Missy exclaimed. "Your sassy comments have decreased, so I assumed you were sad about David or expecting."

"I wish he was here," I wailed, flailing dramatically onto the table, tears mixing with the plant carnage. Surely now sporting bits of foliage in my hair, I sat up, suddenly feeling ridiculous.

Missy came over to me and brushed the greenery out of my hair, stooping down to kiss me on the forehead. "It's not bad that we have some positive things to focus on in this time of turmoil and peril. A new baby, the fact that we're going to be cousins. Shoot, you knew that, right?"

I nodded, knowing that she was correct. I hadn't been trying to act crazy, but I now knew how true it was that pregnancy hormones could wreak havoc on a female. I needed to learn to embrace my feelings and enjoy them.

I was starting to have difficulty buttoning my pants, and my mother insisted on sewing me some maternity clothes even though I assured her I could wear loose-fitting sundresses. A few days after the announcement, she had shown up with a collection of pregnancy-friendly bell bottoms with a little panel I could adjust from the inside with a button as I became larger. I appreciated it since all the maternity clothing in the Sears catalog looked similar in style and cut to the toddler section. Why they thought pregnant women didn't deserve to be fashionable was beyond me.

It was still so strange and surreal. Two years ago, I would have never imagined my business would be successful, and I would be married and pregnant on top of that. I never thought I would have wanted either of those this early on, but it seemed impossible when I thought of not having David in my life.

I'd run into a few women from high school who already had one child and were now pregnant with a second. I knew that it wasn't abnormal for people to marry right after graduation; I never thought I would be one of them, and I was glad David changed that for me.

I missed him terribly, but I used that sadness as motivation to work harder every time I felt sad. If Bee's were even more successful when he returned, our transition would be smoother. All the revenue that didn't go towards rent was going into an account, and I now had enough money for a hefty down payment on a storefront.

My grandfather was going to continue to help me search for a location, as a young pregnant woman today was unfortunately not taken very seriously.

I'd made the mistake of arriving for a showing by myself. I made sure to dress professionally, but when I showed up, the commercial Realtor asked: "When is your husband going to be here?"

"Well," I answered carefully, "Considering he'd have to fly here from Vietnam, we could be waiting here a while."

The man continued to speak to me as if I was a sub-par human until I finally got fed up. "I think the space is beautiful, and I have enough for the down payment to purchase. Unfortunately, you will have to tell the owner that they could have sold it today, but the cockroach in the building changed my mind."

"I didn't see a single cockroach, young lady. I can assure you I'll send an exterminator out if you choose our location," he said, suddenly kinder, the thought of the money burning a hole in my pocket tempting him into submission.

"I'm staring at one in a suit with a horrible toupee right now," I said sweetly to him before turning and leaving the building.

Since then, Grandpa had been going to my viewings with me. We hadn't had any other issues other than one Realtor, creepily assuming my grandfather was my husband. We'd corrected him and then tried not to be too disturbed during the rest of the tour.

Grandpa was getting married in a few weeks, and they were going to do something simple, like David and I had done. Theresa wanted Missy and me to be her matrons, and she'd asked me to do the flowers.

I was excited for them to have companionship. The more time that passed, and the older I got, the more I realized that's what relationships were mostly about. Humans craved social interaction, which was becoming more and more apparent to me.

Grandpa remarrying wasn't diminishing the relationship my grandfather had with my grandma. They'd known each other practically since birth. I knew that my grandma would always want my grandfather to be happy, which made me feel better about the whole situation. Theresa's husband had already been deceased for a decade, so she was a very independent woman. I knew that they would do a great job of keeping each other company and loving each other, and it made me happier the more I thought about it.

I felt a little flutter in my abdomen; I knew from my research that it could be normal gas or the baby. I placed my hand on my belly, "Keep buzzing, my little bee," I said lovingly. I paused for a moment, reveling in the fact that my body was growing a human, a companion created out of David and my love for each other. I went to change into my professional outfit, hoping that the building we looked at today would be the one, the official Bee's Flowers.

27

~Rachel~ July 2011

To: *StrictlySophieInDublin@gmail.com;*
RachelBee2007@yahoo.com
From: ChadW303@hotmail.com

> *Sophie, Rachel-*
> *I apologize for telling you this in an email and not on the phone. Landon was killed in Afghanistan yesterday while examining a car for an IED. We're all devastated, and I know you will be as well. I'm sorry. I will call you as soon as I can, or you can try to reach out to Caleb or Trent for more information. Please come to the service, if possible, those details to follow.*
> *I love you both,*
> *Chad*

I put the letter down, tears streaming down my face. "What's wrong?" Courtney, my roommate, asked as she came over to me. I handed her the letter and collapsed onto the couch. How was it possible that just as they were working on pulling the troops out, one of my dear friends didn't make it home alive?

I felt guilty, thinking that we'd gone to the bar for a few drinks and dancing last night, as we had several times since turning 21. At what point during the night was I having fun while Landon was taking his last breath? "I'm going to be sick," I said as I rushed past Courtney, who had just finished reading the letter, and ran to the bathroom.

I was sitting on the floor, leaning against the porcelain tub, letting the cold harshness of the tile shock me back into rationality. I heard a knock on the door. "Rach, babe, are you okay?" Max, another of my roommates, asked as he slowly opened the door.

"No," I wailed, tears streaming down my face.

Max came in and held me as I fell apart.

"I need to call Sophie," I said after I couldn't cry any longer. Max helped me up, guiding me to my room. Both Max and Courtney offered to sit in there with me, but I needed to feel my grief with someone who loved him as much as Sophie and I did.

For three years, we were continually emailing and meeting up on occasion. We'd shared so much: lots of pictures, advice, victories, and support. We were now one less, and I knew that anything Sophie and I felt, the others in our group would be feeling to the maximum. Since elementary school, Chad, Caleb, Trent, and Landon had been friends.

"Hello, lovie," Sophie answered in her Irish brogue. I knew instantly from the tone of her voice that she hadn't read her email yet.

"Hi, Soph," I said, wanting first to assess where she was before immediately coming out with the horrific news. Though Sophie and Landon had a special online and in-person connection, the relationship was not sustainable, and Sophie had been in a committed relationship for the last year. Still, I knew that she'd always have a special place in her heart for Landon and the connection they shared. It reminded me of Chad and my bond.

Chad. I bet Chad was heartbroken. I needed to get it together, for Landon, for Sophie, for Chad. "Where are you right now, Soph?"

"I'm at Ian's flat," she said. "We're going out to the pub later to hear some music."

"Sophie, my love, Landon has been killed."

I heard Sophie's choking sobs through the phone, "What do you mean? Not our Landon? No, I don't think so. What do you mean, Rachel?" Her tone got louder when she said my name, which broke my heart further. She sounded so primal.

I heard the phone drop and Ian's voice in the background. He was questioning her about what was going on. I could hear her crying loudly, which caused me to cry harder, grieving for my friend and the fact that I couldn't be there to hug Sophie in her time of grief. As Ian picked up the phone, I heard a scuffling sound, "What's going on, Rachel? What's happened to Landon?"

I filled him in, and he assured me he would work on getting her a flight out here in the next few days. I promised to contact him as soon as I found out the funeral details.

I called Caleb first, and we cried together. Caleb didn't know much more about it except that he'd died immediately, which gave me some peace. He told me they were going to be flying his remains back.

"They won't have any choice but cremation, which I think he would have wanted anyway," Caleb said between his periods of crying.

"What about his parents?" I asked. The last I heard, his mother was doing well, living in a sober living facility, and had contact with Landon again, but his dad was still drinking daily.

"This has the potential to break his mother," Caleb said honestly. "She's going to need a lot of extra support. His dad was already not doing well. This will most likely not help his desire for sobriety."

Trent happened to be in Fort Collins, visiting his girlfriend's family for the weekend, and when I called him, we decided it would make sense for them to come to my house. We hung out often when they were in town, and I was glad we'd be able to grieve together.

Time passed in a fog, and I couldn't comprehend whether a few minutes or several hours went by before the doorbell rang. We all embraced, letting our tears fall freely onto each other's shoulders. Trent's girlfriend, Stephanie, had also grown up with Landon, making the grief much more substantial. We sat around reminiscing, telling funny stories we'd either seen firsthand or read about in emails, where I heard most of the stories.

Trent's phone rang. "It's Chad."

My heart felt sick with sorrow, and I couldn't imagine the pain of what he was going through right now. He had a lifetime friendship with Landon just like the others but had been closer to him in the last few years because of their Air Force connection.

He and Trent spoke for a few minutes before Trent said, "I'm at Rachel's. Yeah, yeah, sure."

He handed the phone to me, "Hello," I said meekly, not knowing if my heart could take his pain.

"Rachel," he said, sobbing. Deep, guttural sounds emitted through the phone. "Rachel, I need you."

"Where do you need me to go?" I asked.

"I'm already on my way down," he said. "I was at a training course in Denver and was heading back to Cheyenne. I'm about a half-hour out. Can I stay there tonight?"

"Yes, promise me if you aren't okay to drive, you can pull over, and Courtney or Max will come and get you. They've already volunteered to be of service for anything we need." I saw Courtney and Max both nod in agreement.

Chad and I had continued to be close in the last few years, and since my nineteenth birthday party, and our hot car make out session, we hadn't spoken about the prospect of a relationship. We'd each had our share of short-term relationships, and I always tried and failed not to be jealous when I saw or heard of a new girl in his life. I still figured if destiny wanted us to be more than friends, it would happen at the right time.

My boyfriend, Blaine, and I had broken up a few months

ago, which was a relief. Blaine didn't appreciate my need for independence and alone time, and I felt like we were keeping each other around for companionship, only prolonging an inevitable breakup.

When Chad had heard my boyfriend's name, he instantly teased me about dating men with lame names. Chad's latest girlfriend had been named Cinnamon, which I joked sounded like a stripper name, and I'd started to refer to her as Sin-A-Mon. As far as I knew, they may still be dating though his friends made it sound like it wasn't serious.

I was about to finish my senior year, and I still loved my major, but I was still reading and writing in my spare time for entertainment. Floral design was becoming a passion of mine, and I was looking forward to an internship with one of the best horticultural companies in Fort Collins, which specialized in weddings, for my last semester.

I now lived full-time in Fort Collins and would be until I finished college. Courtney and I had met in one of my electives, creative writing, and we'd just clicked. Max was one of her friends from the dorms, and we got along so well that we all ended up moving into a house together. Max and Parker were currently seeing each other, so it was just a bonus that I got to see Parker more frequently.

Sean and Drew had gotten married about six months ago. I was happy for them but relieved that it hadn't been me walking down the aisle. Knowing the pressures and the future they faced with growing up so early didn't cause any envy on my end. I hoped for both of their sakes that it worked out. I didn't send a congratulations message or card, and I was okay with that.

Stacia was the epitome of an emotional teenager, though instead of getting sad or dramatic about things, she just got snarkier. Her teachers seemed a little fed up with her constant joking, so my parents were working on breaking some of these habits before high school. Amber and Luke were still her constant companions, and surprisingly, there didn't seem to be any romantic interest amongst any of them yet. I wondered if that was coming down the tracks in high school, though.

There was a knock on the door, and in walked Chad, looking defeated and heartbroken. I hugged him. It was as if he had no strength left to walk. His body weight enveloped me, feeling like a thousand pounds. I helped him walk inside, where he fell into Trent.

We sat together in my front room, crying, bringing up memories of Landon. Courtney and Max ordered pizza and brought down pillows and blankets. We all eventually fell asleep crowded together, sharing stories, grief, warmth, and the little strength we could muster.

The morning was harsh, sunlight streaming through the windows, not letting us forget the death of our friend. Trent and Stephanie left shortly after we woke up, and Chad and I, for once, sat together with nothing to say.

"I think I need a drink," Chad said abruptly, breaking the prolonged silence.

"It's nine in the morning," I stated.

"I don't want to think about anything. Can we get a drink?"

I looked at Courtney and Max, sharing a couch and a blanket, a head on each end. Courtney shrugged as if saying that was okay. I guess there were no rule books for a best friend's death.

"I'm here for whatever you need," I said, standing up. "I'm just going to go get dressed."

Courtney dropped Chad and me off downtown, and we went to a breakfast place that served mimosas as there weren't any bars open. I was a little worried about what lowered inhibitions would do to either of us right now. I took a few sips of the mimosa, and the warmth that spread throughout my body relaxed me. I knew why Chad wanted to be doing this right now, but I wasn't sure how it would go.

We ordered food, but neither of us were interested in eating, instead pushing our breakfast around on our plates.

"I never thought this would happen," Chad said after

ordering a second mimosa.

"I know," I nibbled gingerly on a piece of toast. I knew it wouldn't be okay if I drank champagne and juice on an empty stomach.

"I should have been there with him," Chad said, misery making his voice almost unrecognizable.

"I know that what you're feeling is valid," I started, "but he wouldn't want that for you."

Chad took a few sips of his second mimosa before answering, "I know."

"We need to honor him and his memory, and I think drinking the day away today is valid, but we will have to face it after that."

Chad held his glass out to me. "In that case, to Landon." We clicked glasses, drinking until we were both left with empty champagne flutes.

Courtney picked us up shortly after lunchtime. I was somewhat intoxicated, and Chad was, for lack of a better word, completely shit-faced.

"But I want a gyro," Chad slurred as I led him to the car and positioned him in the front seat.

"The gyro cart is open at night," I informed him slowly. "It's still daytime."

"I want a gyro," Chad said again, mispronouncing it, "ji-row."

"Dude, we can order food when we get back to my house," I assured him. I was starting to get hungry and needed to soak up all the alcohol currently residing in my body.

"Dude," Chad said. "You just called me dude. Don't you know you're going to marry me one day? You can't call your husband, dude."

Courtney's eyes shot to mine in the rearview mirror. We exchanged looks of shock.

"You're drunk and being silly," I said, glossing over the comment.

"No, you're funny, and you're drunk," Chad slurred.

"Courtany isn't drunk, are you Court-a-ney?"

"No sir," Courtney replied. I made a drunken mental note to thank her for how well she was handling us in our current state.

We were two blocks from the house when Chad, singing loudly to Katy Perry's "I Kissed a Girl," stopped abruptly. "Pull over!" He exclaimed, and Courtney screeched to a halt. He attempted to haul himself out of the car gracefully but was too unsteady, and I hopped out of the vehicle as quickly as I could without falling. He was already out of the car by the time I got to him. He dropped hard onto his knees and heaved, vomiting out what smelled like pure alcohol.

Once he'd finished throwing up, I tried to assist him to his feet, but he held his hand out to me. "No, please. I can do it."

He got up on his own, and Courtney drove us the remaining two blocks.

As soon as we got inside, I noticed blood spotted the knees of his jeans. I led him into the bathroom and gave him two options: "I can clean your knees up, and you can brush your teeth, or you can hop in the shower, but I'm not leaving the room just in case you fall."

"You want to see me naked," Chad joked with me, forgetting that he was violently ill in the street just ten minutes ago.

"We need to take a nap, and if you're going to be in my bed, you need to be not bleeding in it." I ignored his naked comment, even though he was correct.

He stood up and attempted to wriggle out of his shirt, almost falling. I caught him and somehow kept him upright. Leading him to the toilet, I kicked the seat down with my foot, and positioned him on it. "I just made up my mind."

I wriggled his pants down, which surprisingly warranted no comment from him. I grabbed a washcloth and put some soap on it before carefully wiping the blood off his knees.

"Ouch," he said in the slow, childish way of the intoxicated.

"Okay, now, let's get a shirt for you to change into." He stood up and tried to wriggle out of his shirt again. I wanted to stop him at first, but it became clear that it may be easier not to fight it at this point. I ran to my room, grabbed an oversized t-shirt that I slept in occasionally, and handed it to him.

"Is this yours? You're letting me borrow a shirt. Oh, do you have the pink one I got you when we met?" Chad asked as he rocked slightly. I shook my head, not knowing where it was currently. Then as if the sadness was just below the surface, needing to come out again, his eyes started to tear up. "You're so nice."

The whole situation had pretty much sobered me up, but any residual drunkenness dissipated quickly after Chad started to cry.

I led him, clutching my shirt, to my room, where I laid a blanket on top of my white comforter, placed a trashcan near the bed's edge, and motioned for him to lie down.

"You lie down, too," he demanded as he flopped onto the bed, my shirt still in his hands.

I tried to make an excuse when he said softly, "Please don't leave me alone."

I crawled next to him, and I tried to ignore the feel of his muscular body as it melded into mine. I made a mental note to switch places with him as soon as he fell asleep to avoid getting any throw-up on my back.

"I love you, you know," Chad said softly into my hair. "I'm gonna marry you someday."

I froze again until I heard his deep breathing, indicating he was asleep over the sound of my beating heart.

28

~Betty~ July 1973

Dear Friends and Family,

I know that this will not come easy, and you may not understand now or ever why I've chosen to do this. I know I'm a coward, and for that, please forgive me.

I've tried everything I can, and nothing is working. These demons are too relentless for me to ignore. I can't unsee the things that I've seen and undo the things I've done. I did what America asked of me, and I fought for this country. I came back, and even though I was injured, I've been treated like scum since I've returned. I hate myself enough; I never needed any reinforcement.

I'm so sorry. Please forgive me. I can't take the pain. I just can't take any more pain.

I love you all,
Frank

"D addy!" Greg said as he toddled quickly through the crowd and into his father's waiting arms. It was hard to spot him amongst all the black, the color of death, of mourning.

David scooped Greg up and held him cheek to cheek, hoping to shield his son from the cloud of sadness surrounding all of us. We walked past the table that had various mementos and pictures of Frank.

"Fwank!" Greg said as we walked by the pictures. I could hardly keep it together, and I didn't want me losing it now to scare my son.

David grabbed my arm, and together we walked into the atrium where the church volunteers had put together light snacks. Greg wiggled out of David's arms, having spotted other children and forgetting about the pictures of Frank on display.

I could hardly look at Frank's parents and brothers. I couldn't imagine the amount of pain they were in right now. Missy had tried to attend the funeral. The surgeon she was dating, whom she'd met at work, had driven her here only to turn around when Missy became hysterical.

Frank had been found at home a week ago. He'd shot himself. He left a note, which didn't do much to diminish the grief. Thankfully we did have some of the answers that we would have been unclear about had he not left it.

It had been awful when our men had left to fight in a war of communism that we didn't believe in, and it had been much worse for them when they returned.

I'd been nine months pregnant and could barely waddle around when I received a call from Missy. Frank had sustained a gunshot wound to the leg, and they were sending him home. For the briefest of seconds, I'd wished that it had been David who'd sustained an injury so that he could get back to me. I instantly felt awful for thinking that and blamed it on the pregnancy hormones.

I'd visited him as soon as he returned, and he was unrecognizable. Frank from before, the Frank I'd known since I was a young girl, was gone. In his place was a shell of a man. His mother had warned me of all of this, thankfully, before my visit.

"He lost his leg," his mother said, sadness overwhelming

the tone in her voice. "They tried to keep it, but there was an infection. He said he felt like a shadow person before his injury, and now he feels even worse. He won't leave the house, and he won't try his prosthetic. He won't bathe. I don't know what to do. Even though he's a grown man, he's still my baby, and I can't do anything to help him." She paused, taking a breath before pleading quietly, "please help me."

I grasped the phone, silently crying, emotions about Frank mixing with the feelings from the war, missing David, and my pregnancy. "I'll be right over."

Missy had declined to see him; she was almost done with nursing school and had verbalized a need to move on.

"I'll always love him, but I can't try to support him in person right now," she said tearily.

Honestly, I couldn't blame her. I couldn't imagine if the tables had turned, and David and I were where Frank, and she currently stood. It could have just as easily been us in their shoes.

I grabbed the flowers I'd been arranging at home that I was going to take to the shop the next day and had tried to prepare myself mentally for seeing Frank. I only worked a half-day on Sundays, so I'd been at Bee's this morning. I was hoping that the baby would come on a Saturday night so I could hopefully be back in the shop by Monday. My mother insisted this was unrealistic, but I was stubborn. I was going to try to get back as soon as possible. My grandfather had built a tiny little bassinet to keep at Bee's, so I could have the baby there with me.

Grandpa had helped me locate the perfect storefront; one we'd stumbled across at the ideal time. There had been a new builder whose hope was that they would eventually develop the area. Since it was in a location of transition, he had offered the shop up for a great price, and I'd been able to put a large portion down with money I had saved in the bank. I hoped that I would have the deed in the next five years. Next door was a clothing shop that had recently been renovated and now held stylish clothing. It helped to have the shop next door, and with my family and Missy's weekend help, we'd gotten the flower shop up and running reasonably fast.

I'd already loved having a storefront of my own, but I missed being outdoors and seeing Karen as often as I used to. Sunday afternoons had turned into our time together.

When I was six months pregnant and working exclusively from the shop, she'd brought her mother in and introduced us. Her mother seemed just as I predicted. She immediately seemed annoyed that Karen had taken her to see me. I asked her if she cared that I see Karen occasionally for lunch or a treat. Her reply was, "As long as you pay for it." I now made it a point to see Karen on weekends, either at the park or at lunch.

My first visit with Frank had been rough. He hardly acknowledged me and snapped at me angrily when I pulled the curtains open in his room and told him point-blank that he smelled. I told him in no uncertain words that he needed to clean himself up and figure his prosthesis out before I delivered the baby because I needed someone to waddle around with me. He shouted that he didn't want to waddle with me.

"I would be the one waddling," I told him sharply, gesturing to my large belly. "I'll return when you want to act more like the Frank I know."

His mother looked at me teary-eyed, almost like I failed when I left. The next day I received a call from her. "He took a bath today. Thank you." A few days later, Frank and his mother drove over, and we all went for a short walk around the courtyard, Frank's prosthesis in place.

A month later, he showed up while Missy was there, and we all enjoyed a nice cordial dinner together as friends. He couldn't handle being out in public for very long, but I felt like it was a start. His mood seemed to be getting better, and he was trying.

At thirty-nine weeks, almost to the day, I'd been at Bee's trying to tie up as many loose ends as possible before the baby came. Mom was there, working on her seamstress work and learning some of the ins and outs of Bee's before the baby came. I reached up to grab a spool of brown paper to move it near the fresh cut flowers when I felt a dribble of fluid going down my legs. I thought briefly about hiding it from my mother, hopefully getting a little more work done, but I knew she would notice if my very pregnant self were on the ground trying to mop the floor.

Labor had been painful, but I kept reminding myself that whatever I was going through, our soldiers had been through worse. I kept telling myself it was temporary. I cursed loudly as contractions took me to the brink, but I delivered our baby boy after what felt like years. David and I had already decided to call him Greg Stanley Bee-Wilson. As the nurses whisked him away to the nursery, my mom commented, "His name fits him."

I wished I had a way to call David, wanting to hear my husband's voice. My mother said she'd work on getting word to him. Suddenly I felt like I was in a haze, with an overwhelming urge to close my eyes. The last thing I remembered hearing was the doctor saying, "She won't stop bleeding," before the darkness enveloped me.

I woke up. My abdomen was tight and sore. Labor had been painful, but it had at least come in waves; this pain was relentless. My breasts also felt like they were going to explode from the pressure. When I rubbed my nose, which was incredibly dry, I found there was a tube going into my nostrils, blowing oxygen.

"She's waking up," I heard Missy say. "Go get her mother."

I'd hardly been able to keep my eyes open, feeling incredibly tired and uncomfortable. It at least disappeared when I was asleep. I closed my eyes again.

I woke up with my mother murmuring next to me, "I'm here, honey. You're okay. You're safe. Greg is safe."

"Where's my baby? What happened?" I asked, my mouth so dry I felt like I'd been sucking on sandpaper.

"You were bleeding, and the doctors couldn't stop it," she replied. "You had to have a hysterectomy."

"What do you mean?" I managed to whisper dryly.

"Your uterus had to be removed. Greg will be your only child."

Tears streamed down the side of my face. David and I had never talked about having multiple children, the war had taken that time from us, and now fate had taken the choice for a big family away from us as well. Even in my weakened state, I knew that there were worse things we could be dealing with right now.

"We'll get through it," I muttered, "Greg, I want to see him."

I fell asleep and woke up to my mom with the baby in tow, my son. They helped set me up using pillows, and I held Greg for the first time. My tears of sorrow quickly turned to tears of joy and hope.

Frank had come around a lot in the first year of Greg's life and was like an uncle to him. David wrote daily, and through letters and pictures, he was able to see his son growing up. He appreciated that Frank was checking on us frequently. Frank was doing better than ever and had even started dating a girl we went to high school with, Monica.

We celebrated Greg's first birthday and then started the countdown to David returning home. It had taken me a while to get back to the flower shop because of my unexpected surgery. During that time, Missy, my parents, my grandpa, Theresa, and even Karen showed up, doing what they could to keep the store running. As soon as I could return, Greg went with me, and I loved being there with him.

Frank had abruptly started coming around less and less, and I got a call from his mom one day. She told me that he was drinking a lot, and she thought he was possibly using drugs. He was becoming more explosive, and when people looked at his prosthetic leg, cane, and limping gait, he'd started to comment on it. It saddened me that he hadn't felt respected after sacrificing so much for our freedom, but I felt that he didn't need to cover up how he was feeling with outbursts and substances. I tried to reach out to Frank repeatedly, but he ignored my attempts.

On a cold but sunny February afternoon, my love returned to us. The joy at having my husband back had been indescribable, and the pleasure of him and Greg bonding in person so quickly was more than I could have ever imagined.

We cried together about the hysterectomy but promised to count the tiny blessings we continued to receive. David hadn't liked to talk about the war, and I didn't blame him. I knew that they had been witness to horrible things and, upon returning, had not received warm welcomes from the citizens they'd been fighting for while risking their lives.

We'd slowly gotten into a routine. David worked with my father on most weekends and taught shop at the local high school. His students loved him, and I felt like that helped with his transition back to civilian life. Karen, now a teenager, was helping me at the shop sometimes after school, and on weekends she was Greg's babysitter. I paid Karen well, partly to make up for all the years I couldn't and partly because I knew her mother needed the money.

Bee's was continuing to thrive and grow beyond my wildest dreams. For the most part, we felt supported in our location, but I did have to force one woman out of the shop after she told me my husband was a baby killer. I'd been so angry it had taken me a full hour to stop shaking. He was drafted and told to go to Vietnam, and he was doing what his country demanded of him, just like Frank and so many others their age.

Missy moved into a cute apartment of her own after David returned, and we'd started renting a little house for now. We'd just gotten back from the community swimming pool when Missy had called us. "Frank's dead. He killed himself," she informed us between sobs.

David and I had been in shock since the phone call. During the service, I just kept thinking that his pain was gone. Instead, all of us would have to carry it for him for the rest of our lives. How was that supposed to work?

29

~Rachel~July 2011

Landon Michael Bolter, aged 21, passed away in Afghanistan while serving in the Air Force. On June 5, 1990, Landon was born to Andrew and Lisa Bolter of Lakewood, Colorado. He graduated from Lakewood High School in 2007 and joined the Air Force.

Landon was a loyal friend and son. He was dependable and compassionate. He enjoyed running, poetry, and music. Landon was a great soldier and will be greatly missed by the members of his squadron. He had hoped to one day travel to Peru and own a dog.

Please donate to the Landon B scholarship fund at Lakewood High School in place of flowers. Services will be held on July 30 at Mountain Peace Funeral Home in Denver, Colorado.

C had woke up from our alcohol-induced nap, visibly mortified. "I'm so sorry. I'm usually not that person."

I stretched, trying to check my bed for signs of further alcohol vomit without Chad catching me doing it. I was relieved not to find any. "Chad, look, your best friend just died. I don't think a single person alive is supposed to deal with that well. Like I said before, as long as this is a one-time coping thing, you shouldn't judge yourself too harshly."

"Why am I holding this shirt in my hands?" He asked,

confused.

"Well, your other one had puke on it," I said.

"Wow," Chad replied, "I don't remember that happening."

I hoped that meant he didn't remember the other stuff he'd said. The problem wasn't that he'd said them. The problem was that I felt the same way. I always had. I still wanted to time it correctly, and I didn't want to end up together because grief and alcohol were fueling Chad's emotions.

All of us met for breakfast before the service, wanting to game plan on how to deal with Landon's parents and best support each other. Sophie was flying in and most likely would get there just in time for the service. It would be a fast and furious trip for her because her boss, though understanding the situation, couldn't allow her more than a few days of leave. She was going to stay with me at my parent's house to spend as much time together as possible without having to drive back and forth to Fort Collins. My parents didn't mind; they loved Sophie.

"How are Landon's parents doing?" Caleb asked as he poked at his breakfast, which we all seemed to be doing. It was strange that normal things seemed to have lost pleasure for all of us. Losing a friend affected us all, and you could tell from the faces around the table that the pain ran deep.

"Not great," Chad admitted. "His mother is refraining from drinking, thanks to her sponsor, but I know she's blaming herself and Andrew for Landon even joining the service. I think she feels like if she'd been a better mother, Landon wouldn't have thought he needed to be in the Air Force to gain that sense of family."

"Ouch," I said, "That's a hard one. It's not Landon's parents' fault that he was killed, but they should have been better parents. They need to focus on the future, though, if they want to get better."

"Agreed," Chad said. "It's a bit of a conundrum for sure."

"He was cremated?" Stephanie asked.

"Yeah," Chad answered, "there wasn't enough left for them to have a choice. He would have wanted cremation."

Trent choked back tears. "Sucks, man. At least we know it happened fast."

Caleb gave him a side hug and a macho kiss on the cheek, which caused us all to smile. Landon would have liked that.

We went to the church, and it was already starting to

fill up with a mixture of high school friends, servicemen and women, and family friends. My mom and dad were there, as were Caleb, Trent, and Stephanie's parents. They left Stacia at home with my grandma. She had been panicked after hearing about his death, and my parents, though they talked through all that happened, felt it would be better to leave her at home.

Sophie showed up just minutes before the service started. She slipped into the pew, giving me a giant side hug. We grasped hands and didn't let go unless it was to wipe our eyes. Chad was sitting on the other side of me, and we kept glancing at each other. He looked so sad, and I wanted nothing more than to hold his hand and comfort him.

The service was beautiful despite the palpable grief in the air. The pastor performing the eulogy did a great job of focusing on Landon and the way he would have wanted to be honored. His parents were in the front pew together, both appearing sober, and though it was apparent that his death had taken its toll on them, there weren't any inappropriate outbursts.

My parents took Sophie to their house right after the service to freshen up quickly and drop her stuff off. She wanted to see everyone, so I knew she'd be fast, adrenaline and sadness overtaking jetlag for the moment.

As soon as the reception started, I saw that Cinnamon was here, Sin-A-Mon, the one with the stripper's name. My heart sank as I realized they were still dating. They had to be, or why would she be here? I saw him go over and greet her. They hugged, and my heart broke.

I chastised myself for the games we were regularly playing with each other. We started as enemies, and we became unlikely friends. I ran into him in another country, which was as likely as finding a needle in a haystack. I'd had one of the most memorable nights with him by my side. After that, he gave me a kiss that left me breathless and starstruck. He called me a queen and had a passionate make out session with me in front of my parent's house. He told me when I was ready. He wanted to be my King. He told me he loved me and would marry me someday in his drunken state.

Yet, I continued to ignore my feelings. I continued to hold out for the perfect conditions. Did ideal circumstances exist? Was there ever truly a perfect time? I knew from the emotions coursing through my body that I didn't particularly appreciate seeing Chad with another woman. Had this not been a funeral, I may have wanted to slap Sin-A-Mon across her beautiful face, which was not like me.

I must have been staring because I became aware that Chad was looking at me. I abruptly turned my face, breaking eye contact. Since it was Landon's funeral, I hoped that my face hadn't projected what my heart was feeling. I was going to have to let this go.

Sophie returned quickly and gathered everyone together, "We're all going out tonight, right? In remembrance of Landon? I think it's only fitting that we go dancing as we did in Budapest."

Even though sadness covered us all like a blanket, I could tell that we felt that honoring Landon with a night together was warranted. "I can drive everyone," Sin-A-Mon/Cinnamon said.

"I can drive, actually," Chad said, "I'm not planning on drinking anything." He glanced in my direction, and a look of understanding passed between us.

We waited until all the other mourners had left before piling into Chad's truck. Stephanie and Trent were going to meet us there as they were heading back to campus later tonight and wanted to drive separately. They'd volunteered to drive Sophie home when they left if the jet lag hit her suddenly.

I climbed into the back of the truck with Sophie and Caleb, and Cinnamon hopped into the front seat. I saw her reach out for Chad's hand, and I couldn't tell if he pulled his hand away to shift gears or because he didn't want to make me uncomfortable. I was hoping it was the second reason.

We got downtown and paid our entrance fee to the club. The energy inside was intense, and Sophie and I went straight to the middle of the dance floor and started dancing. I looked over at her, and tears were streaming down her face. I knew that their relationship status might have turned out differently if they lived closer. I didn't doubt that she loved Ian. I knew they were a great fit, but she'd confided in me her feelings about Landon. I wondered if she ever told him how she truly felt, and if not, I wondered if she regretted it.

Caleb, Stephanie, and Trent joined us, and though I noticed that Chad wasn't on the dance floor, I wanted to live this night for Landon. Soon, tears were streaming down my face too, and I took turns hugging and jumping with my people as we tried, as best as we could, to recreate our phenomenal night together.

I went to find water and saw Chad sitting by himself at a table. I knew I needed to be a better person in all of this. Just because he still had a girlfriend didn't mean that I couldn't be there as a friend and support him. It wouldn't be fair to tell him that I loved him and was ready, not while he was with someone.

I sat on the bench across from him, "Where's Cinnamon?"

"I told her to leave," Chad admitted. "I appreciate her trying to be a friend, but I need to mourn my own way."

I gulped, knowing again that I needed to try to put my focus on Landon. Yet I couldn't get the feeling to go away that I needed to tell him how I felt. Hadn't we just learned that life was short? I thought about bringing up my questions casually to save myself face and prevent rejection. Landon's voice came into my head suddenly. I knew he would have wanted me to ask what I wanted to ask.

"Is Cinnamon your girlfriend?" I asked Chad quietly.

"Huh?" He asked, looking at me and pointing to his ear, the din from the club making it hard to hear.

I moved, transferring to the bench next to him, "Is Cinnamon your girlfriend?" I repeated, closer to his ear this time.

He looked at me, sadness breaking away for a moment, a giant smile appearing. He got close to my ear, "Nope," he said, and the feel of his breath in my ear gave me goosebumps. "Why?"

I hesitated before going for it, "Because I love you and I'm ready." Wow, I'd gone all the way, and there was no turning back.

Chad looked at me in surprise. He slid off the other side of the bench we were occupying, and my heart sank. He was going to leave. Maybe this wasn't the right time or the right place for me to be making it about us.

Instead, he came to my side of the bench and bent down so we were face to face, causing an obstacle for people trying to walk the aisles freely. Chad didn't seem to care.

"I love you too. Landon and I talked on the phone last week, and he told me I needed to tell you how I felt. I've lived without your answer long enough, and I can't do it anymore. Life is too short, and I want to spend it with us trying together."

I nodded, feeling happy and full of love. I knew it had been there all along. Now was the time to try. Now was the time to open my heart to someone worthy, to someone who loved that

I was independent, to someone who respected me, to someone who supported me without question. He stood up and swept me into a hug.

Caleb, Trent, Stephanie, and Sophie joined us, carrying bottled waters. "What's going on here?" Sophie asked, joining us in our embrace.

"I need to kiss my girlfriend," Chad said, the first hint of a smile appearing.

"It's about bloody time," Sophie said before moving out of the way.

"I've been waiting to do this again since your birthday party," Chad said softly in my ear. He touched my face gently, caressing my cheek with his hand before pulling me closer.

We kissed perfectly, the way they kiss in movies, which put all the other kisses before this one to shame. By the time we pulled apart, our friends were staring at us.

"Damn," Stephanie said, "Why don't we kiss like that, Trent?" Trent laughed and dipped her into a kiss of their own. Sophie grabbed a random man walking by and planted a peck on his cheek. We all laughed as he grabbed Sophie's arms, going in for a real kiss, but Sophie pushed him away.

We gathered around the table, and each grabbed a bottle of water. "I'd like to offer a toast," Chad said, "To our best friend. We all know he's watching over us at this very moment, making sure we make the best of life and love." Chad looked at me with dark, amber eyes, and my heart quickly pulsed.

"To Landon," Sophie roared.

"To Landon," we shouted in return. We clicked our bottles of water together and drank them down. We got back to the dance floor and danced, hugged, cried, and loved the night away in honor of our sweet friend.

30

~Betty~ July 1973

> *Dear Miss Betty-*
> *I want to thank you for all that you have done for Karen. We didn't have parents who were ever very interested in being involved. As we grew up, I had to think of a plan to better myself to show my sister what it looked like to work hard and become something great.*
>
> *It may have looked like I was leaving Karen on the outside, not including her in my baseball. I was never the greatest in school, but I've always known I had the potential to excel in sports. My hard work has paid off, and I received a scholarship to play for CSU in Fort Collins.*
>
> *I tried to convince my mom to let me take Karen with me, but since I can't file as her legal guardian, she must stay here for the time being. I feel better about this, knowing she has you.*
>
> *Things haven't been the same since my father died in the war, and though I feel like my mom is trying harder, she doesn't always know how much we need her. I would like to ask you to remain a support person to Karen, and please let me know if anything is going on I need to know about with her. I hope to find a job right away to*

save for a car, so I can come and see her on the weekends.
    Thank you again for all that you have done.
    John

"Welcome to Bee's Flowers. How can I help you?" I asked as I approached the woman who had just walked into my shop.

"Beeeee Fowers," Greg said, his greeting for the customer.

Things were slowly getting back to our version of normal, a version with my husband in it but not Frank. It had been so hard to see what the war had done to our young men. In many ways, it had caused a rift in all our lives and our culture, and I just hoped we'd someday recover from the damage. Soldiers were returning broken; all they'd seen and done impacting them in ways we couldn't even fathom.

The ones returning from Vietnam were severely affected, many stricken with survivor's guilt. But many of the young men who the lottery didn't select also felt the effects of not serving. Though alive, the draft dodgers felt shame about letting others fight while they chose to run away.

It had a ripple effect on the families as well. It had been challenging to start my marriage with letters instead of in-person contact and support. Thankfully, it allowed us to develop who we were both separately and together. I'd already known that David had a heart of gold, a great sense of humor, and loyalty before he left. Writing letters to each other allowed us to get to the core of who we were and how we felt without the added pressures of everyday life.

The transition when David had come home, though happy, came with a set of challenges we hadn't expected. We'd gone from going steady to being married with a child while only knowing each other as husband and wife through letters. I learned to be a parent while separated from David, and my husband learned to be a parent to a child he loved without the benefit of bonding with him in person.

I knew that David loved Greg and that Greg would learn

to love him, but it had been a time of adjustment. David had been nothing but patient, but I couldn't have imagined being in his shoes with so much love inside, just waiting to be shown but having to dole it out slowly as Greg adjusted to us all being together.

Greg was extra clingy at first, adjusting to the fact that another person had been inserted into our daily routine. The first morning I woke up to find Greg missing from his crib. The two of them eating breakfast together had given me indescribable joy. Greg laughed as David fed him Cheerios and made funny faces at him. I'd started to have more and more mornings like that, waking up alone to the sounds of laughter from my son and husband. Becoming the family we were always meant to be was the best feeling in the world.

We were all used to having Frank in our lives, and I was saddened about the thought of him not getting to see Greg grow up, of Frank never getting married and having a child of his own. I kept reminding myself that he had been in pain and that though we had to carry that for him now, he no longer suffered. I was thankful for the pictures and memories that reminded us of the person he had been and all he had sacrificed.

My parents or grandparents hosted dinner every week, and either David's or Frank's parents frequently joined us. They were understandably having a hard time, and I hoped they could start to heal, seeing us keeping Frank's memory alive.

"David, we're home," I said as I walked through the door. We were saving to purchase a house now that we had finished paying off the storefront, and we'd made success with a lot of saving and penny-pinching. The area had, as promised, started to become busier in the last year, and owning the building was going to be a game-changer in the profits we yielded, not just now but in the future.

"I'm back here," David said as he poked his head out from the back bedroom.

"Daddy!" Greg shouted as he ran into his dad's outstretched arms. David scooped him up and planted a kiss on his cheek.

"Me next," I said, moving closer to my husband and kissing him.

"This was on the front door," David said, handing me a folded-up piece of paper.

I read the letter and then handed it to David. He read it before commenting, "John and Karen think you are one cool cat."

I nodded, "I am a cool cat." I fingered the bee pin, the one I still wore almost every day, my talisman.

"I feel like there's something we can do to help."

"What do you mean?" I asked.

"Well, your dad and I've been working on a little side project. We don't need another car, so I thought we could give it to John. They could benefit from it."

I looked at my husband, my kind, thoughtful David, and my heart felt like it was close to bursting with love. "I think that's a great idea."

We called their house later, wanting to get permission from Karen and John's mother to give him the car. We knew that there was no way of knowing all that she had been through and how she was day-to-day, so our intention was not to show judgment or step on her toes.

She didn't answer immediately after bringing up the car, and I feared that we'd offended her. I heard quiet cries on the other end, "You are some of the first people who have reached out after the death of my Richard. I am not too proud of a woman to deny that we could use some help. Maybe someday we can repay you?"

"Part of giving a gift is not expecting a payment," I replied, heartbroken that we hadn't reached out sooner. Why would we have ever thought that this was acceptable? "Honestly, Karen has helped me so much. Please consider this an even trade if you need to."

She paused a moment before replying, "Okay, thank you."

We planned to drive the car over later that evening. As soon as we got off the phone, I hugged David. "Wow, that feels so good. I'm glad she agreed. She said she wouldn't say anything to ruin the surprise."

We drove to my parent's house to pick up the car and stayed to visit. My grandpa and Theresa were over there, and we caught up on the last week. Theresa had moved in with my grandfather after the wedding, and it had been smooth sailing. They complimented each other well.

"How's Missy doing?" I asked. Though we were still close and always would be, we didn't talk as much as we had when we were roommates. She was engaged to the surgeon she'd been dating, and they were working on moving her stuff into his home in preparation for the wedding next month. I was to be one of her bridesmaids.

"She's getting excited about the wedding, that's for sure," Theresa replied.

"I'm excited too. I'm relieved that she didn't ask me to do the flowers so I could have fun with my family. It's still crazy to think we're related," I laughed.

"I know that the florist won't compare to you in any of our books," Grandpa said, "but we all appreciate the chance to be together."

We got the car from my father's garage, and David followed me to Karen and John's house. I brought a bouquet for their mother. It had been three months since their father's passing, and I hoped she'd enjoy the flowers, a little something to help brighten her day.

I'd also gotten a locket for Karen. Her picture was on one side, and on the other side was John. It was a picture I'd taken years ago, when they were still just young children, always at the park. I hoped it would help cushion the blow of his absence, that, and the car that he could use to come and visit more often.

We pulled up to the door, and his mother answered, expecting us. "These are for you," I said to her. "I'm so sorry that we didn't bring them earlier."

"I appreciate it," she said with the hint of a smile, and I realized this was the first time I'd ever seen her happy. She was beautiful, and Karen was a younger, almost identical version of her. "Karen has filled me in on all you have been through. It seems like this war hasn't left anyone intact."

I nodded. "I agree."

She opened the door and gestured for us to come in. She went to the kitchen to grab a vase. "Your flowers are beautiful. I always admire them when Karen brings them home. I don't think I've ever received flowers before."

I wondered what had made her into an absent parent. Was there a bad connection with her husband? Was there a lot of stress from his deployment? Whatever it was, it did seem like John had been correct when he said that she was trying harder now.

"Karen, John," she said loudly into the hallway, "Can you come here, please?"

"Coming," I heard Karen reply, and in a few moments, they joined us.

"Hi," Karen said, surprised to see us standing there. She came and gave David and me both a hug, and when Greg reached out for her, she scooped him into her arms.

"Kawen," he said as he nuzzled in for a hug.

John waved to us awkwardly.

"Well, I'm sure you're wondering why we're here though you are both too polite to come out and ask," I said as their mother gestured for us all to sit.

"We have something special for each of you," David said. "I wanted to extend my appreciation," he nodded toward Karen and John. "You're both a big part of my wife's life and helped support her in my absence."

I pushed the jewelry box over to Karen, and she gently unwrapped it. She took the locket out and gasped, "It's beautiful." She looked inside, tearing up after seeing the pictures. "Thank you so much; it's perfect."

Her mom helped her clasp it, and Karen went to admire it in the bathroom mirror. We waited for her to return before heading outside.

"This one's for you," David said, gesturing to the car, a beautiful refurbished 1963 Buick Riviera. When David purchased it, the front had damage from a car accident, and with some gentle bodywork and a tune-up, it looked as good as new.

John gawked at us in surprise, "What do you mean?"

"The car, it's yours. We want you to be able to come to see your family whenever you can. It is our pleasure to do this. Please, take it." David held out the keys. "We want you to have it."

John continued to look shocked, but a smile brightened his face from ear to ear.

"I'll make payments to you," he said, eyes looking shiny.

"No, no payments necessary," I replied.

"Well, one day, I'll do something for someone else to make this a worthy gift," John said.

"I don't think we'd argue with you about doing something charitable in the future, but it is by no means a requirement." David said as he led John towards the car. "Let's go for a test drive."

Part Four

Fern

Sincerity
Humility
Bonds of love

31

~Rachel~ August 2011

To: ChadW303@hotmail.com
From: RachelBee2007@yahoo.com

Chad-

I'm so excited to see you this weekend. I've been thinking about you a lot too. I know Cheyenne is close to Fort Collins, but this will be my first time there. Dinner sounds fantastic, and I can't believe that you learned to line dance. I can't imagine Chad from Budapest participating in organized dancing. If you say that it's fun, I'll trust you.

I'm having fun with you too, King, and I agree that it has been helpful having been friends first. Since I've been your friend for so long, I will mention that I think King and Queen are cheesy nicknames (in a good way), but since I love you, I'll roll with it.

We've seen each other at our worst, and I like that neither of us feels like we must pretend to be someone we're not. The fact that you can still care about me when you know that I avoid doing laundry for as long as humanly possible, and you do it twice a week says something. The fact that I can be around you when you eat, even though you chew with your mouth open, also says A LOT! Usually, that makes me want to punch people in the face, but I find it *endearing with you.*

I understand you may have to go overseas. I knew that was a possibility before starting this relationship. I will love and care for you, whether in person, through emails while we are an hour away, or through the mail while you are on the other side of the world.

Landon, what can I say about that guy? I miss him a lot. He was undoubtedly part of the reason we got together. I feel like he would have wanted this for us, and I don't doubt that seeing us together makes him happy. I wish he were around to see it in person, but I'm sure he's dancing in the clouds, showing us love from above.

I hope you have a great rest of the week, babe!
Love, your Queen Bee,
Rachel

P.S. In signing this Queen Bee, I texted my grandma to ask about a random queen bee fact. They are all a little bleak. Did you know a queen bee will never leave a hive, and when she is no longer fertile, the worker bees kill her and create a new one using a jelly secreted from a gland in their heads? Yikes! The only good thing I found was that she has attendants who feed her and clean her all day. I'd sign up to be the receiver of that service!

I had spent some time in Denver with my family after Landon's death and was now heading back to see them for a few days before school started. I was a week from beginning classes and was working on getting organized. I couldn't believe my senior year was here. It felt like the past few years had gone by in the blink of an eye, and I was ready to be working in my chosen profession and no longer a student.

Landon's death had changed us all, and though it brought us together again, I couldn't believe he was gone. The ripple effect was still leaving its mark on all of us.

After a few fast days, Sophie had returned home, and we were trying to communicate more frequently, not wanting to lose that momentum. She'd had a hard time when she first got back, questioning whether she should have just given up her plans so she could be with Landon. I reassured her that he loved her but that she'd deserved to follow her own dreams. I wanted to inquire more about what transpired between them, but it was still too fresh and raw. Wondering what could have been different wouldn't change what had happened.

I was trying to reach out to Caleb and Trent more often.

I knew that being childhood friends had meant so much to them, causing the grief to be more intense. They'd experienced so much together, and I enjoyed seeing the email strings of memories they were emailing back and forth.

Chad and I were taking things slowly, as slowly as two people who had feelings for each other for as long as we had. It was hard not to run up to Cheyenne a few times a week; it was only a one-hour drive, yet I knew that rushing things wouldn't help. I loved him, and I knew that he felt the same. We had three years of friendship to back those feelings up. I didn't want us to mess it up by being around each other non-stop. I also knew and respected that we each needed to deal with the loss of Landon separately so our being together couldn't ever be blamed on the grief.

During the week, we exchanged emails, texts, and video calls. It all felt so natural, which scared me. We had our own lives, yet it felt like they combined well without much effort when we saw each other.

All our friends were excited that we were together. "Finally," was the most common response. I agreed with them; getting to act on our feelings was new and exciting. At the same time, I was so glad that we hadn't rushed into trying to get to know each other right after Europe. I felt like our relationship could have fizzled out quickly if we had.

I was packing my backpack to go to my parent's house when the pair of granny panties tumbled out onto the floor. Someone had perched them on a notebook I had in there, poised in just the perfect position to fall out.

"Max, Courtney!" I screeched into the hallway.

Courtney poked her head out of her bedroom, "What?"

"This," I replied, "How long have they been in my backpack?"

I heard Parker laugh behind me. He and Max poked their heads out of the hallway bathroom; Max had hair dye on his head, always the experimenter. "That was me," Parker admitted. "I put them in your backpack weeks ago."

I laughed as I walked back into my room. The granny panties had come back into existence after I moved in with Courtney and Max. Parker had been over one day and told the story of them being my talisman.

"My grandma got a cute little bumblebee pin that she

always wears, and I got a pair of control top undies."

That night I'd gotten the idea to hide them in the house, remembering my family placing them in my backpack for Europe, and the next day I'd hidden them discreetly inside Max's lunch bag.

He'd come home and told me the hilarious story about his co-worker going to grab a string cheese from the bag and finding the panties instead. "I'm hiding them in Courtney's stuff next," he informed me. It was now a running joke with everyone we hung out with participating. I knew I'd have to get Chad at some point in time.

My grandma still wore her bee pin, and a few years ago, Stacia and I had gotten her a few different floral pins to accentuate the bee. As far as talismans went, I felt like hers was a good luck charm for her. Bee's Flowers continued to be successful, and I looked forward to spending a few days there during my time in Denver.

I was excited to see family more often. I'd enjoyed being in Fort Collins for the last few years, but I missed seeing them regularly. I felt lucky to have a family that loved each other so completely. I felt proud that my parents and grandparents made their friends like family.

We had an "Aunt Karen," who wasn't my aunt by blood and who'd always been around in the periphery. My grandma had known her since she was small, and Karen's brother, John, an ex-pro baseball player turned professional coach, donated to a charity every year in honor of my grandparents.

I shoved the panties back into my backpack. I would figure out who my next victim would be when I returned. I packed a few outfits and loaded Old Blue, who was surprisingly still running reasonably well. I put in an Adele CD, planning on belting out the songs on the drive.

Stacia was out front when I got home, wearing a bikini.

"Whoa there," I said as I got out of the car. "Does dad know you own that thing?"

"Can't handle that I have bigger boobs than you now, can you?" Stacia saucily sashayed towards me.

I grabbed her arm and pulled her in for a hug, "I missed you, now put some clothes on."

"I missed you too, Rach," she said with a smile, ignoring my clothing comment.

I placed my arm over her shoulder and guided her toward the house. "So, why are you in a bikini?"

"We're doing a car wash to get some money," Stacia said as she walked over to the stairs and grabbed a pair of shorts and a towel. "Amber and Luke are waiting for me."

"Why can't you do something that requires more clothes, like a lemonade stand?" I asked.

"I'm not five anymore, Rach," Stacia said as she got on her bike, draped the towel over her shoulders, and pedaled away. "I'm becoming a lady, and you can't stop it, Rach."

I laughed. She stopped at the end of the block before pedaling back. "If you come to Luke's driveway later, I'll give you the sister discount on a car wash. Old Blue there is looking pretty dingy."

"Okay, but you better keep those shorts on," I agreed. I blew her a kiss as she pulled away.

I loved and hated that she was growing up. She wasn't a weak person with a gentle personality, so she was strong enough not to need her bigger sister continually looking out for her. I knew that in getting older, she would be facing the issues that came with growing up: heartbreak, insecurities, uncertainties, successes, and rejection. I would always be there for her, no matter what, and I hoped she knew that.

I went inside, and my parents were sitting down to eat lunch. We visited, and I got the scoop on Stacia. She'd recently started her period and was handling it reasonably well. She even called Luke out after telling my mom she needed more feminine products, "What?" she'd said in reply after hearing him mutter something about it being gross under his breath. "Even your mom gets her period, dummy." That had shut him up.

"Your great-great-grandfather isn't doing very well," my mom informed me. "He is getting more frail and more forgetful, and your grandma is pretty distraught about it. You need to make sure you visit him while you're down here. His heart failure is getting worse, and time is limited."

I knew life consisted of time that was running out. Landon's death made me want to show appreciation for my friends and family and spend as much quality time with them as possible. It seemed so strange that I could say my great-great-grandfather was still living while Landon's family would have to say he passed before his 22nd birthday.

I called my grandma after lunch, "Can I come to the shop?"

"You never need to check with me, silly," she said. I could hear Creedence Clearwater Revival in the background.

I was getting into Old Blue to head to the car wash and then to Bee's when a text came across my phone: *I just got your email. I feel so lucky to be your King. I love you.* - Chad

I smiled, my heart happy, as I headed away from my parent's house.

32

~Betty~ August 2011

Dear Betty-

I'm glad you had a great 4th of July. We visited John down in Phoenix at training camp and had the most fabulous time. He is just as good at coaching as he was at playing baseball. I'm almost prepared for school to start again. It's incredible how fast the summers fly by, especially when the school years sometimes drag on. My students keep me young, mostly. Well, some of them do.

I followed your advice and planted lavender. The bees have been coming like crazy! I also spread a wildflower mix, bringing in a ton of butterflies.

Mom has enjoyed sitting out there and watching the garden. She is tired from the chemo, but the oncologist says the prognosis is good. It is impressive what the flowers and the sun's warmth do to a person. She always comes in reinvigorated. I will be doing the BRCA testing, and if need be, I will get a mastectomy. I appreciate your offer to come out to visit. Maybe if that transpires, you can come and help?

Speaking of helping, John wanted me to ask what this year's charity will be. He wants to do another local one, so let me know which one you would like him to make a check out to. Johanna is getting so big. I tell you what; she gives these boys a run for their money. She pitches fast and hard, just like her dad. Hopefully, by the time she's 18, they'll allow women in the major leagues, but I won't hold my breath for that one.

As always, thanks for the pictures of your family. I love and miss you!

Karen

"When is your wife due?" I asked Devon, our flower delivery man, as I grabbed the container housing flowers from him.

"Any day now," he replied. "We're beyond ready. She can't sleep at night; therefore, I'm also not sleeping."

"Have you tried honey?" I asked.

"Honey?"

"It causes a release of melatonin and stores glycogen, which will help her blood sugar. I know she probably feels large and uncomfortable, but it's worth trying." I said as we walked towards the flower cooler together.

"At this point," Devon replied, "I would try absolutely anything."

I laughed; I didn't pity her. It had been many years since I went through pregnancy, but the discomfort wasn't something I felt like any female ever really forgot.

I heard the jingle of a bell from the front door. "Grandma, you got a bell just like I recommended!" I heard Rachel exclaim.

"Yes, ma'am," I said as I started to put flowers into the cooler. "I don't know why I didn't think of that before. It didn't matter as much when the store was smaller."

"Hi, Devon," Rachel said as she joined us near the cooler. "Do you need help with the truck?"

"That would be great," Devon said as he handed the last of his load to me. "The sooner I get home, the sooner I can nap. I need a little sleep before this baby gets here."

"Yes, you do," I agreed. "Try the honey in the meantime and keep us updated!"

Devon waved to me as he walked into the alley with Rachel behind him. I loved that she had such a go-getter attitude. She took after me that way, and I knew it would serve her well in the flower business. Lately, I'd thought that if she continued with this career, I would pass the shop onto her someday. Stacia, too, if she was interested. Stacia was always great when she came to hang out with me in the shop, but at 13, it was hard to tell where her passions lay. She took after me in the level of sass she could expel from her tiny body, while Rachel had inherited my absolute love of flowers.

Rachel came back a few minutes later, the last of the flowers in hand. She joined me at the flower cooler, and we put them away with only the music in the background.

"Okay," I said after everything was in its proper spots, "I need a hug now." I wiped excess water from my hands onto my apron before embracing my granddaughter. "Tea?"

"Tea sounds amazing," Rachel answered.

I went and prepared tea with honey and milk, just like my grandfather used to do for me, and we sat at the counter, hands warmed by our cups, and talked.

"Are you excited to be done?" I asked, finding it hard to believe that my oldest grandchild would be a college graduate in no time.

"Yes," Rachel replied. "I want to start working right now. Did you feel like that when you got out of school?"

"You have no idea," I replied, slurping from my teacup, which is how I'd consumed my tea since finding out that it accentuated the taste. "I don't know if I've ever told you this, but my parents wanted me to go to college so badly that when I didn't apply to any, they signed me up for secretarial school. Could you imagine me as a secretary? The first phone call that didn't go well would have sparked my mouth, and I wouldn't have had a job any longer!"

Rachel laughed. "I can picture it now, Betty Bee, secretary for a day."

"I threw my letter of acceptance into the trash after disguising it so my mom wouldn't find it."

Rachel laughed again. " Of course, you did. So, you started your flower cart right away?"

"Yes, my grandfather built it for me as a surprise right before I graduated. He made me pay him back for it, though. He was the first one who believed I could do it," I started to tear up, knowing that time with him was running out. He had somehow lived to be a hundred. The fact that he had been active as long as he had been had helped him remain independent and healthy longer than most. Unfortunately, I didn't anticipate him living much longer.

Rachel moved closer and patted my hand, "He's had a

great life."

"I know," I said, wiping tears from my eyes. I knew I was lucky to, at this age, have a living grandparent. My parents had passed before him, which had hurt so badly, but it had helped still having him around. I would miss him terribly.

"Tell me more," Rachel said.

I composed myself for a moment before speaking, "I would walk around with that cart in the parks in the morning and the restaurants at night. I met Karen the first day I was out there; she was so young, with missing teeth and a lisp. She has been important to me since then. It's how I met your grandfather. I was so obsessed with success that I didn't think I could let anyone in. He changed my mind quickly. It still feels surreal that he was in a different country the first two years."

"Vietnam?" Rachel asked. "I knew that he was there, but I guess I didn't realize it was right away and for that long! Was he gone when my dad was born?"

"Yes, he was," I informed her. "We were forced to get to know each other and learn how to parent together through letters. At the time, it felt devastating, but we were so lucky. Many of our soldiers didn't come back, and some of the ones who did were beyond broken. Like Frank," I gestured to the picture of him and David in fatigues that I'd taped on the cash register back in the early 70s. "I've kept that picture there to remind me to always be kind, to remember that people go through hard things. It reminds me of how hard I worked to support our family while David was away and remember that we can learn how to cope and survive in the hard times. We are strong people, us Bees. I grew up in a time when my hyphenating our last names was questioned by some and applauded by others. It isn't because I didn't want to join with your grandfather. I wanted to be able to carry that strength within me to pass on to all of you. By joining our last names, I like to think that you have legacies behind you from both of us."

Rachel looked at me with obvious adoration. "We've always wanted to be just like you. Stacia and me, both."

"You girls are who you are supposed to be: a little of me, a little of David, a lot of your parents, a lot of each other. I couldn't be prouder. You are becoming amazing young women." I stood up and swept Rachel into a hug. I heard the bing of her cell phone. "Who's texting you?"

Rachel looked down, and a discreet blush bloomed on her cheeks. "Chad."

"It is about time! Sean was high school cute, but Chad is handsome. Those muscles, that-"

"Grandma!" Rachel interrupted me, "I love that you are sassy, but please don't scare me by talking about my boyfriend's butts anymore."

"I was going to say deep voice," I said innocently.

"I like him a lot," Rachel replied, plopping back down on the stool, and adding a little more honey to her tea.

"I know you do. He likes you, too," I said. "If you could see how you two look at the other when you think no one is watching, you wouldn't question it again."

"I'm not questioning it," Rachel admitted. "He thinks he's going to deploy, and I worry about that. What if we aren't strong enough to survive the distance?"

"Rachel, didn't you hear anything I just told you?"

Rachel looked at me. "Yes, I heard you. There's no guarantee that it will go as well as it did for you."

"You know from experience, unfortunately, that there are no guarantees in life. My grandfather is one hundred years old, and Landon died in his early twenties. It would be best if you lived like tomorrow isn't guaranteed. How does it make you feel if you think about Chad not being in your life?"

"Devastated," she admitted.

"Well, then I think you both owe it to yourselves and each other to at least try."

Rachel nodded. "I love him, Grandma."

I nodded back. "I know. He loves you too."

We were interrupted by the jingle on the door, indicating I had a customer to attend to now.

"Welcome to Bee's Flowers," I said cheerily.

33

~Rachel- November 2011

Absence
She felt his absence as if it were a layer of clothing
Clothing that had been stripped away, leaving her naked
Naked, they clung together, gripping and grasping
Grasping for him in the darkness but feeling the air
Air, but not him
He, who had shown friendship
Friendship that became love
Love that became unconditional
Unconditional terms for which they both agreed
Agreed to learn how to live this way, this life
Life with uncertainties
Uncertainties of the future, except
Except their hearts beating synonymously as one being
Being together, even in the absence

Rachel, age 21

C had called me on a cold November morning, the gloomy kind where staying inside, snuggling on the couch with a cup of hot chocolate, a book, and a blanket were priceless. "I got my orders," he said sullenly.

"Orders, what orders?" I asked.

"Deployment orders. I'm leaving," he said. "It's most likely going to be seven months to a year."

"Are you going somewhere safe?" I asked, dropping the book I was reading, Landon coming to mind.

"My brothers and sisters in other branches have it way worse than me. I can't say that anywhere we're deployed could be 100 percent guaranteed safe. Our job in the Air Force is to support aircraft, so there is always a potential for danger. I'm happy to do my part to serve, obviously, and since Landon died serving our country and our branch, I want to do the right thing. You happen to make everything more complicated."

"I'm sorry? I don't want to make anything harder for you."

"I assure you, my Queen, it is the kind of complication I would gladly deal with to have the opportunity to be your boyfriend. It's that I don't want to complicate your life. You have the chance to progress. You are finishing school and graduating, and I can't imagine you having to spend the remaining time you have there worried about me."

I sat for a moment, trying to ponder the things my grandma had talked about. She mentioned how strong we were, how she and my grandpa had spent the first two years of marriage apart yet were still one of the happiest couples I knew.

"I don't know what you're trying to say here, Chad. Is it going to be hard? Yes. There will be bad days and better days. Would you prefer to do this with me waiting on the sidelines cheering you on or solo?"

He sat there for a moment, causing anxiety to brew up inside me. I tried to have faith in us and our relationship. I wasn't going to jump to conclusions and assume he no longer wanted to be with me.

"I want to do everything with you by my side," he replied softly. "I love you, and I need you in my life. I was allowing you to change it back to a friendship level if this will be too much for you."

"I'm going to make you a deal; if there is ever a time being in a relationship with you becomes too much, we'll talk about it. I don't need you to protect me, and I am perfectly capable of doing complicated things. I love you, Chad, and I believe you are worth it; we are worth it. I love you."

"I love you too," he replied, and I could hear the relief in his voice.

"Also," I replied, "I like my independence, so this will just give me a chance to get through school and study hard without you and your body, voice, and laugh as a distraction."

He laughed. "Speaking of bodies, when can I see you again?"

"I could come now?" I said, willing to trade my cozy morning for a priceless day with my boyfriend.

"Okay," he replied, "But we're going to get a hotel somewhere and go out for a fancy dinner and sit in the hot tub after and drink wine and enjoy all that we have to offer each other off base."

"Deal," I agreed, excited about the thought of an intimate night with my boyfriend. Often, we found ourselves surrounded by others, which was fine, but this would be amazing. "Give me an hour," I scrambled off the couch, ran to my room, and grabbed my backpack. I packed my cutest bikini, my laciest underwear, and my most form-fitting little black dress, throwing it on a hanger so it wouldn't wrinkle, and got into my Subaru.

Old Blue had finally taken a turn for the worst, and I'd been devastated when the car mechanic had informed me that repairing it would be more than the car was worth. I'd taken pictures from every angle and framed them to remember every sticker and every moment I'd had in my five years in the car.

I drove north towards Cheyenne, and per usual, the moment I crossed from Colorado to Wyoming, the weather instantly changed from overcast to gloomy and windy with intermittent sleet.

Chad had called right before I left to tell me which hotel he had reservations at, and I'd programmed the directions into my phone. By the time I got there, the receptionist at the front desk informed me that he'd already checked in.

I felt nervous, just as I did every time we were alone. It was the best kind of scary, the kind I got every time I was about to climb on a roller coaster. There was always the knowledge that it would be fun and exciting, but with a layer of vulnerability surrounding it.

I knocked and heard Chad's voice from the other side, "Just a minute."

He answered, and the room felt hot the second I entered. "It's steamy in here."

223

"Yes, it is," he replied matter-of-factly. "Right this way." He led me to the room, which contained a plush-looking king bed. Attached was a large bathroom with a hot tub located to the side. It was currently filled with warm water, the steam source, and was brimming with a bubble bath.

Around the perimeter was a bouquet of mixed flowers, two wine flutes, and a bottle of wine. We were both more mature than many of our 20-something peers, and tonight seemed to highlight that fact. My body tingled with anticipation. It seemed natural to be intimate with Chad, transitioning from friends to lovers. Though it all still felt brand new, every intimate moment was exciting and full of pleasure.

Chad grasped my hand shyly; usually not one to be timid. "Want to get in, or is that too assuming of me?"

"Of course, I'll get in," I replied. I felt like I was inside a rom-com right now.

"If it seems too strange, we can wear our swimsuits," he said shyly again. "It may be nice to have something to take off you."

The heat and anticipation spread throughout my body. Holy cow, this was happening. We'd been intimate before, but again, this seemed so grown up.

I nodded, unable to speak, tongue-tied with nerves.

"I already have my trunks on," Chad said, "So why don't you change, and I'll get in and make sure the temp is okay."

I nodded, still speechless, excited, nervous, and incredibly turned on at all of it.

I changed into my bikini and mimicked running into the bathroom, "Cannonball!" I shouted as I pretended to launch towards the tub. Just like that, all the nerves I had disappeared. Chad's laugh reminded me that I loved this man and that he had never done anything willingly to harm me throughout our friendship. Everything that occurred tonight was bound to be pleasant with my friend, boyfriend, and lover, whom I loved deeply.

The tub was perfectly warm with bubbles and the scent of roses. Eventually, talking led to washing and taking off, as Chad had mentioned. We took our time, enjoying every moment, remembering in the back of our minds that in a few months, we'd only have words to sustain our relationship, no actions.

We were both famished by the time we were dry and

dressed up. We walked down to the lobby, where there was a steakhouse, and ate ourselves silly. Afterward, we went back to the hotel room, and Chad removed my little black dress, kissing every curve of my body as he peeled the dress down and off.

After, we lay intertwined, laughing and joking with each other. I'd never thought of sex and humor working together, but the more I thought about it, the more it was probably essential with someone you hoped to be intimate with for a long time. It would eventually become boring if it were all heated glances and perfect kisses. I put on a pair of Chad's sweatpants and his shirt, and we curled up in bed and watched movies, still feeling like we were in a romantic comedy of our own.

I slept in the crook of his arm and pictured us doing this forever. I focused on the fact that we would have a tiny bump in the road that we could handle together, and if we chose to, this could be our future. Everything about him felt like my future.

34

~Betty~ November 2011

Missy-

    Hello dear friend,

    I hope this letter finds you well. I fear that Grandpa's health is declining. I know it doesn't come as a surprise to any of us, 100 is quite the milestone, but it's hard seeing his memory fade more every day. He gets short of breath with activities that used to come easily to him, and they have had to increase his oxygen. I hope you can find the time to go and visit. We'd love to see you, Nicholas, and Frank. It has been too long. I know that time passes in the blink of an eye and that the longer we live, the more tragedy we see. I miss my oldest friend, and though Grandpa doesn't know me very often, he may remember you. I can tell you are the spitting image of your grandmother from the last pictures you sent.

    I look forward to hearing from you soon!

    Hugs and kisses,

    Elizabeth

"Hi, Grandpa," I said as I entered the room, knocking first to announce my arrival. He was sitting in the recliner chair that faced his window. Under the wrinkles, he looked like the same man. He still had a full head of hair that was more salt than pepper these days. I was so thankful for the nursing staff in the memory unit. They were so great with him, and they'd helped us set up an apartment that resembled the house I visited so frequently until dementia took over, causing it to be unsafe for him to remain in his home.

It sometimes saddened me to see everyone who lived in the facility. It seemed there were often smiles, but there was a fair share of scared residents or ones constantly trying to leave the facility, not knowing why they were there and who they were surrounded by at any given moment. I couldn't imagine how frightening it would be not to remember things that we all took for granted.

He didn't reply, just continued to stare out the window.

"Are you cold, Grandpa?" I asked.

As if snapped into a reality, he turned to look at me, "Oh, hello."

"Hi, Grandpa," I replied, pulling a chair over to the window. I grabbed a blanket on the way to place on his lap.

"Where have you been?" he asked sadly.

I swallowed harshly, not wanting to be sad in front of him. I just wished he remembered so he didn't think he hadn't received visitors. I tried not to take it personally, but it was hard sometimes not to, "I've been here every day, grandpa. I wrote it on your calendar over there. I'm Elizabeth."

"Betty, Betty, Betty Bee, Bug," he started. He looked at me and beamed, "My Bug."

I couldn't stop the tears from streaming down. He hadn't called me that for a long time.

"Yes, Grandpa, I'll always be your Bug. Let me tell you about Bee's Flowers, my flower shop. Today is Sunday, so I closed at noon. It was a pretty good day; I decorated for Thanksgiving."

I knew that in minutes, he could forget who I was and why I was there, but I sat and enjoyed that, for the time being, he knew me.

Theresa had passed away ten years ago, peacefully in her sleep. He talked about how blessed he'd been to have two great women love him. He stayed in his house and managed to cover up the forgetfulness for quite a while. David went to check on him one day, and the stove was on full blast with no pot in view, and my grandpa was still in his pajamas. He thought David was an exterminator, coming to check out a pesky raccoon that "must have gotten into the trash." The trash cans in the backyard were overflowing with garbage, which was another abnormal finding.

We'd found the best memory care facility that we could. It was sad that he couldn't spend the remainder of his time in our house. Knowing it wouldn't have been safe didn't make it any less heartbreaking.

I sat with my grandpa, together, my hand enveloped in his, until he started snoring in his recliner. I spent a few minutes tidying up his room before leaving. I found his favorite nurse on my way out, "He remembered me for a few minutes." She threw her hands up in victory for me and promised to let me know how he was doing later that night.

I hoped that Missy would be able to make it down with her second husband, Nicholas, and her son Franklin, Frank, for short. Missy hadn't had an easy time for the first few years after Frank's death. Her first husband, we'd found out, had been very demeaning, always making her feel unworthy. She'd eventually ended the marriage, seven months pregnant, when she found him with another nurse on the unit in a supply closet. She'd named her baby boy, Franklin, in memory of Frank.

She remained single until Frank was leaving for college, and then she met Nicholas, a very lovely divorcee with no children. He'd been a great husband to Missy and a great friend and father figure to Frank. He loved golf, which had automatically given him and David something to connect with right off the bat. We tried to see them once a year since they didn't live to far away, in Arizona. I hoped they could rearrange their schedules and get down here for a few days in case Grandpa's health declined quickly.

I received a text from Rachel this morning that Chad was going to have to deploy, and David and I planned on calling them later so we could give them some advice. I knew that they could do it, especially with advances in technology, but they were going to have to commit to the fact that it was going to come with some challenges.

I liked Chad and always had. I'd liked Sean well enough, but I didn't think they would have had an exciting life together. I wouldn't have cared if she'd chosen a mundane life, but I had, in all honesty, been ecstatic when that teacher of hers had thrown Rachel for a loop. She had come back as a combo Rachel/Raquel woman, part planner and part adventurer, and I felt like Chad brought out the best of both qualities in her.

"Honey, I'm home," I said as soon as I entered the front door. David was in the kitchen, mixing some spaghetti noodles and sauce. I walked up to him and kissed him.

"Hello, my beautiful Bee," my husband said with a smile.

A sob caught in my throat. "Grandpa knew me today. He called me by my nickname too."

"That's great," David put the spoon down and came over to comfort me.

"I know it's temporary, and I wish it weren't. I know that's me being selfish. I miss him terribly."

"I know, honey, I know. You are so lucky to have the relationship you two have. Not very many people can say they've had that kind of relationship with a family member. I know we've emulated this with Greg and now with our granddaughters. They come to you all the time."

"That is true," I agreed.

"It's impossible to live forever," David continued. "That's why we have memories."

"Yes," I said. What he was saying was making me feel a

little bit better. "I've just been so spoiled having him around for this long."

"I agree," David said before continuing. "How many kids, except for Stacia and Rachel, get to say that their great-great-grandparent is still alive?"

"None that I know of, honestly," I admitted. "Look, everything you say is correct. I'm just going to miss him, that's all."

"We're all going to miss him," David said. "I tell you what, let's eat and then call Rachel and Chad. We need to give them advice on how to get through this. I think he has the potential to be the one for her."

"So do I," I admitted as I got plates from the cupboards.

After dinner, we called Rachel. "Hello, honey. You're on speakerphone with your grandfather and me."

"Hi, Grandpa!" Rachel said. "You're also on speakerphone. Chad is with me."

"Hi, Chad," we echoed.

"We heard the news today," David said. "I wanted to start by saying again, thanks for serving our country. I've been there, and I know that it is a huge sacrifice."

"Thank you, sir," we heard Chad's reply. "I feel honored to walk in the shoes of those who served before me, such as yourself."

"Don't try to kiss ass, Chad," I said jokingly, causing both Rachel and Chad to laugh. "In all honesty, we just wanted to call you both and give you a little pep talk. We've been where you guys are, and it's scary. You must ask yourselves constantly if it's scarier doing it without each other."

"I'm pretty sure that's what I said to you," I heard Rachel say to her boyfriend.

"Yes, yes, you did," I heard him reply.

"I knew I liked you, Chad," I said again. "I like you more and more every time I encounter you. We know you guys can do this."

"Lots of letters," David pitched in. "There's no such thing

as too many letters."

"Noted," Rachel said.

"Lots of honesty," I said.

"Noted as well," Rachel said.

"Wait, are you taking notes?" I asked, picturing it. Of course, she would be.

"You know me too well," Rachel said.

"She's writing everything down," Chad added, laughing.

"Letters, communication, honesty, and make each other a priority. Anything else, honey?" David asked.

"You guys have got this. We believe in you, and we're both available at any point in time if you need us for anything."

"Noted," Rachel said, laughing. "Anything else?"

"I love you guys," I said.

"Me too," David added.

"I love you guys too," Rachel said.

"Ditto!" Chad exclaimed.

We hung up, "They're going to make it." I said.

My husband nodded in agreement, "Yes, they are."

35

~Rachel- 2012

January

Dear Chad,

     Hi, honey. I just got your last letter. The pictures of the helicopter were so cool. I can't believe that you get to ride in those things. Part of me would love the exhilaration of it, especially since the door is wide open. The other part of me would fear throwing up, especially since the door is wide open. I also enjoyed the picture of the camel and was honestly a little sad and disgusted that you saw a dead one on the side of the road. I know all animals die. I'm just used to seeing elk or deer, not a camel.

     School is still going well. My internship starts next month, and I'm so excited. I have been working on my bride-speak. I guess that brides can be kind of high-strung. If all goes well with my internship, my grandma said we could discuss branching out and doing wedding flowers for close friends and family first and then maybe as a regular service for Bee's customers.

     I know that I started the granny panty battle by leaving it in the side zipper of your bag, but I never expected that you would be so committed that you would mail it to Courtney with explicit instructions on where to hide them. I was obviously beyond surprised to find them in my jacket pocket, and I pulled them out while I was at my job, thinking they were mittens. It was epic.

Courtney is doing well, and she says, "Hi, I hope I didn't disappoint you with the panty placement." She is dating a new guy, Noah, and Max and I both approve, for once. He is a drummer in that local band she likes to see play, so it works well. Max and Parker are going strong. They are trying to convince me to go to Arizona for spring break, but I told them that they wouldn't appreciate me third-wheeling.

I'm glad that the weather is staying manageable and that you have air-conditioned tents for when it starts warming up. As you know, it is cold and snowy here one day and the next it is 80 degrees.

Also, I know that you think it's hilarious to send me pictures of camel spiders, but if you plant another one of them amongst the normal pictures, I will never have sex with you again- that is a promise.

I love you!

Queen Rachel

Dear Rachel-

I almost died today, not because of anything military-related but because of the no traffic law thing again. I was riding with another airman, and we almost ran off the road. We're fine, just thinking that we will probably stay safe on the base for a while.

To answer your question, I am hoping that I'll be back right before your birthday. I want to get back to you just as badly as you want me to.

It was unfortunate that you sent me a grasshopper picture sandwiched between the cute picture of you sledding. If you ever do that again, I'll put a real camel spider in your next package- I promise. I almost screamed in front of my squad, and now they know my weakness. They may or may not have left a plastic grasshopper in my bed recently.

Yes, there are scorpions here. We check our shoes and bedding before getting in, which is how I discovered my grasshopper friend. I did scream with that one in front of everyone, and yes, it was a soprano-worthy performance.

I'm sorry to hear about your great-great-grandfather's health. Hospice, though scary sounding, can be a beautiful thing. I don't know if I've talked to you about my grandma and my experience with her before she passed, but it brought us a lot of comfort. I bet they don't get very many 100-year-old patients.

I miss you terribly. I can't wait to hold you again. I couldn't be going through all of this with anyone else. You are my Queen, and I feel honored to be your King.
Love you lots,
Chad

P.S. I can't believe the amount of commitment you showed in sending the granny panties to my division. They didn't exactly hide it discreetly; they hung it on my bunk like a damn flag. They managed to find a fan somewhere, and it was blowing in the breeze. It was impressive.

February

Dear Chad-
My G.G. grandpa passed away peacefully last week. I've been busy with family stuff, so I apologize for not writing about it sooner. It was, as you said, very peaceful. My grandma, though sad, is glad that he isn't in pain anymore. He had progressed so severely that they had to spoon-feed him at the end. He leaves behind quite a legacy. I learned some more stories about how important he was to Bee's Flowers becoming a real business. Can you believe that when he helped my grandma get her storefront, one of the Realtors thought they were married? Gross!
Stacia wanted to write you something, see below:

Chad-
What's up, dude? Rachel told me about the dead camel, gross! I hope never to see that. I want to travel someday, too, just like you and Rachel have. What is the craziest thing you've seen other than that? Have you seen any sheiks? Maybe I'll befriend a sheik someday but hire someone to hide the dead camels from me; I don't think I could handle that.
Miss you!
Stacia

Chad-
Okay, I'm back. I've been staying in Denver for the funeral, and I'm getting lots of family time. I was also able to see Trent and Caleb. They are doing well, and they said they've been sending you letters too. I was saddened to hear that some soldiers didn't get any mail. Is there anything we could do?

Chad-

Stacia again. Please let me know if soldiers need letters. I have to do a project for school that has to do with being a good citizen. I could arrange for my class to adopt your squadron. I'll enclose a form that we could use for the pen pals. Let me or Rachel know.

I stole the pen from Rachel, and that big streak in the paper is evidence of the sister-to-sister violence that occurred during the pen power struggle, sorry.

Stacia

Chad-

Okay, I guess it was unnecessary to write "Chad" again, for the fifth time in this letter. Hopefully, you are equal parts sad for me and happy that my family and I are so entertaining.

I love you, and I hope my birthday is an accurate prediction for your return. My grandma wants to take the whole family, including you, somewhere special when you return.

Rachel-

I'm so sorry to hear about your great-great-grandfather. I've included a letter for you to give to your family with my condolences.

Please let Stacia know that having her class adopt us would be fantastic; there are guys here who are lonely. I feel guilty sometimes getting mail so often, and I think that everyone deserves something to look forward to, big or small. The little sheets that she sent where everyone could write a little bit about themselves were brilliant. I'm glad the kids will be sending one in return as well.

I've been having a hard time sleeping. I feel bad not being able to support you all in this. I know that it is part of the deal, not being able to be present for every tragedy, but it's still hard.

I love you,
Chad

March

Chad-

Oh, My Goodness. You are the best boyfriend ever! I am impressed with the fact that you used the granny panties as your notification to me about the mini vaca you are sending Stacia and me on. It's been a long time since I've been to Glenwood Springs, and we are both stoked to sit in the hot springs and relax together for a few days. You're correct that some sister time was in order. I'm also impressed that you were able to collaborate with my parents on this. Yes, I think it's fantastic that you guys write to each other as well. It means a lot to me.

I'm sorry that your commanding officer pulled you aside to ask you about the underwear. I'm glad he had a good sense of humor about it. I can only imagine that it looks quite strange to ordinary people, normal people without control tops as their spirit animal. As odd as it sounds, every time I see them, it reminds me that life is what you make of it. If we can send granny panties back and forth across the country and smile, then I feel like we're lucky.

I keep dreaming about you, and it always feels nice to wake up and feel like I was just in your presence, even if only in a dream state. It's all the better if we kiss or more ;)

Anyway, I can't believe we are two months into us being apart. I think it helps that we've always had a relationship where we don't see each other all the time, and we're more capable of filling that gap.

Tell me more about life down there; I love picturing it all.

I love you. Thanks again for the vacation. I'll send pictures and will be pretending that you are right there by my side the whole time. XOXOX
Rachel

Queen Rachel-

I'm so glad you enjoyed your vacation. The hot springs made me think of Budapest as well and meeting there again. I do have a tiny confession to make about that; I looked you up on social media.

I never got your last name when we were on the plane, though in hindsight, you had mentioned your grandparent's flower shop. I looked through a ton of Rachels that attended your high school. I finally stumbled across your profile and was grateful that you had posted where you were stopping on your travels. I found out that you were staying in Budapest towards the end, but I wasn't sure exactly what day that would fall on. I, of course, couldn't have predicted that we would be in the same place at the same time, and I knew the second we stumbled across each other that there was the potential for something special there.

Since we're admitting things, I had also started dating a girl right before I left for Europe. I broke up with her a few hours after getting off the plane. I hoped that I would run into you again, but if I didn't, I didn't want to spend any more time with someone who I couldn't talk to as easily as we had on that flight.

Most of the girls I've been with since I met you have been superficial relationships, and I've never felt that connection that we have. Therefore no one else stood a chance. You made me feel something from the moment I met you. Some call that love at first sight, though in our case, it wouldn't qualify as the first sight because our first encounter left something to be desired on your end. I can't believe you still talked to me on the plane that night. You didn't have to; I was obnoxious. I'm so glad you spoke to me that day.
I miss you, and I love you. I can't wait to get back to you,
King Chad

April

Chad-

Howdy handsome! How are you? I'm doing well. I appreciate you opening up the night we met. I can't imagine any of what you were going through was easy, and I appreciate you trusting me with your feelings.

Yeah, I'm glad you thought it funny that Landon told me years ago about the social media stalking. I found it very cute. I also fully acknowledged after our plane discussion that you were probably obnoxious because of what you were dealing with after the death of your parents.

My family says hello! I'm happy to hear that you all are still writing to each other. Stacia says the letter adoption project is going well. She showed me the pictures you sent her of the soldiers with the care package they put together. Everyone looked so happy. They should be sending photos soon from the care package you sent back. Please make sure the granny panties aren't hidden in there, ha ha ha! I miss you terribly. This Queen needs her King.
Love,
Rach

Rachel-

Well, I am starting to feel the heat of Kuwait finally. If this is just the tip of the iceberg, I may be in trouble. I am currently recovering from a lovely stomach bug, and I tell you what, feeling hot and nauseous in an already warm place is not fun.

I tried to tough it out and still go to work, but I had to run outside and throw up in the sand, which was not my most shining moment ever. Writing about it is making me feel worse, so I'm going

to rest, and I'll write another letter tomorrow.
Xoxo Chad

P.S. I was going to send the granny panties back, but I now fear they germ-ridden. I'll try to sneak them into the wash- which could be interesting.

May

Chad-

Hello, my King. Wow, big move sending the granny panties to my grandma. She embarrassed the shit out of me. It was hilarious. She pretended to be fixing my hair, and I ended up with pigtails going through the leg holes of the underwear. Stacia kept me distracted, so it took me a while to realize what exactly was going on. She snapped a picture of me. Did you see it? It was on social media. I'm still recovering from the comments our friends left. Just know that I am planning to get you back in the worst way possible.

I'm counting down the days until I see you. I can't wait to give you a big old kiss. I cut my hair so you may not recognize me when you return. I'll make sure to hold up a sign so you can find me.

I'm glad that work is going well for you. It's excellent that you have a job you love and that it is something you can do whether or not you are in the military. If only they had horticulturists in the armed services. I think it would be good for morale, honestly.

I wish you could be there for my graduation too. Don't worry, we'll have plenty of time to celebrate all those things when you return: graduation, my birthday, my grandparent's grand reopening of Bee's. I can't wait for you to see the store! They've done some fantastic things with the expanded space.

I love you and don't doubt that you are looking forward to not being in 100-plus degree weather anymore.
All my love,
Rach

Rachel-

Hello, my Queen. I can't believe I get to see you next week! I felt like it would never happen. I hope we can figure out how to see each other a little more while you are between jobs. I think it's super cool that you will be part-time at Bee's. I agree that it is probably a good idea to also work part-time at another flower shop so you can learn how they run their store.

I'm excited that all our friends can come down to see me while we're in Denver. I miss everybody. Your parents are sweet for agreeing to let us stay there. I appreciate it. The first thing I want to do after I kiss you silly is eat some cheesy, delicious pizza. Not that the cooks don't make it here, but I miss my pizza joints from home.
I love you. I miss you, and I can't wait to see you,
XOXO
Chad

36

~Betty~ May 2012

Ms. Betty & Mr. David-

Hello, from warm, sunny Kuwait. Until coming here, I never thought it was possible to feel trapped inside a sauna 24/7, but alas, I am now becoming all too familiar with this feeling. I can't complain, it is comfortable with air conditioning inside our tents, but I'm reasonably sure at any given point in time, Hades is cooler.

Since I can't be at Rachel's graduation, I wanted to know if you could do me one last favor and gift her back these panties, her talisman, after her graduation. You would not believe how much joy and laughter we have all gotten from hiding these in random places with each other and with Rachel and her friends. As you both know, during these times, it is the little things that matter.

I'm looking forward to seeing every one of you when I return, and I want you to know that even if Rachel and I had never decided to try this as a couple, I've always thought of you all as family. I appreciate that you always make me feel welcome.
Chad

P.S. I would love pictures of her reaction. I want to add them to the picture book we started with people's responses to the panty escapades.

"**H**urry up, David," I yelled inside the front door. "We've got to go."

"Coming!" David shouted back from our bedroom.

We were on our way to see our oldest granddaughter graduate college. I couldn't believe it.

I grabbed the bouquet I had sat by the front door and plucked some petals that didn't pass inspection. I had taken extra time to put all of Rachel's favorite colors and flowers into the arrangement.

"I'll meet you in the car," I shouted back to David.

"Okay."

I pulled the car out of the garage, leaving the door open for my husband. I thought about all that had happened since I was her age. She would be 22 in a few weeks. I was essentially a single mom at that age. I was only in contact with David through letters, and I was learning how to be a parent to a little boy without my husband. I was successfully running my own business and was working like a maniac to pay off my storefront.

I thought back to things I wish I would have done at that age, and my only regret was not traveling. Thankfully, that was something I could do anytime, and since David and I had worked so hard in our adult lives, we could afford to travel later in life.

I thought about Bee's Flowers at the start, when I was selling flowers out of a tiny cart. We'd always saved money aggressively and recently purchased the small storefront next to us so we could do some expanding. We'd had a grand re-opening last week, and with Rachel's help, we were planning to do more design and wedding work. The re-opening had gone well, and we'd brought in more money than I would have ever thought possible in one weekend.

I thought about all Rachel had done so far in her life: traveling, college, work. She was also learning to maintain a long-distance relationship with Chad. I was thankful they'd met each other, and it seemed like they had the potential to make it.

Chad hadn't just been writing Rachel, he'd been writing the whole family, and when my grandfather had passed away, he'd sent the most beautiful letter to us. I knew that Chad didn't have a family of his own anymore, and I loved that he was allowing us to be a family to him.

The door opened, and David entered. "I couldn't find one

of my shoes."

"I just hope we find a place to sit," I replied.

"Our son is saving seats for us," David assured me. "I texted him already."

We got there with time to spare, and as promised, Greg and Cheryl had saved us seats.

"You guys ready for Chad's reunion?" I asked Cheryl while we waited for the ceremony to start.

"Yes," she replied. "Chad's been great for her. It's nice to see her in a relationship where she doesn't compromise who she is and what she wants. He writes to us at least once a week. How neat is that?"

"He writes us too, which I appreciate," I said. "How many young men would take the time to check on the whole family."

We were interrupted by the music from the procession.

"Her graduation cap is the bright one with flowers on it," Cheryl whispered.

We were able to easily spot her and her decorated cap, and though we knew she couldn't see us, I hoped she could sense us sending her love and sense how proud of her we all were.

The commencement was good, but it was hard not to drift off as I thought about what Rachel's future looked like post-graduation. She'd moved out of her house in Fort Collins last week and was going to live with her parents while looking for an apartment. She would work part-time at Bee's and help me get the design program up and running while also working part-time at another flower shop. I was excited to see her in action.

We cheered for her loudly when the announcers called her name. "That's my sister!" Stacia exclaimed loudly, causing those around us to chuckle. Despite their age differences, they had such a great relationship.

After the ceremony, we took some family pictures around the grounds before heading back to Denver and to Greg and Cheryl's house for lunch. It made me recall my graduation and luncheon at my parents' house; Frank had stopped by, and we'd all visited. I missed my grandpa, parents, and Frank, and I would never stop in my efforts to carry on their legacy and memories.

"I'm so proud of you," I told Rachel as soon as we arrived at the celebration. I'd pulled her to the side, wanting to give her my present in private because I felt like only us flower people would genuinely appreciate it.

I handed her the graduation gift. She tore off the floral powder pink peony wrapping paper and smiled. "You knew just what I needed, Grandma."

She untied the apron, which resembled the tool belt of a construction worker. Instead of a hammer, this apron housed floral scissors, bunch, branch, wire cutters, tiny little jewelry pliers, ribbon shears, and a folding knife. Every device that a floral designer could need.

"It looks beautiful on you," I said, beaming after she tied it around her waist and twirled for me.

"I don't want to take it off. I feel so official now."

Stacia joined us, "Does this mean I have to get into the flower business?"

"Yes," Rachel replied, sarcastically at the same time as I said, "Not if you don't want to."

"We are all about free choice in this family," I said with a laugh.

"I guess I could at least work there sometimes," Stacia admitted, "Or stop by for weekly dance parties."

"Well, weekly dance parties are a given," I replied. "Let's get back to the rest of the family."

The girls followed me, and we overate with the family, laughed a lot, told stories, and had an epic dance party. These moments meant so much to me, and it hit home with what David talked to me about before my grandfather passed. It is in the making of memories and enjoyment that we have together that we can carry on, leaving that legacy even in our absence.

Back at home, David and I ended up discussing that very thing. We talked about Rachel returning from the hospital, loving the tiny bundle so much. We spoke about Stacia coming home and poor Rachel thinking that Stacia would be old enough to play with her right off the bat.

"We're so lucky," I said.

"I know," David agreed. "Can you believe our family is going to keep growing? It will continue and expand long after we're gone."

"It's crazy to think about all the changes that are happening. Someday we'll have great-grandchildren, and if we're lucky like my grandfather, maybe we'll someday get to live to be 100 and see our great-great-grandchildren. Everyone in my family has had children early in life, making that possible."

243

"Let's not get ahead of ourselves," David said, "I prefer to take it one day at a time."

"I do too, and I want to have some things to look forward to when we're older. If you think about it, we've been working hard in some capacity since I harassed you into buying flowers the night I met you. I want to have an end goal. You know how goal driven I am, right?"

"I had no idea," David replied with a laugh. "I'd love to see more of the world with you, and I think we owe ourselves some adventures. Did you have something else in mind?"

"Maybe we could see the world in an RV someday," I replied.

"Will you ever be able to let go of Bee's?" David asked.

I touched the bee pin on my shirt. "Yes, when the time's right. I hope we get to pass it on to someone who will love it as much as I have. I don't want to force either of the girls to take over, but it would be amazing to keep it in the Bee family."

"We'll just have to see what happens," David said as he grabbed the remote control from the coffee table and turned on the Colorado Rockies game.

I grabbed the book I was reading and sat on the couch next to my husband, enjoying being in the same space together. I hoped that either of my granddaughters would be so lucky in the future. Marriage wasn't easy, and anyone who said it is wasn't being honest. But, it was a lot easier when you were married to your best friend.

When Greg had told us he wanted to marry Cheryl, we had talked to him about the pros and cons of marriage. We hadn't tried to convince him not to get married, but we wanted him to know how serious it was entering into a lifelong commitment. We had never doubted he was making a great decision when he proposed to Cheryl. We were lucky to have her in our lives, and I was glad Greg took our conversation seriously, making sure she was the right one for him before they made it official.

Cheryl was a great wife to Greg and a great mother and daughter-in-law. My hope for my family was that they would all have the luck we had in the relationship department. If not, we would always be standing by for support if, and when, they needed it.

37

~Rachel~ June 2012

From: RachelBee2007@yahoo.com
*   To: Caleb.Long@universityofcolorado.org,*
Trenton.Dunn@universityofcolorado.org,
Sk8erBoyStylin'@aol.com,   Max.A.Million@hotmail.com,
CourtneyS80525@yahoo.com,
Stephanie.Turner@universityofcolorado.org;
StrictlySophieInDublin@gmail.com
*   Subject Line: Chad*

Hi everybody! Chad's coming home. He got the final word this morning, and I thought it would be easier for me to let everyone know. He's excited and in good spirits.

It wouldn't be the same without a party, so we're going to have a surprise shindig for him at my parent's house. We all know Chad loves pizza, so I thought we could order some, and if you want to bring a drink or a side to share, that would be great. If we end up having a few drinks, my parents would prefer that you stay at their house—SLEEPOVER!!!!

Sophie- I know you said you were maybe making a solo Vietnam trip with you and Ian breaking up, and I would never expect you to come here for a welcome home party. If you can't make it here,

I insist that you send us pictures when you get back so we can all live vicariously through you!

Also, to all of us but Trent (the only one crazy enough to go straight through to grad school), CONGRATS!!!!! I think we should also celebrate graduations; it was easier said than done to try to make it to everyone's parties.
I love you all! Thanks for being such great friends. I'm lucky to have you!
Rach

P.S. If you tell Chad about the surprise, I'll end you.

"Chad!" I exclaimed as I spotted him from the escalator at the welcoming area of Denver International Airport.

I waved my sign at him, causing him to erupt into laughter.

I'd written in bold, black marker: *Kings sometimes need control tops*. I contemplated tacking the panties on there — the ones I'd unwrapped, again, at my college graduation in front of everyone. This moment was too great to want to embarrass either of us right off the bat. Stacia had recommended I put something about controlling the family jewels, but I felt that would be equally humiliating.

I ran into his arms, and his lips pressed into mine. Our first kiss and all the kisses we'd shared since then had been heavy on my mind. Experiencing it again in person was indescribable. I dropped the sign, no longer caring about the joke, only about the feel of my boyfriend's lips and body as we held each other.

We broke apart and realized people were staring at us; a few clapped quietly. Chad was in uniform, and I appreciated that people no longer treated military personnel like my Grandpa David had been treated when he returned from Vietnam.

We walked together to the car. "Stacia wanted to come," I remarked.

"That's sweet," Chad replied as we got to my car and put his duffel bag in the trunk.

"I had to be selfish; I wanted you all to myself for a while."

"I want that more than you know," Chad replied. "I love that your parents think enough of me to let me stay with them for a few days, but I don't know if I can do the things I've been fantasizing about doing to you for the last six months under their roof."

I swallowed, trying to calm the heat spreading through my body. I wanted time alone with him badly too. I tried not to think about the house full of people waiting for us for Chad's surprise welcome home party.

"There is a reason I'm wearing a skirt," I said to him, my voice heavy with intention as anticipation coursed through my body. "I think it will be easy to sneak away for a few minutes at my parent's house."

"You're killing me right now," Chad said. "I've never been one for public displays, but if I were wearing civilian clothes, we would be pulling over sooner than your parent's house and resolving this issue."

The heat and anticipation, already at a barely manageable level, increased. Chad leaned over to kiss me, and when his hand traveled up my thigh, stopping at my panty line, I was practically melting.

"Okay, soldier," I said, turning my thoughts again to the people at my parent's house, waiting. "We need to get to my parent's house. To be continued?"

"That sounds like a plan," Chad replied, sitting back in the car seat. "Actually, no, I need a distraction. I want you so badly it hurts."

"I'm right there with you, honey," I murmured as I backed the car out of its parking spot, heading towards my parent's house. I tried to focus on all the people that wanted to see Chad. Me stopping for a quickie in the car would be selfish.

We caught up on the car ride, always touching, and once again fell into the regular rhythm of talking, joking, and flirting with each other. It felt as if no time had passed, and I loved being able to discuss things that had happened to each of us while we were apart. It was always so different talking about it than reading about it in a letter.

I had forced everyone to park down the street so that Chad wouldn't see any cars. He knew that I loved surprises, so I wouldn't put it past him to be thinking that I was cooking something up. I pulled into the garage, opening the squeaky door to signal everyone that we were arriving.

I tried to take my time gathering my purse and opening the trunk so people would have a chance to hide.

"Mom, Dad, we're home," I called as we entered through

the downstairs door to the garage.

"We're up here," Stacia called. I could hear the excitement in her voice.

I walked up the stairs and smiled. They'd done a great job decorating with a giant banner that said, "Welcome Home Chad" and red, white, and blue balloons. All our friends, except for Sophie, were standing in the kitchen, as were my parents and grandparents.

"What's going on?" Chad said, a smile from ear to ear on his face as he walked up behind me.

"Surprise!" Everyone yelled.

Chad smiled as he started to make his way around the room.

"We missed you, brother," Caleb said, grabbing his friend in for a big hug. In the car, Chad told me he'd felt a sense of guilt coming home from deployment when Landon didn't make it back. I couldn't imagine how that felt but assured him that Landon would want him to live freely. He had been such a sweet soul. Though it made his absence that much harder, it helped to know that Landon cared so much for his friends.

Chad made a full circle around the room, hugging everyone. There was a knock on the door.

"Must be pizza," my dad said, leaving to greet the delivery man

"Pizza!" Chad exclaimed, "you all know me too well." He enveloped me in a hug from behind. It felt so natural having his arms around me.

"Some alone time would make this day even more perfect," Chad whispered into my ear, and the breath from his mouth plus his comment gave me chills.

"Look what I found outside," my dad said as he walked up with some pizzas in hand. Samantha and Clint were trailing behind him, each carrying a box.

"Sam! Clint, hi!" I exclaimed, going over to hug each of them. It had been a year since I'd seen her. She'd transferred to New York for an internship at an art gallery while she finished school. I hadn't seen Clint since my surprise birthday party, but I knew that they talked often and were trying their hand at dating again. Samantha said Clint was even contemplating transferring to New York.

"You guys want some food?" my dad asked, opening the

pizza boxes.

Chad inhaled deeply. "I smelled this pepperoni in my dreams. It's crazy missing something so simple."

I grabbed a slice and cracked open a beer. I whistled, getting everyone's attention before we all started eating. "I want to say that though this is about Chad, I'm so happy to have all my favorite people here. We do have a few missing members of the crew and I would like to raise a toast to each other and to those that we don't get to see today. I would like to toast for Sophie's safe travels as she journeys to yet another exotic location. And Landon deserves an extra special toast because we miss him dearly. I have no doubt he's here today in spirit."

"Hear, hear," Chad echoed, raising his drink.

Everyone followed suit, and we clinked each other's drinks, thoughts of our two missing members on everyone's minds. I hoped that Sophie was out there on a spiritual journey that would bring her closer to Landon and provide her with the closure I felt she desperately needed to move on with her life.

We socialized together while Stacia put on some music, intent on playing DJ, and we all danced around, acting like we didn't have a care in the world. My grandparents even joined in, my grandpa doing a great interpretation of John Travolta's famous dance from Pulp Fiction.

"My uniform is too hot," Chad said after a few dances. "I'm going to change into comfortable clothes."

I nodded and waited a few minutes until everyone appeared distracted before walking downstairs. "It's me," I said quietly after knocking on my bedroom door.

Chad answered in just his boxers, me catching him mid-change. I rushed over to him, and our lips crashed together. It felt slightly wrong that we were in my parent's house and that practically everyone we associated with was upstairs. Still, we were adults in a committed relationship who loved each other and hadn't seen each other in half a year.

"Rachel, are you sure you want to do this now?" Chad asked, obviously sensing my hesitation.

As if my primal brain had taken over, I reached over to him and peeled his boxers off. I didn't take the time to remove my skirt, just my panties. In seconds we were coupled together, and it was as if all the yearning, sexual frustration, and tension accelerated everything, and in a few minutes, the build-up was over; both of us relieved.

"Wow, that was the best ten seconds of my life," Chad said softly in my ear, "I hope that wasn't a letdown."

"That was at least thirty seconds," I joked back with Chad, "I'm beyond satisfied. That was perfect." I kissed him slowly, nipping at his bottom lip. I stood up and adjusted my skirt, "I'm going to slink into the bathroom and hope no one sees me."

"Good plan," Chad said, "I'll rush upstairs, so hopefully, they won't have time to put two-and-two together."

I shimmied my way out of a tiny crack in my bedroom door and made myself more presentable in the bathroom. I went upstairs where Chad was already deep in a conversation with my grandpa about something.

"There you are," my grandma said, "I was looking for you."

"Pizza didn't quite agree with me," I lied. I was a horrible liar.

My grandma looked me up and down, "You look like you have a case of indigestion, all right." She winked at me, and I worked on keeping my face straight.

"Why did you need to find me?" I asked, trying to distract us both from what she was implying.

"I know this process can be pretty overwhelming, and I wanted to make sure you're doing okay."

"It doesn't feel real yet. It's nice that we haven't spent much of our time together in person, so it wasn't as big of a deal for us when we weren't together. I feel like that's how it should be if you've found the one."

My grandma looked at me and smiled. "So you think he's the one? Does he know that you feel that way?"

"He knows I love him," I replied. "I haven't exactly asked him if he was planning on us being together forever, but I hope so."

"I've seen how he looks at you, and I think he feels the same."

"I hope so," I said. "He's my best friend."

"That's the kind of partner I've always wanted for my family. Just make sure you tell him how you feel."

"I will," I said. I watched him laughing with Grandpa and hoped he felt the same way I did.

38

~Betty~ July 2012

We are happy to announce that we have a new floral designer on staff. Rachel Bee-Wilson has a Bachelors in Horticulture with a minor in Floral Design. Samples of her work are available on the website, and references can be provided upon request. Stop by the store today to schedule your consultation, or sign up online.

Ad for Bee's Flowers, Denver Tribune

"Yes, Mrs. Connor, I will make sure to have our wedding consultant call you as soon as she gets in," I said as I made a note in the notebook I had in front of me. "I do apologize. I know she was supposed to call you thirty minutes ago, this is not normal practice for her or Bee's Flowers. I promise we will make up for your time." I paused, letting her finish getting her frustrations out. I understood why she was frustrated. I also meant what I told her, Rachel was never late. I needed to get through this phone call because internally, I was freaking out that something had happened to my granddaughter.

I apologized to Mrs. Connor again and was just about to call Rachel when I heard the back entrance open. I sighed with relief, seeing Rachel. Then my relief changed to annoyance. She was almost an hour late, if she weren't my granddaughter, I would have to have a serious discussion with the employee. I couldn't give her special treatment because we were related.

I was about to reprimand her when I noticed the look on her face. It was a look I'd never really seen on her before. Her eyes were puffy, indicating recently shed tears. Her hair was frizzy and not brushed, and she had pulled it into a raggedy ponytail. She looked like someone in shock.

"Rachel? Sweetie, what's wrong?" I approached her, putting an arm around her and guiding her to a chair.

"Nothing's wrong, Grandma," she said, though I could tell from the look on her face that there clearly was.

"Did you know that bees communicate with each other through dancing?" I asked her. "They call it the waggle dance. I think we, as Bees, communicate through dancing too. I have never seen you turn down a dance party. Do you want to dance it out?"

She attempted a smile, but I saw the falseness behind it.

"Okay, honey, please tell me what's going on. I was worried about you. I tried calling you a few times, and your phone went straight to voicemail."

"My phone's turned off. Chad keeps calling me," Rachel replied sadly. "I should have called you. I'm sorry."

"Why would you not want Chad to call you?" I asked. "I thought things were going well."

"They are, but I found something out, and now have some decisions to make."

"Rachel, I'm here if you want to talk to me," I said, walking towards the back of the store. "I may not always know the right answer, but I've been through a lot in my life. I'll grab us some coffee, and you can think about whether or not you want to talk about what's bothering you."

"I'll skip the coffee, it's been making me sick lately," Rachel said glumly.

I paused in my tracks. "I couldn't even smell coffee without throwing up at one point in my life. Are you pregnant, Rachel?"

She stiffened in her chair; her pause told me everything I needed to know.

"Oh, Rach, you are. Are you okay?" I sat next to her and pulled her hand into my lap.

"No," she said, teary-eyed. "Chad wants to marry me."

"Okay," I said, knowing whatever was going on was going to need to be dealt with carefully and with consideration. I remembered how emotional I'd felt while carrying Greg. "How do you feel about what's going on?"

"I remember us sitting down like this when I was about to graduate high school," She sniffled. "I knew what my life plan was. I've let go of most of that. I want to have the baby, that is non-negotiable for me. We're going to have the baby, but I wanted it to happen differently. I wanted to have an established career; I wanted to be married and have a house." She sniffled again before a sob escaped. "And," she sobbed, "a dog." She started crying harder, "I don't have a dog yet."

I patted her back and let her cry. I couldn't judge her for the feelings she was having. I remembered crying over not having any ground beef in the apartment once when I was pregnant. Missy had never let me forget about how upset I'd been.

She started to settle down, and soon the sniffling stopped. "Can I have some chamomile tea? The kind great-great-grandpa used to make you?"

"Of course," I said as I stood up. The shop phone started ringing, "Do you feel okay answering that? It may be the wedding consult from this morning, Mrs. Connor."

"Mrs. Connor, I forgot! I'm so sorry," Rachel sounded like she was going to start crying again. I waited, unsure if I would need to handle the phone call, but she took a deep breath and got up to answer it.

"Bee's Flowers," she answered. "Hello Mrs. Connor, I was just about to call you. I'm so sorry about missing our phone meeting, but I have some things in store for you that I think you and your daughter are going to be excited about."

I made eye contact with Rachel, and she gave me a thumbs-up sign and gestured for me to go to the back.

I went to make tea as I processed what she'd told me. I understood the emotions that were behind carrying a child. You could never be completely ready to have a baby, no matter what. Finding out you were going to be a parent could be overwhelming, and I knew that from personal experience.

I did not doubt that Rachel and Chad would both be great parents. The fact that he wanted to marry her was significant, but I hoped that if he wanted to go through with that, it was for the right reasons.

I made tea for us and headed back out to the front.

"I agree, I think that will be a great combination. I look forward to getting some samples put together for you. For the inconvenience of this morning, I will personally pay for one of the bridesmaid's bouquets." She paused. "Yes, I'm sure. The pleasure was all mine. Take care."

I walked over to her and handed her the piping hot cup, "Things smoothed over well it sounds like."

"Yes, once I started talking to her about the colors we could use and echoed the flower choices she wanted, she forgave me pretty fast," she sat down and blew into the mug. "I'm sorry I was late. I've had a shocking morning. I hadn't been feeling very well the past few weeks, and with Chad being back, I guess I hadn't been tracking my periods as well as I normally do. I've been taking my birth control regularly, sorry if that's too much information, so I didn't think this is what it could be. I told Samantha what I was feeling, and she recommended I take a test, which I did this morning, and it was positive. I called Chad, and he said he wanted to get married. He didn't panic at all, which freaked me out. I don't know what to do."

"Well, the fact that he didn't panic is great. So he wants to be involved?"

"Yes, he said he wants us to be a family."

"What do you think?" I asked.

"I love Chad and couldn't imagine doing this with a better person. I want to make sure that he would want to marry me even if a child wasn't involved. I think that's something that freaked me out this morning, that I realized I could do it by myself, with or without Chad."

"I've done both," I said matter-of-factly. I paused and drank some of my tea. "From someone with some experience, both come with its own sets of challenges. I agree with you, though; if you are going to be making a lifelong commitment, you want to make sure it's for the right reasons. Do your parents know yet?"

"I found out, called Chad, and came here. I'll tell them soon; I just needed to process. I wasn't planning on telling you today, but it feels better talking about it."

"Do you need to go home and deal with this?" I asked.

"No, I'd prefer to be distracted. I need some flower therapy."

"Okay," I agreed, "but if you change your mind, I can handle it today. Mrs. Connor was the essential thing today. Would you agree to turn your cell phone on, though? Regardless of what you decide to do, Chad is probably nervous about not being able to get a hold of you. Now you must think about more than yourself.

"You're right. I'm being selfish. I'm sure he's freaked out," she said as she reached into her pocket.

The bell jingled, and a group of customers came in together. Rachel walked over to help, seeming to be happy for the distraction.

Rachel assisted the customers as I finished my tea. She helped them make some bouquets and showed them the merchandise section of the store, which we were currently trying to expand. After adequate browsing time, they came to check out, flowers and some cute little summer decorations in hand.

"Here's my card," Rachel said as she assisted in ringing them up. "I'd love to be a part of your wedding planning. We try to keep up on the latest trends, so contact me anytime, and we can work on getting something exciting and new together for you."

I thought back to the beginning of Bee's, how we'd been able to cater to the hippie movement. I thought about Woodstock and Flower Power. Every year the business had to change and evolve to fit the times. It seemed crazy that the flowers people wanted and coveted changed. Having Rachel, and her college degree, provide expertise for weddings was proving to be very beneficial to the business.

Rachel was straightening up the flower station that she'd used to make the bouquets when we heard the door ding open. I heard Rachel gasp.

"Chad?"

"You're okay," he said, rushing over to her side. "I've been trying to get a hold of you for hours. I was so worried about you." He hugged her.

"My phone," she gasped as she pulled it out of her pants pocket. "I meant to turn it on, and the customers came. I must have forgotten. I'm so sorry, Chad, that was selfish of me. I should have never worried you. I was freaked out, sorry."

He hugged her and kissed her boldly on the lips. "We're going to have a baby. The rest will work itself out. It's going to be okay."

She kissed him back and then as if they both remembered that I was there, turned to look at me. "Did you tell your grandma?" Chad asked.

"No, you just did, though," Rachel said and when she saw the panic on Chad's face quickly interjected, "I'm kidding, I'm kidding. Yes, I told her. She told me to turn my phone on, but I got distracted. How did you get here so fast?"

Chad looked at her, sheepishly. "Well, let's say that there was a lot of speeding involved. I've never been so nervous in my whole life."

I looked at them knowingly. "I think you two have some things to talk about. Why don't you get out of here? I've handled this store myself for most of its existence, and I can handle it today. I love you both, know that."

They both looked at me, "I love you too, Grandma."

Chad looked at me. "I'm going for it; I love you too, Grandma."

I hugged them both. I didn't envy what they were feeling right now. My heart soared though at the thought that I was going to be a great-grandma!

39

~Rachel~ August 2012

Dear Rachel-

     I know that I didn't handle it very well when you told me you were having a baby. I acted like a butthead, and I'm sorry. If you decided to call me Stacia Buttface for the rest of my life, I would deserve it.

     Here's the deal. I'm a teenager, and as you know, I am horrible at controlling my emotions. I want to be honest with you and tell you that I was jealous when you told me, and it came out as anger. I'm sorry. I feel like I just got you back after you moved away for school. I pictured us getting to do lots of sister things while you're living here. Mom has assured me that you will still be able to do a lot with me. I looked it up on the Internet, and since I'm not too fond of sushi and wouldn't be drinking alcohol with you anyway, we're okay.

     Not getting to have coffee with you will bug me. I know you're going to tell me that I shouldn't be drinking it, but I'm about to start high school, and I tell you, it tastes pretty great and gives me energy.

     I just want to make sure that you'll always be around and be the bossy big sister that you are. I plan on still being your hilarious little sister,

Love you,

Stacia

P.S. Dude, I'm going to be an aunt?!

"**W**hat do you mean, you think you hear two heartbeats?" I asked the nurse-midwife, who currently had a wand pressed to my belly. "Could it be an echo or something?"

Chad didn't say a word, just stared at us silently.

"Well, there's only one way to find out," she removed the probe and wiped the cold jelly off my stomach. "We will take you across the hall and do a quick ultrasound. If we can see two heartbeats, then you're expecting twins. Someone will be here in a few minutes to take you over there." She exited.

"Two babies, twins. I just found out about one baby. How can there possibly be more than that?" I asked Chad as I sat up on the exam table. I started to breathe faster, two babies. TWO BABIES?!

"We need to stay calm, babe," Chad said, though his face looked pale, which I wouldn't have thought possible. "Let's take some deep breaths together. It's going to be okay."

An ultrasound technician came to get us a few minutes later. She smiled when she found us breathing in and out slowly, forehead to forehead. "It's hardly ever news people expect."

"I still think it was probably an echo," I said, which caused the technician to smile. It looked fake, and I knew then that we were having twins; the ultrasound was just a formality.

The tech guided me to another exam table. She put new jelly on my belly and moved the ultrasound wand over my abdomen. This method didn't produce any sound, just pictures.

"Two heartbeats," she confirmed after a minute, angling the screen so we could see the little flutters on it. "Congratulations, you're having twins."

Chad and I rode back to my house in shock. Three weeks had passed since we had found out we would be parents, and the focus had been on figuring out what to do from here. We planned on taking as much time as possible to figure out the logistics.

I honestly felt more nervous than Chad about the whole thing. I was excited, but I was also nervous. I knew that Chad was ecstatic about the prospect of a family, but I was scared that he'd proposed on the phone because he felt he needed to. I didn't want him to feel obligated to marry me; that was something I was keeping to myself for the moment; we had bigger things to figure out now.

We pulled up to my house, and it was one of those moments where I'd hardly been able to remember the drive home. We sat in front of my parent's house, wanting to process the news together before bringing anyone else into the mix.

"Two babies," I said again. I felt like most of my vocabulary in the past thirty minutes had consisted of those two words. I couldn't call them twins; twins seemed singular.

"Yeah, two babies," Chad said. He started to laugh. "Well, you told me that you had this perfect dream when you were eighteen. How's that working out for you?"

I sat there for a minute, thinking about the perfect existence that I'd thought I'd wanted. I tried to picture it to see if I would have been happier. Was a life with maximal control and predictability the way I should have gone?

I thought about being married to Sean, who Parker informed me was already separated from Drew. I thought about our relationship in high school: we got along well, but short of a little excitement when we first met, it hadn't been exhilarating or passionate. I thought about how happy I was with my floral career and how satisfying it felt. I thought about working with my grandma, who I was now working for full-time. I thought about being single for most of the last four years and how it had allowed me to become an individual. I thought about how I wouldn't trade my life as it was today for anything.

"You know what, Chad," I said. "I feel like my life is pretty damn amazing. Let's go in and tell my parents that they have two babies to be excited about, twins."

"Twins!" my mom exclaimed as she came to hug both of us.

"Twins," my dad said, sitting down abruptly at the kitchen table.

"Freaking twins?!" I heard Stacia exclaim from the stairs where she'd been eavesdropping.

My parents asked if we wanted to talk about the plan. Chad seemed very willing, but I wanted to do a little more processing first. I knew exactly who I should call, someone without a filter who would tell it like it was, Sophie. I left my parents and Chad to talk and went downstairs to my bedroom to get my friend's guidance. As the phone rang, I crossed my fingers that she was done with her workday and would be able to talk to me.

"Hello lovely, what's up?" Sophie said from the other end of the world.

"First off, I loved your pictures from Greece; I hope to make it there someday. Maybe we need to reprise our trip again." I paused, knowing that we were both thinking that we would redo it without one of our gang's key members.

"Speaking of Landon," Sophie said softly, "I was putting together some picture books post-Ian, and I found a picture of Landon and me at his promotion ceremony. I don't know if I ever told you this because, at the time, we were trying to see if we could make a relationship work in private, but I saw him when he was stationed in Germany. Someday I would love to talk to you more about it, but I'm still love-sick about him and Ian, even though Ian was a little bit of a wanker."

"I'll send Ian an overseas kick in the bullocks," I paused, thinking. "Bullocks means balls, right?"

Sophie chuckled, "Yes, it means balls."

"So, yes, kick him in the bullocks," I said cheerily.

"How're things going with Chad?"

"That's what I wanted to call you about. I'm knocked up, and we're having twins."

"Holy shit!" Sophie screamed over the phone. "Are you messing with me?"

"Nope," I replied, "I wanted to wait to tell you until I knew what we were doing. I've talked to my friends here, and though they give pretty good advice, I sometimes feel like they are telling me what I want to hear."

"Shoot," Sophie replied.

"We found out a few weeks ago, and Chad immediately wanted to propose. I love him. I just don't know if I want to get married because we're having children. I want to do this with him, and I would love for the babies and me to be his family. I also know I can do it myself if I need to. My grandma took care of my dad by herself for his first year while my grandpa was in Vietnam."

"You have a lot of options here," Sophie started. "You could do this in different towns but stay in a relationship, you could move in together. You could get married or do this separately. The biggest question is whether you want to do it with or without a physical relationship with him."

"With him, without a doubt. I love him." I replied without hesitation.

"Your kids are going to be adorable!" Sophie said. "Hopefully, they have Chad's nose, no offense, your eyes, your elastic skin. God, I would kill for that and his skin color."

I laughed; I was interrupted by a knock on my door. My dad poked his head in. "Lunch is ready."

"I'll be up in a minute," I said to him. After he was out of earshot, I wrapped up my conversation with Sophie. "I don't know what feels stranger, being 22 and having your dad make you lunch, or being 22 and having to discuss arrangements for myself and my children with my boyfriend in front of my parents."

"Contact me when you figure it out, love," Sophie replied before pausing, "You will figure it out."

I walked into the hallway when my father stopped me and silently motioned for me to go back into my room. I wasn't sure what he needed to talk about, but I followed him back in.

"I came down a minute ago and overheard the part of your conversation where you mentioned Chad proposing. I don't want to get involved in anything, but I don't know if it would help you to know that Chad spoke to your mom and me about wanting to marry you in his letters to us. Marriage is something he has been thinking about since before the pregnancy."

I sat for a moment, happy to hear that and curious to know what my parents said to him. "What did you say?"

"When the time was right, we would love to have him as part of the family. He's going to be in our lives no matter what. We don't require marriage to love you both and your babies, and we'll be here for you either way."

I nodded, tears welling in my eyes. "Thanks, Dad. I needed to hear that. I'm not sure what the decision will be, but just knowing we have your support is helpful."

We hugged and headed up the stairs.

After careful discussion, we decided that Chad would continue with his request to move to Colorado Springs. We would give him time to adjust, and in the meantime, we would look for a house that was midway between Bee's and his work. We would decide the rest later, but for now it seemed that everyone was on the same page. Chad left temporarily to run some errands before coming back to spend the weekend with us.

Stacia sat next to me, a look of sadness clear on her face. "I wish you were going to be closer. Now I'll have to miss having you around, and I'll miss out on having babies in the house."

I laughed, recalling how much I'd yearned for a baby and how repulsed I'd been when Stacia cried constantly. "Believe me," I said, "You'll have a lot of time with us. Us not being here full-time will allow you to enjoy them when they're here. Mom and Dad will help watch the twins, and Grandma Betty has also said that I can bring them to the shop for a while since that's what she used to do with Dad."

"Amber said that her sister cried all the time until she was four," Stacia reluctantly admitted.

"Yeah," I said, "you're going into high school, and you're going to be meeting boys and doing more grown-up things. You don't want to have the babies and us around for that."

"Speaking of boys," Stacia changed the subject abruptly, "Luke has been a little different with me lately. I sometimes notice him making googly eyes at me, and sometimes he gets moody and leaves abruptly. I think he might like me, which would be super awkward."

I smiled. I'd known it was only a matter of time. Stacia and Luke had big personalities, so it would be interesting to see where it would all end up. Poor Amber was just along for the ride with those two.

"What are your feelings about the situation?" I asked my sister.

"Well, he's bossy. He's also super cute, so we'll see what happens," she replied.

"It will all work itself out," I said to her, using the advice I felt I'd heard a lot recently. I was happy that I continued to get better and better about going with the flow as time went on.

"I know," Stacia said with a smile.

40

~Betty~ January 2012

Dear Rachel-

I know that you've heard of the legacy of the Bee family. We come from a long line of beekeepers. My ancestors were rumored to be able to charm the bees, extracting honey with very few stings. The last name, Bee, has been carried down from generation to generation. We are a family of hard workers, just like the honeybee.

I'm so excited that you will be adding two little Bees to the family. Did you know that worker bees are female? As their name states, they also do all the work. I'm happy that you have a partner that I have no doubt will share the load.

Chad is like family to us, and I look forward to seeing all that is in store for both of you. We are here to support you always. Did you know that male bees only inherit genes from their mothers, while female bees inherit both their parent's genes?

I've included a picture that may seem random. The VW bus is symbolic of a time I was facing a lot of the things you are facing: first love, new career, motherhood, the vast unknown. Let this picture remind you not to lose yourself in all of this. Don't forget to keep your identity even when it seems like being a mother is your only title.

If you are ever having a hard time, know that you have a whole hive behind you, Chad, and those babies. We love you all dearly. Rachel, we're proud of the woman you've become, the risks you've taken, and the person you are becoming. I can't wait to have the first dance party with you, Stacia, and your little girls. I hope they'll like Justin Timberlake as much as I do. Hopefully, a new album will be out by the time they're walking.

Love,
Grandma

"Where should we put the presents?" Samantha asked as she popped in the front door of Greg and Cheryl's house.

"Right here," I said, holding the door for her as she lugged a large gift wrapped in cute floral paper into the entryway.

"Wow," Samantha said, "This is heavy without a baby in it. No wonder moms can carry so much; they develop big muscles."

I laughed in agreement. The equipment from when Greg was little was different from what my granddaughters had and different from what my great-granddaughters were going to own.

Rachel had made sure Chad knew all about what he could expect with two daughters flowing with Bee's blood, a lot of character.

"Oh, believe me, I'm well aware of what I have in store," Chad admitted. I felt like he'd been glowing with pride since he found out she was pregnant, and it became even more prevalent when he found out the babies were girls.

I went into the bedroom to finish the letter. I took out the picture of Frank's VW bus, the one we'd driven to Woodstock in, and enclosed it in the envelope. There had been so much life between then and now. I'd experienced twists and turns yet still had many things to be thankful for despite the tragedies. The list of bad was still there, as was life, but the list of good was so long that I couldn't revisit every good moment even if I wanted to. I heard laughter coming from downstairs and went to join the group.

Chad and Rachel had moved into an apartment closer to Bee's than Chad's job because he insisted on her having a shorter drive. It was nice to know that he thought about little things like that. We'd all gone over there on a Sunday a month ago and decorated the nursery, and Chad, David, and Greg assembled two matching white cribs. We helped hang cute little flower and bug decorations on the walls, and the quilt I grew up with, the one with flowers and bees on its surface, was hanging above their cribs.

Her mom and I had arranged for a similar theme today. We'd decorated the house with Gerber daisies in bright yellows and pinks. We'd strung pastel streamers and even gotten a honeybee pinata that Stacia had insisted would be hilarious to break. We'd filled it with baby items that would all go to Rachel.

I got to the dining area and saw that most guests were there. Rachel looked beautiful in a flowing mint green sundress. I thought about the sundresses I wore when I was pregnant. Maternity clothes are much more stylish these days. She was glowing, and her belly protruded like a watermelon from the center of the dress.

They were trying to keep the babies in utero as long as possible, but twins usually came early, and they'd planned accordingly. Chad came upstairs, Trent and Caleb trailing behind.

"How are my girls doing?" He stopped to give me a hug and a peck on the cheek before going to Rachel. He placed a hand on her stomach lovingly before kissing her.

"Yuck," Stacia said teasingly to Chad, and he swiftly swept her in a hug.

"Your girls are exhausting me already," Rachel joked as she put a hand on the small of her back.

"Maybe the Queen should be using her throne," Chad said, gesturing to a chair that had fake flowers and vines intertwining the legs and top. "I decorated it myself."

"If you insist, your majesty," Rachel said with a wink.

"Okay, smartass," Chad said as he assisted her into the chair. She swatted him on the butt, which incited a "Gross" from Stacia.

Cheryl and I helped corral everyone, and we gathered the men to play the games. We started with a baby food guessing game. Thankfully, the trash can was nearby and uncovered, so it wasn't quite as catastrophic when Trent threw up his green peas. After that, Rachel looked a little green as well but managed to keep it under control.

Next, we played the candy bar diaper game, and this time Chad was the one looking nauseous. "Get over it," I said. "You and Rachel will have much less pleasant presents left in the diapers from here on out."

"That's what I'm afraid of, Grandma," he said.

I beamed. He'd started calling me Grandma since the day at Bee's when I'd found out about the pregnancy, and I appreciated it.

The men tried to participate in the gift-opening portion of the shower, but all the men except Chad eventually broke off from the group to revisit the food table. My husband was claiming they were going to work on cutting the cake before the pregnant woman died of sugar withdrawal.

I could see the excitement on Chad and Rachel's faces as they opened each gift, each offering from their beloved friends and family to be used in the rearing of their new family. I could also see their excitement reflected on Cheryl's face. She would be a fantastic grandmother, and she'd already done so much shopping at the outlet malls that I was confident the girls had enough clothing to last until they were four.

Rachel opened my letter, and when she'd finished reading, she looked up at me with love and adoration. "I love you, Grandma."

"I love you too," I said in return.

She went to open the next gift, a beautifully wrapped pink box. I saw Chad perk up. I knew what was in the box. I was excited.

On top was a card with steps: Step 1: Unwrap the present 2. Hand the box to Chad 3. Read the card aloud.

Rachel looked excited but apprehensive as she carefully peeled the paper away, handed the box to Chad, and removed the card from its envelope. "I'm supposed to read this aloud. It says, 'Rachel- My Queen, I can hardly control my heart when I look at you."

There were giggles as Chad removed first a crown and then the granny panties from the box. He placed the crown on her head and fastened the panties onto her throne, resulting in more laughter.

She continued, a smile on her face. "'I'm so happy that we are going to have two little Bees of our own.'"

He removed two delicate stackable honeybee rings from the box. "'I want to promise always to be the partner you want and deserve. I want to provide you and the girls with comfort and joy. I want you to have these two promise rings as a symbol of my intentions. I intend to be the best boyfriend, partner, and father you and the girls need. Someday, when you are ready, I want to be your king."'

He attempted to place the two rings on Rachel's ring finger, "They're a little too swollen," she laughed. Chad pulled a delicate chain from his pocket.

"I had this for backup," they smiled at each other as he slipped the rings onto the chain and fastened it around her neck. "Finish the last part."

"When you feel the time is right for me to be your king," he pulled a crown out of the box and placed it on his head, "' You can leave the crown somewhere to symbolize you're ready. You could leave it out thirty years from now or tomorrow, and I will be just as happy.'"

Rachel's face glowed. She pulled him in for a kiss. "I love you, Chad. Thank you for this, all of this."

She continued to open her presents, Chad close by, a comforting hand on her back, belly, or hand as they continued unwrapping.

They had such a bright future. I couldn't wait to watch them as the babies were born, as they became a family.

Epilogue

Rachel- March 2012

Beeeee Happy

Rachel Bee and Chad Harper proudly announce the birth of their daughters, Stella and Marie Bee-Harper. Stella, weighing 5 pounds, and 7 ounces, was born calmly, with barely a cry at 9:23 am. Marie, weighing 5 pounds and 6 ounces, came 10 minutes later, at 9:33, with a scream loud enough to announce her presence. The family has had a great time bonding and getting to know the twin's personalities. Stella seems content with almost everything and loves swaddles and swinging. Marie has had some colic and likes to be driven around in the car when she is cranky, listening to Jimi Hendrix.

"**M**ake sure you grab the pictures," I said as another contraction hit. I braced myself, grabbing onto the wall as my belly became tight, pulsating pain up and down my body. Chad put an arm out to help make sure I didn't fall.

"The pictures are in our bag," Chad reminded me once the contraction passed, and I was able to focus.

"They told me to have some positive things to focus on, and if birth continues to be this painful, I will need as many things to focus on as possible."

Since becoming pregnant, I've been focusing on the stories we all leave behind us and what we go through to become the people we are at one time or another. Pictures are a relatively accurate representation of who we are in one snippet of time. Sophie's picture of Landon reminded me of this. The image of him standing proud as she pinned something on his uniform, surrounded by soldiers, had made me reflect on how short life was. He didn't know that his life would end abruptly, but he was willing to risk that happening to serve his country.

I thought of the picture my grandma gave me, which symbolizes not only that period, but her independence, her venturing out and trying to find herself, her starting Bee's, and meeting my grandpa. I could picture her in front of that van at Woodstock, selling flowers, emanating sass and independence while having the calloused fingers of a hard worker.

I thought of a picture I'd taken from Chad's scrapbook of a helicopter. It made me think about meeting Chad on an airplane. How shortly after we'd taken the next step in our relationship, he left on an aircraft to work on planes. It reminded me that our relationship would take many forms but always be held together by parts and pieces. Even when the pieces required maintenance, we'd do all we could to maintain them for our girls and each other.

"Holy SHIT!" I said as another contraction rippled through my body.

Chad guided me into the car as we headed to the next leg of our journey.

Betty- March 2013

Our little Bees are Turning One,
If you could join us in some fun!
Please join us at 1 pm on Saturday to celebrate the 1st Birthday of Stella and Marie Bee-Harper. Instead of toys, please bring a book.

"**H**appy Birthday to you, Happy Birthday to you, Happy Birthday Stella and Marie, Happy Birthday to you."

The song ended, and Stella looked at the family and friends there with a sense of curiosity. Marie kept trying to grab her candle, which Rachel and Chad were trying to prevent. They each blew a candle out for the girls and left them to destroy their cakes. Stella's was a yellow cake with little bumblebee decorations, and Marie's was a flower.

The girls had been such a joy in our lives. Rachel and Chad were natural parents, taking care of every need, even on the days when neither parent slept more than a few hours. Cheryl and Greg were natural grandparents, and the girls had taken an extra special liking to their grandfather. He had a secret hold that only he had perfected that could put them to sleep. Stacia was also incredible with them. She would come to Bee's sometimes simply to see them since Rachel brought them there while she worked.

Rachel and Chad cleaned the girls after the cake and started to open presents.

"There is one left," Stacia said after all the gifts had been unwrapped and appropriately admired. She brought the box over. It was addressed to Chad.

He looked at Stacia, surprised, and she shrugged her shoulders. He peeled the paper off and opened the box. His smile broadened as he pulled out the crown from the baby shower.

Rachel looked at him, "What do you say we make this kingdom thing official?"

He scooped her into a hug. "We're getting married!"

BEE HAPPY

The music cued up, and they all took their positions, ready for the first few beats of the song to begin. The music started. They all looked at each other as they began to bob and move along with the beat. Stella grabbed Marie's hand, and the sisters bent their knees up and down in the cute yet disjointed way toddlers danced. They looked even cuter wearing their pale-yellow matching flower girl dresses, which matched Stacia's.

Stacia grabbed Rachel's hand, and together they imitated the twins dancing. The toddlers both giggled as they realized what was going on. Rachel looked like a queen in her long-sleeved floor-length wedding dress. Grandma Betty stooped down, grabbed each of the twin's hands, and they all swayed to the song's rhythm.

Chad and David approached in their tuxes and joined the circle. After a few moments, Greg and Cheryl came over, strutting to the song's rhythm. Together, as a family, they danced.

ACKNOWLEDGEMENT

I want to thank, first and foremost, military families. The sacrifices that are made when someone is in the service are vast. I touched on a lot of the subjects, but only superficially. I hope I did justice for the service members and their families. Thanks to my brother, Bret, and his wife, Shante, who allowed me to put them on the original book cover. Bret returned from his second deployment shortly after I finished the book, and Shante was just like Betty in this book, taking care of my nephew, Cayde, in my brother's absence. It has been incredible watching them grow as people, as a married couple, and now as parents, all while separated for long periods. They are inspiring.

Thanks as always to my husband, Mark, and daughter Serenity. Thank you for allowing me to follow my dream; it means the world to me.

Thanks, Dad, for reaching out to your graduating class from 1969 and providing information on the lingo and KIMN radio. You all are groovy! Thanks, Mom, for informing me about independent women in the late 60s. I love that when you and Dad married, Dad had bell bottoms and a vest, and Mom had a black flower sundress and a flower crown. Through you both, I added some personal details to my research. Again, I hope I did justice for your generation.

I owe a HUGE thank you to Amy Elliott. I was originally writing this book from Rachel's point of view, and I kept getting stuck. She told me exactly what it could use: a dose of Grandma Betty. Thanks to my first readers, Autumn (my loudest cheerleader), Angela (my favorite critic), Connie (you are so sweet), and Donna (thank you, thank you). Thanks to all who volunteered to be first readers. I appreciate it: Megan, Amy, Abi, Andrea, Wendy, Lois, Jen, Bonnie, and Carrie.

Please follow me on all social media accounts for the latest news. The best way to support an author is by leaving a review, and I would love your feedback. Thanks for reading this and for the continued love and support!

Finally, and most importantly. This book touches on some hard subjects, such as PTSD, death, alcohol and drug use, and suicide. If you or someone you know is having a hard time, don't hesitate to seek support. Crisis Hotline: 866-314-0214

BEE OUR GUEST

A BEE'S FLOWERS NOVELLA

Stacia
+
Marco♡

CORLET BOELMAN

SNEAK PREVIEW

The Bee family saga is far from over. Turn the page for a preview of Bee Our Guest- Stacia & Marco, a Bee's Flowers wedding novella. Available now.

CHAPTER ONE

"I don't know if I can do this!" I said into the phone receiver. "I'm probably going to be shitty at this marriage gig."

There was no response on the other end of the line. I knew that my sister wasn't saying anything because I was correct. I was not wife material.

"I love Marco with my whole heart, don't get me wrong, but I may as well tell him to leave and find someone else. I'll miss that amazing butt of his and how he works those hands if I do that. Oops, is that too much information to give you? Sorry, Rach."

There were a few seconds of silence before I heard a voice on the other end of the line. And it was not the voice of my sister.

"Aunt Stacia? It's Stella. Mom ran a quick errand for the wedding and left her phone here."

Shit.

Ashamed, I took a sip of my lukewarm coffee. Coffee was always my solution to awkward situations. Who was I kidding? Coffee was my solution to life, and the fact that it wasn't hot anymore was just the icing on the cake.

"Hi, Stacia," my brother-in-law, Chad, said in the background.

"You're on speakerphone with me, Stella and Marie.

Oh. My. God. Great. I was guilty of cursing, talking about Marco's butt, and pleasure-producing hands while on the phone with my brother-in-law and my nine-year-old twin nieces. I'm sure they'd heard their fair share of curse words, most of them probably from me. It didn't help me feel better about that or anything else they just heard me say.

"Is it too late to say that this was a wrong number?" I asked innocently.

"Yes, unfortunately, we're past the point of no return." Chad's deep laugh helped ease my embarrassment. I had known him since I was ten, and he was used to me after all these years.

"Am I still on speakerphone?" I said.

"Not anymore. I don't think I've ever grabbed the phone away that quickly before," he said with another chuckle.

"Please tell the girls that I'm sorry and don't let Rachel disown me. I would have at least censored the sexy parts if I knew they were on the line. I seem to be making a mess of things lately."

"I'm disappointed in you, Stacia," Chad said sternly as if reprimanding one of the girls.

"You and everyone else, most likely."

"Seriously, stop it right now. You're amazing. What are you doubting? Why're you doing this to yourself?"

"Are you sure you want to delve into my insecurities? How much time do you have? This could take hours. Years even."

"Come on, Stacia. You realize that we all know that you use sarcasm when you're trying to avoid talking about your feelings, right?"

"Dammit, you're onto me," I said in the most sarcastic voice I could muster.

"I'm here for you if you need me. I know how it feels to be married to a Bee woman, and I wouldn't change it for the world. I've known you for more than half of your life, and I can tell you that Marco feels ecstatic about marrying you. He's told me how excited he is, and it's all we've talked about the last few weeks."

The thought of my fiancé speaking to Chad about us made my heart patter. I know he loves me and that I need to get out of my head. My past sometimes gets the best of me at the most inopportune times. "I just," I sighed. I took a sip of my ever-cooling coffee and took a moment to think. "I just feel like it's too good to be true. Marco is such a great man. The whole Luke-slash-Amber situation messed with me. I've dealt with it and become a better person, but it made me doubt my ability to make someone happy long-term. Why would he want a woman like me? I can be a sarcastic ass. I'm also strong-willed and stubborn to a fault. Why would he want to deal with that for the rest of his life?"

"Listen, I know that finding out your best friend and your boyfriend were having a baby together was traumatizing. How could it not be? Your sass is endearing. Also, isn't comparing Marco to Luke like comparing apples to oranges?"

Why was Chad so damn good at making me think?

"You're right. This all boils down to being a mess of emotions right now, which I'm not used to. I'm excited about the wedding and ecstatic about marrying Marco. Who wouldn't want those dimples, blue eyes, and perfectly tanned skin in their life? I already mentioned the butt and other things, so I won't mention those again."

"Yeah, I would appreciate that," Chad said. "I love Marco in a brother-in-law type of way. But now I can't unhear some of the things you said, and I feel like I'll be obligated to check out his rear, which could be super awkward, so let's quit mentioning those things."

I laughed at the thought of Marco catching Chad looking at his ass. I would pay to see that.

"Everything you're feeling, including questioning both of your decisions, is normal. It would be best to embrace that this might be a rollercoaster ride of emotions. This has been fast and furious for you two, especially with Marco unexpectedly getting his dream job. Rachel and I took years to make it all work before we walked down the aisle, and even with that amount of time under our belts, we thought long and hard about making that commitment. We decided we wanted to be together for all our future adventures. You've made that decision, but you can change your mind at any time."

I felt awful hearing those words aloud. I wasn't going to change my mind. I wanted to make sure he didn't want to change his. I was confident about Marco being my husband. I simply wanted to be certain I was worthy of him, especially since I'd already dealt with the heartbreak of a broken engagement.

Luke, Amber, and I were once the best of friends. We'd been inseparable since elementary school. When Luke and I became an item in high school, it barely changed the dynamic. We were still the fearless three, with Amber occasionally throwing a boyfriend into the mix. We all moved to San Diego together to attend college. A few months after starting school, Luke and I became engaged.

One day I walked into the apartment we all shared to find them huddled together on the couch.

"We have something to tell you," Luke said before my world, and my heart shattered.

My older sister drove from Colorado to take me back home the next day, leaving behind a broken engagement and irreparable friendships. After finding out that the two people I thought would never let me down had started sleeping together after we moved to California, what else was there to do?

Luke and Amber were now married, and they had a daughter. I tried not to think about how old their child was. She was already pregnant when they told me about their affair, so it was easy to do the math, give or take a couple of months.

Deep in my heart, I was glad that the best friends I grew up with were happy, but the betrayal was still there. It felt less like a sharp knife and more like a dull needle as time went on.

"Your sister just got here. Do you want to talk to her?" Chad asked.

"I've been with her all day at work. She knows how crazy I'm being. I'll just take it out on the pavement," I replied.

Running was something I used as a healthy form of release. It helped me excel in soccer, and other sports, when I was younger. Recently, running was helping me with my PTSD diagnosis. I'd been attacked in my family's flower shop last Halloween, and it had taken time to get back to feeling like myself. With the help of counseling, I'd found some healthy coping strategies. When I was running, I was able to focus on my feelings while also getting some of my nervous energy out.

My phone dinged as I was changing into my running clothes.

My daughters are now scarred for life. Chad also might be. He asked me if I could rate Marco's butt for him. I can't begin to imagine what your conversation was about, nor do I think I want to.

I laughed.

Would you expect any different from me?

Nope, which is why I love having you as my little sister. Are you okay? I thought we talked about this today. You and Marco are great together.

I know. I drank too much coffee, felt a little twitchy, and got into my head. I was looking up information on changing my last name, and I freaked out.

Are you going to hyphenate?

Of course, I am. It's our tradition.

You don't have to.

I know. I couldn't imagine not having the Bee's last name.

Okay, well, I'm here for you anytime. We have some wedding flowers to discuss when you're ready. Love you!

I glanced down at my engagement ring, something I did every time I wanted to remind myself how real we and our love were. It was rose gold with a vine-like band and a yellow diamond, reminding me of a flower. I loved that he knew me well enough to get me something dainty and unique. He knew that I grew up loving the flower shop but not caring as much about the flowers as my grandma and sister. Somewhere along the way, that had changed. If coffee was the energy force for me, flowers were the lifeblood that made me happy. Having a ring that symbolized our commitment while reminding me of my family roots was a bonus for me.

I tied my laces and headed out the door. After my run, I needed to buckle down and complete some wedding and travel preparations. Marco was working at his flower delivery job today. He was spending extra time there to get his coworker and best friend, Benny, up-to-par on the business's ins and outs before we left. After that, he would start packing up some of his apartment. He was an artist and had a lot of belongings, and I hoped he'd make some headway soon.

I'd undergone a lot of transformation since the break-up. I met Marco when I was nervous and afraid of being in a relationship. After what I'd been through, I was terrified of falling in love again. His calm, relaxed demeanor and kind heart quickly tore down all the barriers I'd built after Luke and Amber's affair.

Marco had been there every step of the way. He'd been there to show me how to love and trust again. He hadn't left my side after my attack at the store, teaching me how to live with the weight of trauma. He'd helped me through the death of one of our friend's daughters. He was there for anything and everything I needed.

He proposed to me on the balcony overlooking the Rocky Mountains after sending my sister and me on a relaxing getaway. Shortly after our engagement, Marco received news that a new publishing company was interested in his photography and writing. They were offering a hefty advance to tour the world for an off-the-grid travel guide.

Marco felt conflicted about being offered his dream job right after such a life-changing event for us. He advocated with the publishing company to bring me along as his paid assistant. Marco, always going above and beyond when it comes to me, sent them a link to Bee's Flowers website. They liked our content and approached us with a counteroffer. They would pay all travel/assistant fees and wanted me to contribute to the guide. I would be responsible for providing a section in each place we visited with local plants and floral arrangements to showcase the horticulture in different regions. The publisher would include those portions in the guide if they liked it.

I had worked at my family-owned flower shop, Bee's Flowers, for a significant portion of my life. Working there didn't exactly give me knowledge of flowers from all over the world, but I could research what I needed to on the trip and bullshit the rest. My sister, Rachel, graduated with a degree in horticulture and floral design, so I could utilize her as needed.

When Marco asked me if I wanted to go with him, I felt conflicted for an entirely different reason. When he posed the question, he made it clear he wanted me to go with him as his wife, which would leave us only a month to plan a wedding and get our affairs in order.

It was nerve-wracking thinking about leaving my family and the flower shop. My grandma only recently developed enough trust in Rachel and me to allow us to take over Bee's Flowers. Once that transition occurred, she and our Grandpa David left to travel the United States in their RV. I didn't fully realize my dependence on the flowers, my family, and the friends that I met through Bee's until I contemplated leaving. My sister was instrumental in assuring me that all these things would still be around when we returned.

We were fast-tracking a wedding and preparing to leave the country for the next several months to a year. As I ran down the familiar streets of Denver, Colorado, I thought about all that needed to happen in the next few weeks. Our wedding was going to be a simple affair. What could possibly go wrong?

ABOUT THE AUTHOR

Corlet Dawn

Corlet (Cor-lay) is the international-selling author of the Bee's Flowers series. Corlet Dawn has written two full-length novels in the Bee's Flowers series, one novella and a children's book about her favorite animal-pigs. The Bee's books can be read as part of the series or as standalone novels. She writes thrillers under the pen name Corlet Boelman.

Corlet lives in Colorado with her husband, daughter, and dogs. She loves being active and traveling as often as possible. Check corletdawn.com for the latest updates, or follow her on all major social media accounts—email inquiries to corletdawnauthor.com.

From a young age, she knew that she was equally compassionate and creative. She uses these qualities in her nursing career and her passion as an author.

She is a Colorado native. In her spare time, she enjoys reading and being active. She is lucky enough to live in Colorado, where there are more sunny days than not. She loves to run, hike, garden, and weightlift. She also enjoys spending time with her husband, daughter, and two dogs. Her dream job would be to travel the world and write books full-time. She has dance parties as often as possible.

Corlet was inspired to write the Bee's Flowers books after being raised with a grandmother, mother, and sister who loved flowers. She often wondered about flower shops and why people would purchase flowers. She started writing the first book ten years ago, but during her nursing rotations, she further explored the idea, and eventually, Bee's Flowers began to form.

She is still determining the origin story behind her name. Her parents tell her a different story every time.

BOOKS BY THIS AUTHOR

Bee's Flowers

Bee-Coming

Bee Our Guest- Stacia & Marco

Harold The Hog

The Face On The Poster

A thriller written under Corlet Boelman